Malavita

WHAT READERS ARE SAYING

"...leaves you wanting to read *Revenge* (if you haven't already—shame, shame, shame on you... go READ it) and the follow up, *Retribution*."
—*Steph's Book Retreat* blog, 5 stars (on *Malavita*)

"This is the first book I have ever read by this author and I have to say I couldn't put it down till I finished it. What a ride I got! Love, action, excitement, crime families—heck, what more could you ask??"
—Amazon reader "cedarblue," 5 stars (on *Malavita*)

"This story truly exceeded my expectations. *Revenge* is action-packed, and when the pace picks up, it does not slow down.... Pick up this book today; it will grab your attention from the beginning. I cannot wait to read the next book."
—*The Romance Reviews (TRR)* site, 5 stars, Top Pick (on *Revenge*)

"Here is to a WHOOPING 5 Stars. If I had to describe this book in about four words, it would be action-packed, sexy, romantic, and adrenaline-rushing.... This would make a kick-butt movie! There were times when I was fanning myself, sitting on the edge of my seat, and so mad I had to put it down. The steamy scenes were oh so delicious!"
—*Bengal Reads* blog, 5 stars (on *Revenge*)

"The suspense keeps the pages moving quickly in book two of the Blood and Honor series. A fast pace, credible characters and a complex plot guarantee hours of entertainment."
—*RT Book Reviews* magazine, 4 stars (on *Retribution*)

"When I compare the quality of the writing, the complexity of the plot, and the development of the characters in this series to other books I have awarded 4 or even 4.5 stars to, this one is clearly worthy of a much higher rating than many of them. Not only do I look forward to reading more in the series, I am also really excited and can hardly wait."
—*Lindsay and Jane's Views and Reviews* blog, 5 stars (on *Redemption*)

"This series is awesome!!! If this series was ever made into a movie, it would put *The Godfather* to shame! I am always pulled into the lives that Dana creates in her books, heart beating so fast it is like I am part of the story line!!! ...I VERY HIGHLY RECOMMEND THIS BOOK. I WANT TO GIVE IT MORE THAN 5 STARS."
—Julie's Book Reviews blog, 5 stars (on *Redemption*)

ALSO BY DANA DELAMAR

Blood and Honor Series: Mafia Romance

Malavita (Prequel)
Revenge (Book One)
Retribution (Book Two)
Redemption (Book Three)
Reckoning (Book Four)

Writing with Kristine Cayne

Total Indulgence Series: MMF Ménage Romance

Her Two Men in London (Book One)
Her Two Men in Tahiti (Book Two)
Her Two Men in Sonoma (Book Three)

Malavita

BLOOD AND HONOR

PREQUEL

DANA DELAMAR

ACKNOWLEDGMENTS

Many people contributed to the creation of this book. No writer goes it alone, and I am certainly no exception.

As always, I can never adequately thank my wonderful critique partner, Kristine Cayne. She kicked my butt when I needed it, gave this book her ever-valuable time and attention, and asked many hard questions. Kristine, I owe you big time!

I'd also like to thank my beta readers, Kim, Ninia, Stephanie, and Trish, for their insights, comments, and catches. You made this book better than it was!

Many thanks to Luigia Tella for promptly and thoroughly answering my questions about Italy. Any errors are my own.

I'd be remiss if I didn't thank Natalie G. Owens and the readers who asked "What happened before *Revenge*?" for inspiring me to write this prequel.

I owe a great debt to Romance Writers of America® and specifically my hometown RWA® chapters, Eastside RWA and Greater Seattle RWA, for providing inspiration, support, guidance, friendship, real-world craft advice, industry contacts, and knowledge that proved invaluable. Thank you all.

Last but not least, I'd like to thank my family, my friends, and most of all my real-life hero, James Davis, for bearing with my craziness. You will always be my honey bunny.

CAST OF CHARACTERS

The Lucchesis

Enrico Lucchesi (LOO kay zee) – son of Rinaldo Lucchesi

Rinaldo Lucchesi – Enrico Lucchesi's father; *capo* (head) of the Lucchesi *cosca* (crime family)

Leopoldo (Poldi) Lucchesi – *capo di società* (second in command) of the Lucchesi *cosca*; brother to Rinaldo Lucchesi

Elma Lucchesi – wife of Leopoldo Lucchesi, mother to Dom Lucchesi

Domenico (Dom) Lucchesi – first cousin to Enrico Lucchesi

Francesca Lucchesi – wife of Domenico Lucchesi

Livio Vela – bodyguard to Rinaldo Lucchesi

Vittorio Battista – *padrino* (godfather) to Enrico Lucchesi

The Andrettis

Antonella (Toni) Andretti – daughter to Carlo Andretti and sister to Dario Andretti

Dario Andretti – son of Carlo Andretti and brother to Antonella Andretti

Romola Andretti – wife to Carlo Andretti

Carlo Andretti – *capo* of the Andretti *cosca* (Milan branch)

Lorenzo Andretti – *capo* of the Andretti *cosca* (Calabrian branch) and father to Carlo Andretti

Benedetto Andretti – *capo di società* of the Andretti *cosca* (Calabrian branch) and brother to Carlo Andretti

GLOSSARY OF TERMS

bacio (bah CHOH) – kiss

basta (BAHS tah) – enough (as in "I've had enough!" or "Stop!")

bella, bellissima (BEHL lah, behl LEE see mah) – beautiful

bene (BEN ay) – good

bocce (BAH chee) – lawn bowling game

buona sera (BWOH nah SAIR ah) – good evening

capisci (KAH pee shee); *capisco* (KAH pee skoh) – you understand; I understand

capo (KAH poh) – head (don) of a crime family (*cosca*); plural *capi* (KAH pee)

capo di società (KAH poh DEE so cheh TAH) – second in command of a *cosca*

cara (CAR ah), *caro* (CAR oh) – dear, sweetheart

carabinieri (car ah bin YAIR ee) – Italy's national police force; a single member of this force is a *carabiniere* (car ah bin YAIR ay)

ciao (CHOW) – informal hello and goodbye

cosca (KOHS kah) – a crime family; plural is *cosche* (KOHS kay)

Cristo (KREES toe) – Christ

davvero (dahv VAIR oh) – really, seriously

Dio mio (DEE oh MEE oh) – my God

dolcezza (dole CHAYT zah) – sweetheart, honey

faida (FEYE dah) – blood feud

finocchio (fee NOHK kee oh) – derogatory slang term for a homosexual

gelateria (jay lah tah REE ah) – store that sells *gelato* (ice cream)

grazie (GRAHTZ yeh) – thanks. *Mille* (MEE lay) *grazie* means "Many thanks."

idiota (ee dee OH tah) – idiot

In bocca al lupo (een BOHK kah all LOO poh)/*Crepi il lupo* (CRAY pee eel LOO poh) – Literally *In the mouth of the wolf/ May the wolf die.* Traditional way of wishing luck. Similar to "Break a leg." Means more or less "I'm going into the wolf's mouth. May he choke on me."

lire (LEER ay) – currency of Italy prior to the Euro. *Lira* (LEER ah), singular.

Madonna (ma DOEN nah) – the Virgin Mary; Mother of God

GLOSSARY OF TERMS (cont.)

malavita (mah lah VEE tah) – the criminal underworld, the criminal life

merda (MARE dah) – shit

'Ndrangheta (en DRAHNG eh tah) – the Calabrian Mafia, or "the Honored Society." *'Ndranghetisti* (en DRAHNG eh tees tee) are "men of honor." A single member is an *'Ndranghetista*.

nocciolato (noh choh LAH toe) – hazelnuts and chocolate

nonna (NOHN nah), *nonno* (NOHN noh) – grandmother, grandfather

padrino (pah DREE noh) – godfather

papà (pah PAH) – dad

passeggiata (pah sayj JAH tah) – evening stroll; a tradition throughout Italy

per favore (PAIR fah VOR ay) – please

perfetto (pair FEHT toe) – perfect

polizia (poh leet TZEE ah) – Italian police

porco Dio (POR koh DEE oh) – literally "pig God;" *very* vulgar religious curse

porca vacca (POR kah VAH kah) – literally "pig cow"; means "shit" or "damn"

prego (PRAY go) – welcome

principe (PRIN chee pay), *principessa* (prin chee PESS ah) – prince, princess

salute (sah LOO tay) – to your health; cheers!

scusa (SKOOZ ah); *scusi* (SKOOZ ee) – excuse me (informal; formal)

sì (cee) – yes

signore, signora (seen YOR ay, seen YOR ah) – sir, madam; the "e" is dropped from *signore* when used with a last name

stronzo (STRON tzoh) – shit, turd, bastard

troia (TROY ah) – slut

troppo (TROHP poh) – too much

vaffanculo (vahf fahn COO loh) – go fuck yourself

zia (TZEE ah), *zio* (TZEE oh) – aunt, uncle

PROLOGUE

1982
Cernobbio, Lake Como, Italy

The phone call, when it came, shattered Enrico Lucchesi's world. His mother, his brothers, all dead. Gunned down in the street by order of Carlo Andretti, *capo* of the Andretti family.

He still couldn't believe it was only him and Papà left. Enrico couldn't cry, couldn't speak past the *bocce* ball lodged in his throat. All he could do was stare dry-eyed at his father, who'd done nothing for the last ten minutes but sob, great shuddering wails that shook Enrico to the core. His father never cried. He'd always told his sons a *capo* had to be stronger, braver, tougher than other men.

But here he was, the great Rinaldo Lucchesi, weeping as if he'd never stop.

Enrico finally found his voice. "Papà," he croaked, reaching across the kitchen table for his father's hand. When there was no answer, he tried again. "Papà."

The slight rebuke in his tone—after all, how many times had his father berated Enrico for softness?—caused his father to look up, to notice him at last. Papà took a shaky breath and wiped his eyes with the handkerchief he always carried. He ignored the hand Enrico had stretched toward him, and Enrico pulled it back, all the way to his lap.

In the wake of those sobs, the kitchen seemed deadly quiet, filled only with the sounds of their breathing. His, his father's, and Dario's. Enrico glanced at the Andretti boy, who'd sat mute and wide-eyed this entire time.

That glance seemed to remind his father of Dario's presence, and a murderous glint came into his eyes. He snatched the boy out of his chair, scattering their playing cards to the floor. Dario let out a yelp of surprise. "*Per favore*, it's not my fault!"

For the past three days, ever since he'd taken Dario hostage in an effort to get Carlo Andretti to negotiate, to end the feud between their families, Papà had insisted on treating Dario as a guest. A guest who couldn't leave the house, but a

1

guest nevertheless. Because that's how civilized men handled things. With honor, with respect.

All that courtesy seemed forgotten now as his father wrestled Dario to the butcher block in the corner and mashed Dario's slender body against the counter. When he pinned the boy's arm to the cutting board, bile rose in Enrico's throat. Dario was only fourteen, tall and gangly, all bones. He was no match for Rinaldo Lucchesi, a bull of a man in his prime.

Enrico was no match for him either, but he had to try. He sprang from his chair, his eyes glued to Dario's wrist, thin as kindling under his father's meaty hand. Papà grabbed the cleaver from the knife block and swung it up in the air. Enrico grabbed his father's arm at the top of its downward arc and yanked it back.

Gritting his teeth, Enrico strained to stop his father. *Dio*, Papà seemed stronger than that marlin Enrico had hooked two years ago on a sport-fishing trip. He'd been Dario's age then, too weak to hold out against the enormously powerful fish for long, but he'd put on muscle since. Not enough though. He was still only sixteen, and his father had to outweigh him by close to seventy pounds.

They seemed to struggle forever, his father grunting curses under his breath, Dario's thin reedy voice whimpering "*per favore, per favore*" in the background.

At last his father said something intelligible, his voice a rusty rasp. "I am your *capo*. Do not interfere."

"You always said we aren't savages."

"Savagery is all Carlo Andretti understands!"

Papà gave him a hard shove, weakening Enrico's hold. Catching a whiff of his father's cologne, Enrico flashed back to a time when his father had carried him up to bed as a boy, cradling him in his arms. Somehow he had to reach that part of his father. Somehow he had to make him see reason.

Enrico's lungs burned and his arms shook, his father's muscles hard as granite underneath his hands. "I want Don Andretti dead too. But crippling Dario isn't going to bring Mamma and Primo and Mario back."

His father let out an inarticulate cry of rage and stilled, no longer fighting. "I must do something. I must show Carlo I can hurt him."

"Not the whole hand. The Lucchesis aren't cruel. You always say that."

"The little finger then."

Enrico swallowed against the acid surging at the back of his tongue. Now that Primo was dead, everything had changed. Someday, when he became *capo*, he'd have to make harder decisions than this. Decisions that meant life or death. Decisions he'd never wanted to make, had never pictured himself making. But Carlo Andretti had killed his brothers, had taken any other future away from him.

He could no longer think like a boy, act like a boy. He had to be a man now.

Enrico nodded and released his father's arm, then stepped away and closed his eyes. He tried not to hear the thunk as the cleaver bit into bone and wood, tried not to hear Dario's cries of pain. Tried hard to think of what he'd done as mercy.

CHAPTER 1

Two years later
London, England

Enrico Lucchesi left his infant son howling in his sobbing mother's arms. Because he had to. Because it was his duty. Because he was engaged to marry another.

Antonella Andretti. Carlo Andretti's daughter. A girl he barely knew.

He took one last look at Nico and Veronica. "Rico, don't go!" she called, following him onto the path that led to the gate of the small home he'd paid for, the only thing he'd been able to leave her, aside from a monthly check.

He couldn't marry her. He couldn't raise his son. He couldn't do anything but return to Italy and his fate.

Veronica ran up behind him, her bare feet slapping on the paving stones, Nico letting out another wail. "Rico, please," she sobbed. "Please."

His throat tight, Enrico turned back to her, waving at the waiting driver and holding up a finger to tell the man he would be a while.

Veronica looked like her world was ending, and it was all his fault. He never should've gotten involved with her, no matter how lonely he'd been. Not when he knew he was already promised to someone else. Not when he wasn't free. He'd just wanted *something* for himself. Something—someone—who was *his* choice. At least for a while. But it had all been a horrible mistake. Except for Nico.

Reaching up, he brushed away the blonde strands that had fallen across Veronica's green eyes. Eyes flooded with tears, all because of him. "I am sorry, *cara*. I must."

Her face crumpled. "You can't leave us. What about Nico?"

His fingers drifted across her cheek. Leaving them was going to kill him. "He has you. And I will be back. To visit."

She shook her head, her voice low, urgent. "You can't marry her. Not when you love me."

The lump in his throat grew. "I told you, *cara*. I have no choice."

"I don't understand. How can your father make you marry this girl? You're eighteen. You're a man. You can make your own choices."

He shook his head. She'd never understand. Even if he explained who he really was—that the Enrico Franchetti she knew was a fiction—she'd never understand the life he led, the rules he lived under. The rules of the 'Ndrangheta, the Honored Society. The Calabrian Mafia. They'd considered him a man for two years now. Ever since he'd taken the vows and become the one thing he'd sworn he'd never become: a man of honor. One of *them*. A Mafioso.

But with Primo and Mario dead, he'd had no choice. His father needed him.

And if Enrico didn't marry Antonella Andretti in four weeks, he and his father would be dead shortly after. Carlo Andretti would ensure it.

Leaning forward, he pressed his lips to Veronica's forehead, then both of her cheeks. "I'll be back as often as I can."

She grabbed his collar with her free hand and rose up on her tiptoes, pressing her mouth to his, the kiss desperate, urgent. He didn't return it. Instead, he gently tugged her hand from his shirt. "Veronica, that is over between us."

Anger erupted over her face, and she punched him in the chest. "Go then! Go back to Italy and leave me. Leave your *son*." She held Nico up so he could take one last look.

Nico was fourteen months old now, his green eyes bright, his chestnut hair curling around his plump cheeks. He waved a chubby fist at Enrico. "Papà," Nico burbled, and tears pricked Enrico's eyes. He kissed his son's fist, kissed his cheeks, and let him go.

Veronica snatched their son to her chest and glared at him, her pale cheeks flooding with color. "You go, Enrico Franchetti. You go, and don't darken my door again."

"I will be back, Veronica." He said the words wearily. At first he'd loved her volatility, her fire. But there was a frantic, histrionic edge to it that had worn thin over time. She'd changed so much from when they'd first met. Had he really known her at all, or had he been too young to see her clearly? Maybe with him gone for a while, she'd calm down, relax. Find someone new.

Though the thought of another man raising his son made his gut twist. Nico was his. *His* son. *His* child.

But Nico was safe here. He'd grow up far away from the 'Ndrangheta. And if Enrico was careful, Nico would never know that world, would never have to fear for his life. Would never know a man like Carlo Andretti.

Carlo Andretti. The one man Enrico desperately wanted to kill.

"You can't leave me like this, Rico," Veronica sobbed. "You can't."

"I do not want to." He raised a hand to touch her cheek, to touch Nico again.

"You have to do something. You have to come back."

He hated seeing her like this. Hated the desperate look in her eyes, hated the quaver in her voice. He'd done this to her with his omissions, his wishful thinking. He owed her and Nico something more. "I will try. Perhaps there is a way out of this marriage."

Her mouth curved into a grateful smile, and his stomach contracted into a ball.

Had he just lied to her again?

He sincerely hoped not.

There had to be a way to win his freedom. There had to be a way to keep his son.

———◆———

Two days later
Blevio, Lake Como, Italy

Since returning home, Enrico had dreaded this moment. He turned to his father as the driver pulled onto the road that led to the Andretti estate. Papà looked drawn, pale. Thin. The sight made Enrico burn. Carlo Andretti had ruined the man Enrico had always admired. "Why are we doing this? All he wants is to rub our noses in shit. Like his damn dogs."

"Rico, control yourself. Don't let him rile you."

Enrico's blood pressure skyrocketed. "Don't let him *rile* me? After what he's done? After Mamma and Primo and Mario? After forcing me to leave—"

Rinaldo raised a finger for silence. "We are the only ones who know about that."

Enrico flicked his eyes at the driver and his father's bodyguard, Livio, in the front seat.

"You don't trust them?" he whispered.

Rinaldo leaned closer. "I do. But men can't speak of what they don't know. Yes?"

His father was right. The fewer people who knew, the better. If Carlo Andretti ever learned of Nico's existence, the boy would be dead, and Enrico and Rinaldo along with him.

"You need to meet the girl. It's customary," Rinaldo said.

"It's also customary that I can refuse her." Before his father could speak, Enrico added, "Oh that's right—I *can't*. I marry her, or Carlo hunts us down like rabbits. Frightened fucking rabbits. Have I got that right?"

Enrico didn't have time to do more than recoil from the slap to his cheek. "Stop it. Now." His father's voice was like iron. "I'm doing this for *you*. So you'll have a future. Instead of a grave. You think I like this any more than you do?"

The car pulled to a stop, and Rinaldo slammed out before Enrico could answer. He rubbed his stinging cheek, shame overwhelming him. His father had always been a proud man who'd never bowed to anyone. And certainly never to Carlo fucking Andretti. But that was before everything that had happened during the last two years. "I'm sorry, Papà," Enrico whispered to himself as he got out of the car and followed his father and Livio inside. The four guards who'd accompanied them in another car brought up the rear. Their weapons weren't drawn, but their alertness spoke volumes. They were in enemy territory.

Carlo's villa wasn't nearly as grand as the Lucchesis' own, but it was well-furnished, as Enrico recalled from the last time he'd visited. Four years ago, before all the trouble had started between his father and Carlo.

They'd come for a wedding—some cousin of Carlo's had wanted to be married on the lake. It was the first time Enrico had met Antonella Andretti. He'd been fourteen, she twelve. A gawky slip of a girl, all large dark eyes and a mass of black hair. Nothing special. He'd barely taken notice of her. And there'd been that one time at school when some very stupid boys had been harassing her and her twin brother Dario. Enrico had stepped in and stopped it. She'd tried to thank him, but he'd brushed her off. He couldn't even remember what her voice sounded like.

He'd find out soon enough.

They were shown around back to a large terrace beneath a huge plane tree, its silver-gray bark peeling. Sunlight filtered through the thick green foliage, dappling the figure of Carlo Andretti, who was sitting at a table and sipping from a steaming cappuccino. Breakfast dishes had been set out for six. Carlo's family, plus Rinaldo and Enrico.

The guards fanned out and took positions around the table. Carlo watched them, but didn't comment beyond the amusement in his eyes.

He rose when Rinaldo and Enrico approached, a smug smile spreading across his face. "*Prego,*" he said, motioning them to take chairs at the table, playing the gracious host. Enrico wanted to strangle him. A bitter taste rose in his mouth and his stomach churned. How could he be expected to just *sit* there and have breakfast with the man who'd killed his mother, his brothers?

Enrico placed a hand on the back of a chair, but didn't sit. He was gripping the painted metal so hard his fingers hurt. His emotions must have shown on his face because Carlo's grin widened. He looked at Rinaldo and said, "So your pup thinks he's a wolf, yes? He thinks he will challenge me?"

Enrico looked at his father. "Papà, *per favore*—"

"Sit," Rinaldo said between gritted teeth.

Holding Carlo's gaze, Enrico took a seat. Carlo chuckled and leaned across the table. "You'll live longer if you learn to be more like your father. Accept your losses and move on."

Enrico took a deep breath and looked away. Someday, somehow he'd make Carlo Andretti pay. What he didn't quite understand was why his father was just *taking* this treatment. Sure, things were bad, but they couldn't be *this* bad, could they? Something had happened. Something Papà hadn't told him.

Carlo smoothed a hand over his coal-black hair and took another sip of his cappuccino, motioning for a maid to pour espresso for Enrico and Rinaldo. Nodding at Enrico, he said, "You've grown. So where has your father kept you stashed these last two years?"

Enrico looked at his father, who nodded. "England. Boarding school."

"Did you enjoy their bland food?"

"Would you?"

Carlo laughed. He addressed Rinaldo. "I like your pup."

"Does that mean you won't shoot me too?" Enrico asked.

Carlo laughed harder and slapped the table. Rinaldo glared at Enrico, but Enrico didn't apologize. "You could teach my boy a thing or two about balls," Carlo said.

The double doors in the back of the house opened, and Enrico turned, his heart speeding up. What did Antonella look like now?

Dario stepped out first. He'd filled out some since Enrico had seen him last. He was followed by his mother, Romola, who stopped just outside the doorway and spoke to someone still inside. Her voice was pitched low, and he couldn't hear what she said.

Was something wrong? Did Antonella not like this idea either? If so, maybe she'd refuse him, and he and his father could make some other arrangement with Carlo to end the feud.

And Enrico could go back to England and his son.

Finally Signora Andretti walked toward them, and her daughter stepped outside. Antonella's head was down, her eyes staring at her feet, her mass of black hair shielding her face. She was wearing a light, flowery sundress with simple sandals. She was quite tan, her legs and arms shapely, her body willowy. Not much in the way of breasts, but that was all right—

She looked up and straight at him, her eyes locking with his.

A pang of disappointment hit him. She was plain, so plain. And she had the "Andretti beak." That overlarge nose that looked fine on the males, but that overwhelmed the faces of the women. Perhaps "plain" was being kind.

Her step faltered. *Merda*. She'd seen what he was thinking. He forced a smile, but she looked away and stalked to the other end of the table where she wouldn't have to talk to him.

He wanted to crawl under his chair. He was a worm. An insect. He'd just upset this poor girl. She'd been teased plenty at school—the taunts had reached even his ears. He'd been among the popular crowd, but despite their wealth, the Andretti twins had been outcasts. As far as he knew, Antonella had ignored the taunts and Dario had remained silent, speaking to no one but his sister.

Well, she'd apparently *pretended* to ignore the insults. Obviously they'd made their mark.

And here he'd gone and made her feel them all over again.

The only good thing was that she was sure to reject him now. And then he'd be free.

Breakfast—an assortment of cold cuts, fruit, and pastries—was served, no one chatting much. Dario kept his right hand in his lap, eating awkwardly with his left. Had Carlo told him to do that, or was the boy ashamed? Enrico's cheeks heated. Here was another Andretti he'd wronged. He should've argued harder with his father. Maybe he could've spared Dario that pain.

But maybe—if he was honest—maybe he hadn't wanted to.

Maybe he'd wanted his vengeance. And maybe he'd taken it in the wrong place.

He pushed his plate away, suddenly not hungry. Perhaps his father was right, and he needed to get a better handle on his feelings. At least when it came to the Andrettis. He couldn't seem to do anything right when it came to them.

His throat clogged, an apology lodged in it. But how could words ever make up for what he'd done to Dario?

"May I be excused?" Antonella asked. Her voice was a lovely, husky contralto, and Enrico found the courage to meet her gaze.

"You may," Carlo said.

She tossed her napkin down and rose, heading up the hill toward the olive grove.

"I'd like to talk to her. If I may," Enrico said, not stopping to second-guess himself. He was going to apologize for something today. Carlo nodded, and Enrico sprang up from his chair, loping after her. She was surprisingly fast, and he had to put in a little effort to catch her. "Antonella," he called as he came up behind her.

"Spare me," she said, not looking at him. He placed a hand on her shoulder and she shrugged away. "Don't touch me."

"*Per favore*—"

"I should've known better. To think I thought you were nice!"

His steps faltered, but hers continued. She split off her present course and veered for the hedge maze to their right.

For a moment, he stared after her. Maybe he ought to leave her be, let her reject him—

But he couldn't stomach the idea of her thinking that he hated how she looked. That he was rejecting her.

Even though he had.

His face hot with shame, he trailed her into the maze, and she broke into a run, sprinting away from him. He charged after her, following her around turn after turn, soon utterly disoriented.

Exasperated, he put on some speed and grabbed her left arm. She stopped and whirled on him, her eyes blazing. "I told you not to touch me!"

The tremble in her voice signaled how close to the edge she was. "Antonella, *per favore*. I just want to apologize."

"For *what?*" she asked, stepping closer to him, her arms crossed over her chest.

His cheeks flamed hotter. What could he say that wouldn't make her feel worse? "For my behavior."

She stepped closer. "For what *exactly?*" she asked.

Oh *Dio*. She was going to make him say it aloud. He couldn't do that.

"I'm sorry," he stammered.

"Sorry for *what?*" Her voice could cut glass. He took a step back as she advanced. "Afraid to say what you were thinking?" she asked, motioning to her face.

"No, I—"

She snorted. "Go ahead, *lie*. Because you're too *kind* to say what you were thinking. How disappoin—" Her voice grew thick and she turned away.

He placed a hand on her shoulder. "I'm sorry I caused you pain. Truly."

"Papà says I'm beautiful. But I know the truth." She wiped her eyes and sniffed, still not looking at him.

"You have beautiful eyes, and your voice—"

"Stop. Just *stop*." She rounded on him. "Life's been easy for you, Enrico Lucchesi. Have you ever even had a pimple?"

He scratched his chin. "A few."

She laughed. "And how long did that phase last? A week?" She gestured up and down his body. "You've always been a god. You don't know what it's like to realize you have a face only a parent could love."

He didn't know why he did it, but he reached out and tweaked her nose. Her mouth dropped open in rage. "What are you *doing?*" she yelled.

"Making you stop feeling sorry for yourself. Your being angry at me is better."

She placed her hands on her hips. "You need me, Enrico Lucchesi, whether you realize it or not."

"I don't need you."

"Ask your father. I did this for *you.* For Dario. For my own father."

"You sound like this was your idea."

She crossed her arms again. "It was the perfect solution." After a moment she added, "It *was.*"

"What do you mean?"

"My father wouldn't stop the *faida* until your family was ground to dust. But he didn't realize what this war was costing him. The men were weary, the merchants were sick of being caught in the crossfire, and the *carabinieri* wouldn't keep looking the other way, no matter how much money he threw at them. The war had to be stopped, and in a way that let both sides save face."

She honestly thought she'd stopped the feud? "Wait a minute. Your father took advice from you? A girl?"

She nodded. "I suggested it, and he listened."

"But... why?"

Her face darkened. "Because he loves me. I was afraid for Dario. Especially after we got his finger in a box."

"*Madonna,*" Enrico murmured. What must that have been like for her? "I'm sorry about that too."

"You might tell Dario that."

"I don't think he wants to hear it."

She shrugged. "Maybe not."

They stood there in silence, both of them looking anywhere but at each other. Finally he said, "Can we start over?"

Her eyes snapped to his. "I will *never* forget the look on your face."

He groaned. "I was caught off guard."

"No. It was an honest reaction. The last thing I want from you now is lies."

He threw his hands in the air. "*Basta!*" Enrico wheeled away from her and tried to retrace his steps but ended up in a dead end. Even though the mid-May day was just pleasantly warm, he was broiling in his suit jacket, so he whipped it off. Then he surveyed his surroundings, searching for anything that looked familiar. Turning around, he saw her standing a few feet away. She'd trailed him, probably having a good laugh at his expense.

"Follow me," she said. They'd gone a few meters before she stopped. "You honestly want another chance?" she asked, her voice low, her eyes darting toward him then away.

Strangely, he did. "Yes."

She smiled. When she wasn't scowling, her face lit up, and her curved lips caught his eye. They were soft, kissable. Plump. She was... passable. Even almost cute. "That's the first honest thing you've said to me today."

How had they gotten to this point? She'd been ready to reject him—she'd been ready to do what he'd *wanted*—and he'd begged her to reconsider?

The smile left her face then, and she pressed a palm into the center of his chest. "But I want to be clear—I'm no pushover, Enrico Lucchesi."

He nodded, letting a hint of a grin touch his lips. "Believe me, I've figured that much out."

They returned to the table in silence, Carlo's eyes on them. "All is well?" he asked, his eyes sliding from Enrico to Antonella. She nodded, but all Enrico could think about was how miserable his father looked. Just what had Carlo been saying to him while they were gone?

This wasn't how it was going to end. He—they—weren't just going to roll over for Carlo. Not if Enrico had his way. His family needed to be avenged.

There was only one problem. Carlo Andretti was a nearly impossible target.

Then a crazy thought struck him: perhaps the men who'd pulled the triggers weren't.

CHAPTER 2

Even though the Lucchesis had left, the atmosphere at the breakfast table remained tense. Papà repeated his question, but Antonella barely heard his words. Enrico had hurt her pride, hurt her—

"Toni?" Her father's sharp voice cut into her thoughts. "What's wrong?"

Nothing a nose job wouldn't fix. But the doctor had said she was too young; she had to wait until she was eighteen. *Dio.* She'd look hideous in her wedding pictures too. Just like in every other picture taken of her. Why hadn't she ended up with Mamma's nose instead of Papà's? "Everything is fine."

He narrowed his eyes at her and pulled out a cigar and his gold lighter. "Walk with me," he said, rising from his chair and lighting up as he headed toward the olive grove, his favorite place for their talks. She cast a glance back at Dario, who still sat at the table, the closed look on his face speaking volumes. He longed for the same connection to Papà that she had. But no matter what she said to Dario, her words didn't sink in. He wanted Papà to be someone he wasn't. Papà would never respect Dario until he met Papà on *his* terms, not Dario's. Papà respected strength and boldness; Dario preferred to observe and study before making a move. No matter that Dario was often right—all Papà saw was weakness and indecision. She hoped that someday Dario would learn, because Papà wasn't about to change.

Her father started down a row of trees, stopping every so often to inspect their fruit or run his hands over their silver-green leaves and gnarled bark. Insects whirred and birds chirped, and a breeze danced through the trees, rustling their leaves. When her father said nothing after a while, her mind wandered back to thoughts of Enrico Lucchesi. He was so much better looking than she'd remembered. He'd grown into a man, with broad shoulders and slim hips, his face taking on firmer contours, his jaw harder, his high cheekbones more prominent. He still had the same chocolate brown eyes fringed in long black lashes, eyes that made her melt. He wore his black hair shorter now, its waves a little more tamed than they had been when she'd seen him last. There'd been that moment in the

11

hedge maze when he'd smiled at her, and his eyes had dropped to her mouth, and she could have sworn he was thinking of kissing her. If only he'd looked at her that way from the beginning—

"Toni, be straight with me. That boy upset you."

She sighed. "A little, Papà. It was nothing."

"Tell me, *dolcezza*." He rested a hand on the nape of her neck and squeezed lightly, then kissed her hair. The scent of his cigar wafted around them. It was comforting to her, that smell.

Tears rose in her eyes, but she blinked them back. "It was a misunderstanding, that's all."

"You know I hate it when you're like this. Tell me."

She sighed. "It's my nose."

He ran a finger down its contours, then kissed her forehead. "*Dolcezza*, we've talked about this. It's a good, strong nose."

"For a man. For a woman, it's hideous."

He placed his hands on her shoulders. "Look at me." She looked up, meeting his gaze. "You aren't one of those women who has to rely on her looks to get by in life. You are meant to be a leader. You are meant to do *more*. And you're beautiful just the way you are."

"You're the only one who thinks so." Her throat closed up and she looked away.

He gave her a little shake. "Any man who is worthy of you will see that too. You're not a decoration, Toni. You're a *principessa*, a *capa*. Like Cleopatra, you were born to lead armies and rule men."

She bit the inside of her lip and let out a snort. "As if the 'Ndrangheta would accept me."

"It's happened before. I can make it happen again. If that's what you want."

"But what about the marriage?"

He waved his cigar in the air. "For now, the marriage suits us. But that may not always be the case."

"*For now* it suits us?"

"This marriage may have been your idea at the start, but it's taken on a life of its own since then. The only thing I can do now—if you don't marry the boy—is restart the *faida*. But that will pit Andretti against Andretti."

Her pulse sped up. "Nonno Lorenzo wants this marriage?"

"I agreed to certain terms, and he agreed to hold me to them."

"I don't understand."

"You think this is *Romeo and Juliet*. It's not. This is the union of two *cosche*. Many families are interested in the outcome. There will be a shift in power."

"I still don't see—"

"If I am not fighting Rinaldo Lucchesi, and he is not fighting me, if we work together again, we may become stronger than some people may like."

"That's a good thing."

"I don't want to be yoked to Rinaldo Lucchesi."

"You were his partner before."

"Before he betrayed me. Before I knew who he really worked for."

"Nonno Lorenzo." *That* was why her grandfather wanted this marriage to go through.

"And if the marriage doesn't happen? If it's not what I want?"

He smiled. "I finish what I started, and Rinaldo and Enrico Lucchesi get what they deserve."

She imagined Enrico and his father lying face down in the dirt, blood flowing from bullet holes in the backs of their heads. She didn't want that. Even if Enrico didn't think she was pretty. Her face grew hot as she recalled her angry words in the maze. She'd really had no right to say them.

She deserved whatever Enrico Lucchesi thought of her; the *faida* never would have started if it weren't for her. Enrico's family wouldn't have been killed if it weren't for the stupid way she'd blindly followed her father. If she hadn't thought it was all a game, a harmless game...

"That won't be necessary, Papà. The marriage is still on."

He almost seemed disappointed. "*Davvero?*"

She nodded. It was best for all involved. Wasn't it?

But what if it wasn't best for her? What if Enrico Lucchesi never looked on her with love, with desire? Was she trading the future her father was offering her for a lifetime of heartache?

She'd give Enrico two weeks. Two weeks to prove himself to her. And if he couldn't do it, somehow she'd persuade Papà to let Enrico and his father live. She owed Enrico that. She owed him some sort of recompense for the horrible wrong she'd done to his family.

She rubbed her belly, feeling sick. Some sins could never be forgiven.

———— ◆ ————

Carlo Andretti watched his daughter walk back to the house. He hated manipulating Toni like that. He hated telling her only half the story.

But he needed her cooperation. He needed her to keep the Lucchesis complacent, to make them think the marriage was going forward, to make them think he'd been tamed.

He wasn't yet strong enough to take on his father. Not yet. But he was close, so very close. In a few weeks, he should be able to eliminate Rinaldo Lucchesi and go to war with his father. To show Lorenzo Andretti which one of them was the master.

Lorenzo thought he could exile him. Lorenzo thought he could use Rinaldo Lucchesi to keep him in line. But Lorenzo was only Carlo's father. Only a man.

Lorenzo Andretti wasn't God. And Carlo would never be a pawn in his father's game of chess.

———— ◆ ————

Enrico's sleep had been nothing but nightmares. Over and over he'd dreamed about how Mamma, Primo, and Mario had died, those images entwined with

Carlo's smug smile, his father's heart-wrenching sobs when he'd received the call, and the shock on Dario's face as he beheld his maimed right hand for the first time. So much horror, so much he wanted to forget.

So much he *couldn't* forget. So much he couldn't leave unavenged.

How had Papà done it? How had he reconciled himself to a life of ghosts circling him, howling for justice?

Something was wrong. The man Enrico knew, the man who'd sired him, wasn't one to take an insult or a blow without dealing out bloody retribution afterwards.

And yet he'd seemingly rolled over for Carlo and shown his belly. And Carlo had seemingly accepted Rinaldo's surrender. Why? Could it be as Antonella had said?

If so, he might have an explanation for Carlo's behavior, but not for Papà's. And he wanted one.

But first, he wanted revenge. If he couldn't get Carlo, he'd get those who'd pulled the triggers. Those men were vulnerable.

The problem was, he didn't have their names. Or the first idea how to go after them. They were all hardened killers. Though Enrico had been well-versed in firearms from childhood, he'd never even aimed a gun at another person. Knowing how to use a gun and killing with one were two different things.

He needed help. And there was one man who could certainly assist him. The question was: Would he? Livio Vela, his father's personal bodyguard, was loyal to the bone to Rinaldo Lucchesi. As far as Enrico knew, Livio had never questioned or second-guessed his *capo*. And yet, if Livio helped Enrico, he'd be outright defying his don. Rinaldo had been very clear with Enrico—he was not to pursue the right to vendetta against Carlo.

It had been easier in England to obey those orders. But if he were marrying Carlo's daughter, if he were going to be able to hold his head up with any sense of pride, Enrico needed to act. And there was no time to waste. In less than a month, he was supposed to marry Antonella Andretti. And once he made those vows, he'd be setting aside any grievances, any claims to justice.

He found Livio smoking on the back terrace and reading the newspaper. "May I have a word?" Enrico asked.

"Of course." Livio folded the paper and set it on the table. Then he took a drag on his cigarette.

"I need your help," Enrico said. Livio grunted and motioned for Enrico to go on. "I need the names of the men who killed my family."

At this, Livio fixed him with a stare and took another drag on the cigarette, holding it between his thumb and first two fingers. He let the smoke out slowly and squinted at Enrico through the cloud, his silver-gray eyes betraying nothing. "You mean to defy your father."

"I mean to right a wrong."

"You'll get yourself killed." Livio drew hard on his cigarette, then tapped the ashes on the flagstones. "Your father would never forgive me if I helped you."

"And I will never forgive myself if I do nothing."

"Do you know how I came to work for your father?" When Enrico shook his head, Livio continued. "The Velas have never been rich. But we have always had beautiful women in our family. So beautiful, that one of them was stolen. Carlotta Vela, my great aunt. She was stolen and raped and beaten savagely by a member of the d'Angelo family. My great-grandfather, my grandfather, and my father all lost their lives in the feud that erupted over this heinous act. Generation after generation of Velas and d'Angelos punishing each other. And I did my part." He took another drag, then crushed out the cigarette. "I killed my first man when I was sixteen, and I did it with my bare hands. He was a d'Angelo, a boy like me, yet he dared remark on how he'd love to fuck my sister."

Livio laid his hands on the table, spreading out his fingers. "You see these scars?" He motioned to his marred and distorted knuckles. "I beat that boy's face until it was nothing but pulp and bone. Because I did it in front of witnesses, the *carabinieri* arrested me." Livio looked down at his hands and flexed them. "Your father made the charges go away. He was my friend then, and he is my *capo* now. You're asking me to break my word."

Enrico sat back. "I'm sorry. I didn't know who else to ask."

Livio said nothing for a moment. He just looked out at the lake glittering in the sunlight. "The names you want are these: Leone Valentino, Guido Ripoli, Cristiano Borelli, and Luigi Gennaro."

"But I thought—"

"I don't regret what I did. Maybe that boy didn't deserve to die. Maybe he did. Maybe he would have attacked my sister. Or some other woman. Who knows? What I do know is he had no respect. No honor. And neither does Carlo Andretti. Killing women and children is forbidden. He disgusts me."

"*Grazie. Mille grazie.*"

"You can thank me by not getting yourself killed."

Enrico's heart was beating fast. "Any advice on how not to do that?"

"Surprise is your best asset in any fight. Learn the men's routines, learn when they are least alert. And be ready to act. Zero hesitation."

"I will." *I hope.*

Enrico's gut tightened. Was he really going to do this?

With a sharp rap of his knuckles on the table, Livio rose and wished him luck. "*In bocca al lupo.*" *In the mouth of the wolf.*

Enrico gave the traditional response. "*Crepi il lupo.*" *May the wolf die.*

———— ♦ ————

Antonella picked up the phone twice before finally placing the call, her heart skipping like a stone across a pond. Enrico had said yesterday that he wanted a second chance. Would he prove her a fool for giving him one?

The phone rang several times before someone answered. One of the maids. Yes, Enrico was home, please wait.

She wiped a sweaty hand on her skirt. This was stupid. Why open herself up to more ridicule? *But if you're going to marry him, you should know him first.*

A rustling came on the line, then Enrico's rich deep voice. He spoke with the beautiful cadences of the north, his diction perfect, less slangy than her father's own frequent lapses into Calabrian. When she identified herself, he said, "So you *did* forgive me." A smile filled his voice.

"I said it, yes?" Her tone was a little sharper than she'd intended. "Sorry. I didn't mean it like that."

He chuckled. "I'm supposed to be apologizing to you, remember?"

She relaxed. He was right. "So, how are you going to do that?" she asked, injecting a teasing lilt into her words.

"There's a beautiful café in Bellagio. Splendore. Have you been?"

"No." Her heart started acting up again, and her stomach joined in.

"Great. Let's take the boat. I'll pull up at your dock in an hour."

"I can't wait." And she meant it. She'd always dreamed of such a day with him. The boy she'd longed for by her side, the wind whipping in their faces as they sped across the lake. It was a dream come true.

Except that her father might ruin everything. She hadn't liked his lack of hesitation when she'd asked him what he'd do if she didn't marry Enrico.

This had better work. Enrico had better be able to see who she was; he'd better be able to see the inner beauty rather than the exterior.

If he didn't, he'd be in trouble. Except this time, she might not be able to save him and his father.

———— ◆ ————

Antonella tore through every outfit in her closet at least three times. None of them would fix her nose. She finally settled on a dark blue sun dress with white sandals. She knotted a white silk scarf at her throat. Maybe it would draw his eyes away from her hideous beak.

At least she could be proud of her hair. It was a glossy, wavy, blue-black, thick and tumbling to mid-back. She'd never suffered a moment's insecurity over it. Grabbing a hair elastic, she pulled it up into a loose chignon at the nape of her neck to keep it from blowing all over while they were on the boat.

Heart in her throat, she raced down the central staircase and hurried toward the rear terrace. "Toni, where are you going?" her father called from the end of the hall.

She stopped guiltily. Should she tell him? What if he said no? "I'm meeting Ilaria."

"You're awfully dressed up."

"We're going to Bellagio."

He came toward her, one hand in his pocket, the other holding his ever-present cigar. He stopped a couple feet from her and scanned her head to toe, his gaze coming to rest on her face. Could he see that she was lying?

"Where in Bellagio?"

"Just shopping. I'm not sure." She glanced at her watch. Enrico would be down at the dock any minute. If she wasn't on time, how long would he wait?

Her father pulled out his wallet and peeled off a stack of *lire* and handed it to her. "Get yourself something nice."

Clutching the money in her hand, she beamed at him and rose up on tiptoe to kiss his cheek.

"Stay out of trouble," he added, his eyes twinkling as he smiled at her.

"Always," she promised with a pang. They were just going to lunch. And Enrico was her fiancé. Technically. He hadn't given her the ring yet, but he would. Wouldn't he?

She hurried along the path through the garden and down to their dock, which was hidden by a copse of trees. When she heard the purr of a boat's motor, her pulse sped up. She quickened her pace, then stopped short just before she came into view. Taking a deep breath, she forced herself to wait a moment. Papà's words echoed in her ears: *Like Cleopatra, you were born to lead armies and rule men.* Would Cleopatra race like a puppy to greet a man? No, she wouldn't. She'd make him wait, and when he saw her, she'd be as unruffled as the Sphinx.

She heard a bump as the boat pulled up at dockside. That was her cue. Taking another breath, she stepped out onto the dock, her sandals thudding on the boards.

Enrico leapt over the side of the boat. He was wearing a beautiful tan suede jacket, cream-colored trousers, and a white Oxford shirt unbuttoned at the neck. His tanned skin and black hair stood out in sharp contrast to his clothes, and when he looked at her and grinned, a thrill coursed through her. "You look lovely," he said as he looped a rope around a post, pulling the boat up tight.

"*Grazie.*" She deliberately kept her pace slow, casual, even though she was so excited she felt like her heart would burst through her chest.

He extended a hand toward her and she took it, for some reason surprised when he started helping her into the boat. Had she really expected him to kiss her hand?

Masking her disappointment, she clambered into the boat, never an easy task in a dress. Her foot slipped on the wet gunwale, and he grabbed her awkwardly by the upper thigh to steady her.

"Careful," he murmured. "Your father would never forgive me if I brought you back in less than one piece."

True. "He doesn't know I'm with you."

His hand tightened on her thigh. "He doesn't?"

"Don't worry."

Once she was safely in the boat, Enrico cast off and swung himself up over the side, landing beside her with a gentle thump, like a cat. A very tall, very handsome cat. He regarded her solemnly. "I'd rather he knew."

"I'm not a child who needs looking after."

"That's not what I meant," Enrico said. He turned away then and busied himself with idling the boat away from the dock. Once they were clear, he patted the seat beside him up front, behind the windscreen. The motorboat was a sleek Riva Aquarama, its mahogany hull polished to perfection, with plush white leather seating in front and along the sides.

She looked around, a little stunned. Her father had a fine motorboat as well, but it wasn't a super-expensive Riva. How could the Lucchesis afford such an extravagance?

"Hang on," he said, motioning to the railing beside her. They took off with a spray of spume.

Wind whipped at her face and she inhaled deeply, her eyes scanning the dark green hillsides and the midnight blue waves of the lake. Was there ever a more enchanting place than Lake Como?

Though the sun was shining fiercely overhead, the wind chilled her bare arms, and she mentally berated herself for forgetting a sweater. When she rubbed at them, Enrico glanced over. "Cold?" he asked, shouting above the roar of the motor.

She nodded, and he cut the motor back to idle while he shrugged out of his jacket and handed it to her. She wished he'd have helped her put it on, or at least have draped the coat over her shoulders himself, but it was still a gallant gesture.

Gallant, but merely friendly. Not at all romantic.

Was this how it would be between them? Civil, polite, but nothing more? On his part, at least.

He started up the boat again and steered them toward Bellagio, at the lake's northern end. She tamped down her worries. What did she expect? They barely knew each other. And there was the little matter of what Papà had done to Enrico's family.

She must never forget that.

The rest of their trip passed without comment, but she continued to feel a slight unease. Would Enrico ever *see* her, truly see her? Or would he always think of her as an Andretti?

Her pulse quickened when the Grand Hotel Villa Serbelloni, so iconic a landmark of Bellagio, drew near. Then she reminded herself. Cleopatra. While he helped her out of the boat, she did not dwell on the feel of his large hand wrapped around hers, his other hand at her waist to steady her as she stepped out. No, she did not dwell on it. The moment she had both feet on the dock, he released her hand and turned away, starting toward their destination, not waiting to see if she followed, not taking her hand.

Not treating her as the slightest bit special.

A lump rose in her throat, but she swallowed to disperse it. Cleopatra wouldn't allow a man to affect her this way.

She hurried after him, then forced herself to slow. How long would it take for him to notice that she wasn't at his side?

A few moments later, he stopped and looked back for her, waiting until she caught up. It took everything she had to maintain her unhurried pace.

When she reached him, he gave her a sheepish grin. "Sorry," he offered, but she said nothing. Didn't even give him a smile. Cleopatra wasn't pleased.

He tried to take her elbow, and though she stiffened, she didn't withdraw it. Inwardly, she smiled. So he responded to the silent treatment. Good to know.

When they reached Splendore, he was a perfect gentleman, helping her out of the jacket, pulling out her chair, making sure she was comfortable, and meeting her eyes and smiling, as if they were truly on a date.

The staff greeted Enrico like he was an old friend, chiding him for being away so long. So he'd been there before many times. When the waiter joshed him about his latest date, she realized that he'd brought girls there before. He must have, back in the days before he'd gone to England.

Whatever appetite she'd had was gone. He was humoring her, that's all. He hadn't selected a special place.

Oh, Splendore was romantic and had a lovely view. But it wasn't a place he hadn't been a million times before. He hadn't chosen it for *her*.

"What has you frowning?" he asked, as he perused the menu.

She slapped hers shut and set it on the table. "How many girls have you brought here?" *Whoa. Not Cleopatra in the slightest!*

"A few. It's a nice place."

"I thought you were trying to apologize."

He gave her his full attention then. "I was."

"You didn't put a second's thought into this."

"Antonella, I'm not sure what you expect from me."

"If I have to spell it out—"

"You do."

That caught her by surprise. "What?"

"I'm obviously failing to meet your expectations. I'd like to know what they are."

She lowered her voice. "I'm your fiancée. You ought to be reminding me of that."

He let out a breath, but clenched his menu, bending the edges of it. "Not by my choice," he said through gritted teeth.

It was the truth, yet still the words hit her like a blow. "Then why are we here?"

"Because I'm not a jerk. I hurt you, and I wanted to apologize."

"You're doing a horrible job," she said, her voice warbling. *Damn it.* She didn't want him to hear that.

He set his menu on the table. "You expect me to forget everything that's happened? Everything I've lost?" Now his voice was the one warped with emotion. "I'm not some unfeeling robot."

"And I'm not just Carlo Andretti's daughter. But that's all I'll ever be to you, yes?"

"What do you expect?" he asked, his voice soft. "What do you expect of me?"

She almost said nothing, almost demanded he take her home. But the look in his dark brown eyes—the ache she saw reflected there—made her pause. She let out a sigh. "I am not my last name."

He nodded and took her hand, squeezing it lightly. "You are right. *You* have never hurt me. But I have hurt you. Twice now." He gave her a wry smile. "Give me a third chance?"

She returned his smile. "This *is* your last one. I mean it."

"I won't need another," he said and pressed a kiss to her knuckles, the brush of his lips making her belly flutter.

———◆———

Judging by the smile on Antonella's face, kissing her hand had worked. Enrico turned back to the menu. What if she *was* right? Was Toni truly more than her last name?

She hadn't been the one to order their deaths. She hadn't been involved at all. But if she'd been telling the truth, she had lobbied for their marriage. Which made her the one keeping him away from Veronica and Nico.

He'd called Veronica that morning from a pay phone in Cernobbio. She'd been glad to hear from him, but had soon dissolved into tears when he'd told her he wouldn't be coming back, at least not for a month, maybe more. Nico had been crying in the background, and the urge to hold his son, to fly to him that minute, had been so hard to resist he'd punched the frame of the telephone booth. He couldn't go to them, not now, not until Carlo Andretti was dead, if he ever was. He couldn't risk his son, not after losing so much.

But this separation—it was hell. Flat-out hell.

He reminded himself to smile at Antonella and fingered the wallet in his pocket, picturing the photo of Veronica and Nico inside. He ought to hide it. It was too dangerous to carry around with him, especially now, when he was forcing himself to court Antonella Andretti. Whatever he might think of her looks—and she did look quite lovely today—she was a very smart and perceptive girl. He'd been underestimating her, hoping that a dose or two of the Lucchesi charm would keep her snowed.

But he'd hardly managed a lick of charm, had he? He'd make a lousy actor. He led with his heart, always.

And that was not what he needed to do right now. He had to muster up another persona, one who could embrace the Andrettis until he could stab them in the back.

Antonella didn't deserve what was coming, no more than her brother had deserved to lose a finger. But then again, Enrico hadn't deserved to lose his mother and his two brothers either. The only one who was going to get what he deserved—a bullet—was Carlo Andretti, and that was all that mattered.

That and making sure Nico was safe.

"What's good here?" Antonella asked, shaking him out of his thoughts.

"I've always enjoyed the linguine with clams. The black truffle risotto is excellent as well."

She ordered an antipasto plate to start, then the risotto. After he ordered the linguine, he cast about for some subject of conversation that wouldn't get him into trouble. He came up blank.

Fortunately, she saved him. "What's England like?"

"Very, very green. And wet."

"Did you enjoy it?"

He nodded. "The food is mostly terrible, but the people are friendly and the countryside is beautiful." He glanced outside. "Almost as nice as here."

"Do you miss it?"

Best not answer truthfully. "My heart belongs here."

"And the girls? What did you think of them?"

His stomach tightened. Why was she asking him about that? "They're very pale."

"That's all?"

"If you're asking something, say so." Not exactly laying on the charm, was he?

"Did you date any?" she asked, fiddling with her place setting.

"I was engaged before I left. Remember?" He tacked on a grin, hoping to hide his anger.

"I was just checking whether *you'd* remembered."

"And if I hadn't?" he asked as casually as he could muster.

"I'd forgive you. Of course."

"Of course." *Tell me another one.*

"I'm serious."

"I doubt you've ever forgiven anything anyone's ever done to you," he said, and she colored. He'd hit a nerve.

"Let's talk about something else."

He took a sip of his cappuccino. "What, then?"

"Are you planning to attend university?"

As soon as I kill your father. "Yes. Economics and finance."

"Interesting."

"And you?"

"That's up to you, isn't it?" she asked.

Anxiety made his stomach churn. He'd forgotten the archaic ways of the 'Ndrangheta. England had made him forget many things he'd rather not think about. Like all the responsibilities he'd someday have as *capo.* "I have no objection if you wish to attend."

"Most men in the business don't want their wives to be any smarter than they are."

He grinned at the saucy way she said it, and when she waggled her black brows at him, he burst into laughter. "My ego isn't so weak."

"The Lucchesis are known for their arrogance."

He bit back what he wanted to say. *And the Andrettis are known for their greed.* "With good reason." He somehow managed to wink.

It was her turn to laugh. "You're right; your ego definitely isn't suffering. You think you can charm me with this?"

"I already am," he said, then kissed her hand again.

She truly was pretty when she smiled. And her nose wasn't so bad. Maybe someday she could get it fixed—

Where had *that* come from? He didn't care about her nose or how pretty she was. Antonella was irrelevant. They'd never be married. All he had to do was string her along and make her think they were. To make her father think so.

"You *are* full of yourself," she said, but she was still amused.

Maybe later he should kiss her. Yes, he should. It would throw her off. But he had to make it believable.

And he knew just the perfect place.

CHAPTER 3

After making a brief phone call from the restaurant to confirm that they'd be welcome, Enrico escorted Antonella back to the boat, careful this time to treat her like a date.

He found it surprisingly easy, once he stopped thinking of her as an Andretti. She was just Antonella, a witty, intelligent girl who was alternately warm and wary. Just as he was.

The trip to Villa del Balbianello didn't take long from Bellagio. As they motored toward the magnificent villa with the terraced gardens—truly the crown jewel of the lake—Antonella sighed. "What I wouldn't give to live there," she said, raising her voice over the engine.

He cut the motor back and idled up to the stone stairway that served as a dock. "Well, we can't live here, but we can visit."

Her eyes widened. "You know the owner?"

Enrico shrugged. "I've met him. My father knows him."

"And he's letting us visit?"

He chuckled. "He's away, off on another expedition. I think the staff are bored. The caretaker said it would be no problem."

She gave him a sidelong glance. "You *do* know how to charm a girl, Enrico Lucchesi."

"I swear to you, I've never taken a girl here. This is only my second visit," he said as he helped her out of the boat.

The stairway passed under a high stone arch and then proceeded up the rocky promontory the villa perched upon. After a short climb, they reached the first level of terraced gardens and were met there by a gray-haired man with a cigarette stuck in the corner of his mouth. "Signor Lucchesi," the man said, sticking out his hand.

Enrico took it, then made the introductions. "This is Antonella Andretti. Antonella, this is Alberto Sporelli, the caretaker."

"*Mille grazie*," she said. "I've always wanted to see these gardens."

Sporelli gestured around them. "Feel free to roam wherever you please. When you're finished, come up to the house for a drink."

"You are very kind, *signore*," Antonella said. She lightly squeezed Enrico's hand, communicating her excitement.

Following the winding footpath, their shoes crunching on pea gravel the color of ripe wheat, they soon left Signor Sporelli behind. The grounds were immaculate, every tree, every bush, every blade of grass groomed and in its place. The whole effect almost put the lovely gardens of the Lucchesi villa to shame.

The path traveled along the perimeter of the rocky outcropping, giving them breathtaking vistas of the lake as they passed beneath old shade trees and strolled by weathered statues artfully placed at intervals. Antonella stopped to admire some beautiful pink flowers on a low shrub, and on impulse, Enrico plucked one off for her.

"You shouldn't!"

"No one will notice." He held it out to her, the intricate ruffles of the petals catching the light.

"I don't want them to get angry with us," she said as she took the flower. She held it up to her nose and inhaled with her eyes closed, a smile blooming across her face.

"Don't worry. What are they going to do?"

She opened her eyes and raised them to his, fixing him with a somber look. "Just because we are who we are, that doesn't mean we should throw our weight about."

Heat rushed to his face. "I never expected to hear that sentiment from an Andretti."

"Intimidating people doesn't make you more powerful. Just more despised." She twirled the flower in her fingers. "My father thinks fear is stronger than respect. But he's wrong."

If someone had told Enrico he'd ever hear such words from a member of the Andretti family, he'd have laughed. "You're serious."

Her gaze turned icy. "I'm not an animal." She tossed the bloom to the ground and stomped off, leaving him gaping like a fish. So much for his resolution to forget who she was. He hurried after her and caught her by the arm.

"Antonella, *mi dispiace*. Truly."

She looked down at his hand on her bicep. "I'm surprised you can even bring yourself to touch me. Haven't you heard? I have Andretti disease. It's incurable."

Her dryness only highlighted the absurdity of their situation, and a laugh boiled up in his chest, a laugh he couldn't suppress. She watched him for a moment, her arms crossed, her gaze cautious, until he got hold of himself. "I *am* sorry, Antonella."

Her lips parted, but she said nothing for a moment. Then her mouth curved into a slow smile that lit up his chest with warmth. "Call me Toni when you apologize."

"Only if you'll call me Rico when you chastise me."

They stared at each other a few moments more, then she flashed him a devilish grin and pointed to where the walkway terminated in a terrace shaded by trees. "I bet I can beat you there," she said, her tone light and teasing.

So she wanted to challenge him? Fine. "I'll even give you a head start."

"You shouldn't." Her grin widened. "And I don't want one."

He pointed to her sandals. "Those aren't good for running."

"Doesn't matter." She crouched down, readying herself.

Amused by her confidence, he shook his head. She was going to get beaten—badly. But it was her choice.

"Go!" she called, then started off, fast as the flicker of a bird's wing, her lithe form moving with a grace and ease he hadn't seen before. He'd been so focused on who she was related to he'd hardly taken notice of Toni. The *real* Toni. The girl behind the name.

He loped after her, having to put some effort into it. Toni was a tall girl, and she ran with all the economy of a long-distance runner—bounding lightly on the balls of her feet, her strides long and elegant. He wanted to just stop and watch. He wanted to catch her. He wanted to—

Kiss her? That *had* been the goal, yes? But that had been to fool her. Now it seemed he'd somehow come to actually want it.

The gap between them lengthened. She was going to beat him. But he didn't care. He was enjoying the swing of her tanned limbs, the luscious sight of her curved hips and ass bouncing beneath the blue fabric of her dress. Her black hair gleamed in the sun, and he wanted to see it down, flowing around her shoulders.

Toni reached the terrace before he did and plopped herself onto a bench in the shade below a large tree. She grinned up at him in triumph. "Told you I'd beat you," she said when he arrived.

He leaned over her and gripped the lacy metalwork that supported her back, caging her in while he caught his breath. "You were distracting me."

"How?"

"I couldn't take my eyes off you," he murmured. Leaning closer, he made his request. "Let down your hair," he whispered in her ear, letting his breath wash over her skin, making her shiver.

She hesitated, then reached up to the base of her neck and loosened the tie holding everything in place, lightly shaking her head to let the thick waves fall free. When they tumbled around her shoulders, he smiled. This close, he could see every lash that fringed her large liquid eyes, eyes that looked away from his with sudden shyness. He gently took hold of her chin and made her look at him.

He studied her face, every bit of it—the flawless olive skin, the high cheekbones, the lush tremble of her lips, the long slope of her nose, the slight bump in it—and he realized something. Antonella Andretti was beautiful. Not in some fairy-tale princess way. But in a real way. Although her cheeks grew pink under his scrutiny, she didn't break eye contact this time.

The molecules of air between them seemed to thicken, time slowed down, his heart ceased to beat. All he wanted in that moment was to kiss her. He started to close the distance, mere centimeters between them—

She slid out from under his left arm and dashed out of reach. "Catch me if you can, Enrico Lucchesi!"

This time she took off across the grass, heading uphill toward the house and a loggia with three vine-covered arches.

Had she known what he'd been about to do? Did she not want to kiss him? Or was she just making him work for it?

He scrambled up the slope behind her, the tinkling music of her laughter causing a grin to spread across his face. She reached the loggia first and pretended to hide behind one of the columns. He let her circle away from him, but when she tried to break away again, he caught her around the waist and swung her up in the air. "Put me down!" she demanded through her laughter.

He set her back on her feet and pushed her up against a column, using his body to pin her in place. Both of them were breathing fast, and this time he didn't hesitate. Framing her face in his hands, he touched his lips to hers, making the kiss a mere ghost of a touch. She trembled against him and let out a soft sound he couldn't interpret. Pulling back, he saw the glisten of tears in her eyes, and his belly clenched. "What's wrong?"

She closed her hands over his, where they cradled her cheeks. "You don't have to," she whispered, her voice breaking.

"I want to." And he did.

"I don't believe you." She looked at the stones beneath their feet as she spoke.

He shifted his weight, pressing his hard *cazzo* against her belly. "Feel that?" he murmured.

Her eyes flew back to his, but she said nothing. Letting go of one cheek, he took her hand and brought it between them, grazing her shaking fingers over the bulge in his trousers. "Do you doubt me now?" he asked.

She stiffened, but her hand tentatively stroked him, and his *cazzo* twitched beneath her fingers, making him take in a sharp breath and her jerk away as if she'd touched a hot kettle. He stepped back from her. *Madonna*. What was he thinking? She was a virgin, and here he was, treating her like some *troia*.

"I'm sorry," he said. "I forgot myself." He started to turn away, but stopped when she placed a hand on his shoulder.

"You just startled me, that's all," she said, her voice low and filled with a heat he couldn't mistake.

Before either of them could say anything more, a small boy came barreling out of the house and tripped as he entered the loggia, falling and skinning his knee. He let out a wail, and Antonella was by the boy's side in an instant, wrapping an arm around him and shushing him. "It's okay," she said, her voice calm and reassuring. "Just a scrape." She turned to Enrico. "Do you have a handkerchief?"

He pulled one out of the inner pocket of his jacket, feeling the raised embroidery of the dark blue monogram of his initials. His mother had done the needlework herself. With a pang, he handed the handkerchief to Antonella, and she folded it into a smaller square and pressed the cloth to the boy's wound.

"*Nonno!*" the boy called, and soon Signor Sporelli appeared in the doorway.

"What's happened?" he asked.

"Someone took a fall," Antonella answered.

Sporelli's look of concern eased. "Taddeo never listens. Does he?" the man added, his voice deepening with meaning as he gazed fondly at his grandson.

"*Nonno, mi dispiace,*" Taddeo mumbled.

"It's all right," Signor Sporelli said and held out his hand to the boy, who left Antonella's embrace with some reluctance. She'd held him for what—a minute, perhaps?—and already he was attached to her.

But Enrico understood the feeling. He understood it all too well.

Antonella Andretti had a way of getting under someone's skin. Somehow she'd slipped past his defenses. Defenses she'd rendered worthless.

———————◆———————

As Signor Sporelli led his grandson inside the house, Enrico offered Antonella a hand up. She rose from the stone floor of the loggia and dusted off her dress, then turned her back to Enrico. "Do I look all right?"

His hand brushed along her hip, leaving tingles in its wake. "You look lovely."

The deepened tones of his voice, the slow, appreciative way he delivered the compliment, started her heart pounding, made her breath catch in her throat. Could he possibly mean what he was saying? Well, he *had* kissed her, and then when he'd taken her hand and placed it on his...

She could hardly believe any of it had happened. But it had. That kiss, so soft, so gentle, so delicious. And then that hardness—*she'd* caused that. *She* had.

It was enough to make her head spin.

Enrico's fingers closed around hers and he tugged her to him. "I'm sorry we were interrupted," he said, a smile curving his mouth.

The fluttering in her chest intensified. Was he going to kiss her again? She'd dreamed of this moment for so long, she felt almost sick with anticipation—and fear. What if she disappointed him? What if he laughed at her?

What if... he was toying with her?

She searched his face, trying to read his intentions. His chocolate brown eyes twinkling, he bent down until his lips hovered over hers. "I promise to be a gentleman," he said before kissing her again, more firmly this time, his lips coaxing a soft sound out of her as an indescribable pleasure swept through her body.

Every place they touched, every bit of skin, lit up as if it were giving off sparks. He slid a hand up to cup the base of her skull, and the other pressed against her lower back, urging her against him once more. But it was his mouth—his wonderful, sinful mouth—that truly undid Antonella. His lips parted, moving against hers in a slow feathering caress that she mimicked, pleased to hear him groan low in his throat and clutch her more fiercely.

His mouth opened wider and his tongue traveled across the seam of her lips. Did he want her to...? He did it again, and she opened up for him, shocked and amazed when his tongue swept inside her mouth, finding hers and stroking it. She'd never have guessed she'd enjoy such a thing, but now she understood why the girls in her class had giggled about it.

She clutched at his broad shoulders, her knees feeling suddenly weak. How had he reduced her to a quivering mass so quickly? She was nothing but raw emotion, raw reaction. It was all so overwhelming, she needed to sit down. She broke the kiss, and his eyes opened. He looked as stunned as she felt. "Are you okay?" he asked.

He hadn't let go of her, and she was grateful for it. "It's just so... *much*," she finally whispered. *Dio*, she must sound like an idiot! Heat raced over her neck and face, making her ears burn.

He chuckled, but he still held her. "I'd forgotten."

"What?"

"My first kiss. It shocked the hell out of me."

Jealousy swamped her. Someone else had kissed *her* Rico. She straightened and held his gaze. "I'm not shocked."

"Surprised, at least?"

"A little," she allowed.

"Want to do it again?" he asked with a wicked grin.

Did she ever. But... "How many girls have you kissed?"

He shrugged, and a shadow flickered across his features. "My share."

"Avoiding the question."

"Toni, a gentleman doesn't discuss other women while he's holding one."

His tone was so arch, he made her laugh, and then his archness dissolved into a laughter that matched hers. He let go, then spun her around as if they were dancing, catching her around the waist and dipping her before hauling her back to her feet.

Someone coughed behind them. Signor Sporelli stood in the doorway to the house, a bandaged Taddeo in tow. "Ready for that drink?" he asked, a broad grin on his face.

Had he seen them kissing? She blushed and nodded, surprised when Rico kept hold of her hand. They followed the caretaker inside and into a light, airy room filled with books, where a tray of meats, cheeses, and olives nestled beside a bottle of white wine and a carafe of mineral water.

Signor Sporelli poured them glasses as they helped themselves to the refreshments, then he raised his glass in a toast, Taddeo aping him with a glass of water. "To young love," Sporelli said, his gaze resting on Toni. Her cheeks flamed again, and Rico laughed.

He put an arm around her as they touched glasses. "*Salute*," he said, seemingly to her alone.

"So you are back from school," Sporelli said to Enrico.

Rico nodded. "Yes. My English is much improved, so now it's time I came back to finish my studies."

Sporelli sipped at his wine, his eyes assessing the two of them. "I'd heard there was bad blood between your families. I'm surprised to see you together."

Antonella looked at Rico, not sure what to say. How much did this man know about who they were?

Enrico nodded. "There was. But now Toni and I are to be married."

Sporelli raised a brow, his eyes searching Antonella's hands. "No ring?"

Enrico set his glass down. "I plan to give it at the formal engagement party in two weeks."

"Ah." Sporelli nodded. "*Bene*. I would not want Carlo Andretti upset with me for letting you run about unsupervised."

Toni watched Rico closely, but other than a tightening of his jaw, he hid his reaction. "Signor Andretti is well aware that we are together."

Guilt stabbed at her. Enrico had been right. She should have told Papà. If word got back to him that she'd been with Enrico, that they'd been fooling around— "My father doesn't need to know *everything*," she said. "Yes?"

Sporelli laughed. "I suppose not." He shook a finger at Enrico. "I was your age once. Behave yourself. *Capisci?*"

With a low chuckle, Enrico relaxed. "*Capisco.*"

But *she* couldn't relax. Somehow she'd managed to forget the gulf between her and Enrico, the secret shame she carried. Should she tell him about her involvement in the deaths of his family?

Part of her desperately wanted to confess. But if she did, the results could only be catastrophic. Rico might reject her. Her father's strategic advantage would be lost, and *he'd* be infuriated with her too. People would die, not the least of them being Enrico.

It was best to remain quiet. For now. Perhaps someday, after the wedding… but would Enrico take the news any better then?

Her stomach knotted up, and she twisted her hands together in her lap. "Are you all right?" Enrico asked, leaning closer, his deep voice a rich rumble in her ear.

"Everything's fine," she said. "But I'd promised to meet up with Ilaria at four, and I just noticed that it's a little past three."

"We must be going then," Enrico said. He turned to Signor Sporelli. "*Mille grazie* for your generous hospitality."

"Any time," Sporelli said. "Tell your father to stop by. We haven't seen him in a while."

"I will," Enrico promised, and they said their goodbyes, Taddeo's a little downcast when he realized they were leaving.

"But you just got here!" he protested, stamping his foot.

"We'll be back," Enrico assured him. "And I'll bring Toni."

Taddeo crossed his arms, his little face screwed up into a suspicious squint. "You'd better."

Enrico ruffled the boy's brown curls. "Try to be more careful, yes?"

They descended hand in hand to the boat, but Enrico had gone quiet. "I don't think Signor Sporelli will say anything to Papà," she said.

"Probably not." He handed her into the boat, then cast off and swung himself up over the railing again with that grace she so admired. "You might want to tie your hair back," he said as he started up the motor.

He was saying all the right things, he was being polite, he was even taking off his jacket and patiently holding it as she worked on her hair. But he wasn't looking at her, and there was a crispness, a clipped quality to his speech, that made her gut tense up.

When she finished with her hair, he helped her into the coat. "Rico, I'll tell him," she said.

Finally he looked at her. "I don't think he'll be happy hearing about it after the fact." He turned his focus back to steering the boat away from the dock and turning them south.

She wanted to comfort him, but he was right, and the roar of the engine effectively cut off any attempt she might have made to reassure him.

They'd had a lovely afternoon, and she'd gotten what she'd wanted. Hadn't she?

But what about Enrico? What did he want? And was he getting any closer to being happy about this marriage?

The grim set of his jaw, the knitting of his brow, and the stiff way he held his shoulders all said no.

———— ◆ ————

Enrico jerked the boat away from the shoreline below the Villa del Balbianello and headed it toward the Andretti estate in Blevio. Antonella perched on the seat beside him, her anxiety palpable. He wanted to say something, to calm her, but the discussion with Sporelli had carried too many reminders of everything that was wrong with this situation.

He was trapped—marrying a girl he liked, but didn't love, marrying into a family he despised, taking on a role he'd never wanted and never prepared for, and worst of all, giving up his son—and all because of Carlo Andretti.

Bracing his feet, Enrico mashed the throttle down mercilessly, the boat's motor kicking up spray behind them like a frightened horse. He wanted to punch something so badly that a bitter taste filled his mouth. The images of his mother and his brothers bleeding in the street filled his vision. They were never going to get their justice, unless he came up with a damn good plan.

Antonella's delicate hand touched his jaw, her fingers smoothing along the muscles that jumped there. He cut the boat back to idle and rounded on her. "You think you can pet me like one of your father's damn dogs and make everything okay?" he shouted.

When she shrank from him, he instantly regretted his behavior. Then she straightened and crossed her arms. "That's not what I was doing."

He inhaled deeply and let it out. "What, then?"

"I'm here for you."

He placed his hands on his hips and looked at the decking lightly rocking beneath his feet, unable to suppress a snort of disbelief. "You know what I was just thinking about?"

"No."

He met her eyes. "I was thinking about the crime-scene photos. What they looked like, dead and bleeding in the street."

She blanched, not needing him to clarify. "How did you ever see those?"

"My father paid someone in the *carabinieri* to make copies."

"Why?"

Emotion clamped his throat shut, and he struggled to say the words. "He said it was so we wouldn't forget."

"Rico, he shouldn't have shown you those."

He pinned her with a stare. "You think I'm a child?"

She shook her head. "No one should see that."

"*No one* should have *done* that." His tone dripped acid.

29

"Rico—"

He held up a hand. "I don't want to hear it."

"Let me finish," she said. "You're right. My father did something unforgivable."

"He broke our laws. Mario was eleven. *Eleven.*" Enrico clawed at his hair and turned away from her, his hands trying to crush the railing. "He was my brother. It was his birthday. If only Papà and I hadn't been sick—"

"You'd have died too," she said.

"We might have saved them."

She embraced him from behind, her small hands resting flat on his belly, her breasts pressing into his back, and damn him, he wanted to turn and kiss her. He wanted to forget again, he wanted to forget everything. "I am sorry from the bottom of my heart," she whispered, her voice choked.

He folded his hands over hers. "I know it's not your fault, Toni. But how can I marry you? How can I bow to your father?"

"You must, Rico. You *must*. Or your family will be destroyed." Her tone was fervent, and a tingle of alarm raced down his back.

He turned around in her arms. "What do you mean, destroyed?"

"I asked Papà what would happen if I broke the engagement. He said he would finish what he started."

How calmly she said those words. Enrico wanted to roar at her. "So that's why you're giving me another chance? Because you're so sure your father will win?"

She didn't blink. "I know he will. The war between our families was costly, but two years have passed. My father hasn't been idle. He has a plan in place. The thing that scares me is that I don't know what it is."

"Why would he tell you?"

She frowned at him. "I told you. He listens to me. He's often said I could be a *capa*."

Enrico blew out in amusement. "Toni, you're smart, I know that. But you know how the 'Ndrangheta is—"

"Yes. Which is why I told Papà he's being sentimental. The best place for me is at the side of a powerful man." When he said nothing, she continued. "All of the influence, without the target on my back."

This time he chuckled. "You expect me to consult you?"

She raised a brow. "You'd be a fool not to. I bet I know a lot more about this business than you do."

"Prove it."

"Your father is nearly bankrupt. If it wasn't for my grandfather, he would be."

What the hell was she talking about? "My father has plenty of money. And what would your grandfather have to do with anything?"

She crossed her arms again, her eyes boring into his. "You had best ask your father. You need this marriage, Rico, more than you know."

He wanted to say she was crazy, he wanted to ignore her. But Antonella wasn't prone to exaggeration or false alarms. In that way, she was the polar opposite of Veronica. Toni's words held a ring of confidence, of truth, he couldn't easily dismiss.

And if the roiling in his gut was any indication, she'd just given him a clue to his father's strange behavior.

30

CHAPTER 4

How did Antonella know about the state of his family's finances?

After dropping her off, Enrico cut across the lake to Cernobbio. But instead of going directly home, he went to see his cousin Domenico. Papà was unlikely to tell him the truth unless he had more proof than the say-so of Antonella Andretti.

Perhaps Dom could shed some light. And help Enrico devise a plan to take out his family's killers. Livio had made clear he wasn't going to provide any additional assistance beyond those four names. If what Antonella had said was true, Enrico was his family's only hope for justice, but he had scant time to achieve it.

Leopoldo Lucchesi, Enrico's uncle and Dom's father, had set up his family in a lovely, yet far more modest, villa close to his brother Rinaldo's. Although Leopoldo was the eldest, a heart defect, discovered in his youth, had made him reluctant to take the reins of the Lucchesi *cosca*, and so the title of *capo di famiglia* had fallen to Rinaldo, while Leopoldo acted as his brother's *capo di società*—his right-hand.

Now that Mamma, Primo, and Mario were dead, these Lucchesis were nearly all the relatives Enrico had left. They'd always been a tight-knit group, but Rinaldo's breakdown after the murders had strained the relationship. *No one likes to be around the ill*, Enrico thought. *It might be catching.*

He tied up at the dock and headed toward the house. As he approached the rear entrance, he heard the murmur of voices, but couldn't see the speakers through the trees and shrubs of the garden. He recognized the voices though: Dom and his wife, Francesca.

"How about we get started on baby number two?" Dom said, his tone teasing.

Francesca laughed. "We have to wait for number one first."

"We can practice..."

Enrico coughed loudly as he rounded a hedge and saw Dom kissing his pretty wife. Even though her belly was swollen with pregnancy, she still looked elegant, her light brown hair pulled back off her face, a loose dress showing off the tanned skin of her arms and shoulders. She turned at Enrico's cough, one of her hands

31

curving over her belly in a protective gesture, and jealousy stabbed Enrico in the gut. Veronica had been the same way—so protective of Nico from the very start. Whatever Veronica's faults, he could never say she didn't love their son—the son he should be with right now.

"Rico," Dom and Francesca said at the same time, then both of them laughed and welcomed him in a flurry of hugs and smiles.

"What brings you here?" Dom asked.

"It's about Papà," Enrico said. "I have some questions."

Dom's handsome face, so very like Primo's, turned somber. He gestured to a nearby table. "We should sit."

Francesca pecked her husband on the cheek. "How about I get you both an espresso?"

"*Grazie, cara.*" Dom returned the peck. They took their seats and once Francesca was out of earshot, Dom said, "What would you like to know?"

"Has he been having money trouble?"

Dom rubbed a hand across his mouth. "I think so, yes." He shrugged. "They don't tell me much."

"But you're an underboss."

Dom chuckled. "Exactly. Underboss. Means what I don't need to know, I don't need to know."

"But someday—"

"Someday you'll be the boss and I'll be your *capo di società*." His cousin's voice was flat. Maybe even bitter?

"I'm not sure I want that."

Dom snorted. "*Il principe* doesn't want to be king? I'll believe that when I see it."

"I'm serious."

Dom's brows cranked down over narrowed eyes. "Rico, cut the bullshit and stop acting like a damn kid. You're back. You're marrying Antonella Andretti. You're taking your place in this family. End of story."

"It's not what I want."

"To hell with what you want. It's what you're going to *do*. You've known it since you took the vows."

The door behind them opened, and Enrico held in his reply while Francesca brought out their espresso. He accepted a tiny cup from the tray with a grateful smile.

"I'll leave you to your business," she said and went back inside.

"See?" Dom continued. "Francesca knows her role. So do I. So do you."

He *did* know. But that didn't make it any easier. "I'm not sure I'm cut out for this."

"You're a Lucchesi, yes?"

Enrico took a sip of his espresso. "Haven't you sometimes wished for a different life? One where you could be sure you'd come home to your wife every day? Where you didn't have to look over your shoulder all the time?"

Dom stared at him like he'd wished for a unicorn. "England made you soft."

Enrico looked away, his throat closing. Maybe it had. Maybe the time with

Veronica and Nico had changed him, their quiet domesticity a cocoon he'd wrapped himself in, a way of shutting out the horrors of the life he'd left behind, if only for a little while. "Not entirely."

"Oh?" Dom raised a brow. "You're going to come here and whine, and then tell me you're not soft?"

"I need your help with something Papà's forbidden me to do."

With a sharp clink, Dom set his cup on the ceramic tabletop. "You're going to do it." A grin spread across his face.

Enrico nodded. "I am."

Dom clapped his hands together. "I take it back. You did find your balls somewhere along the way."

"The problem is, how do I do it? I know their names, but I've never killed anyone."

Dom sobered and sipped at his steaming espresso. "I'm not going to ask how you got the names. Your source is reliable?" When Enrico nodded, Dom continued. "Well then, the first job is surveillance. We've got to know their habits."

Enrico laid a hand on Dom's forearm. "I need your help, but these are *my* kills. My family, my vengeance."

"They were my family too," Dom said, his voice low.

"I know. But I want to do this for Papà." He removed his hand and picked up his cup again. "Besides, the men will never respect me if they don't think I have it in me."

Dom smiled. "*Sì, il mio principe.*"

Enrico ignored the ribbing. "So, a big thing I'm having trouble figuring is the timing. I have to finish before the wedding. But these are trained men. When I start picking them off, once two are down, the other two will be on guard, and that's going to make it difficult to get to them quickly, if at all."

Dom nodded, thinking. Finally he snapped his fingers. "You need to do them like this," he said, holding out a hand and using his fingers to illustrate. "One first, then two the next day, then the last one on the day after that."

"Two in one day?"

"*Four* in *three* days."

Enrico let out a low whistle and passed a hand over his hair. "Sounds impossible."

"Sounds crazy, you mean."

But brilliant. If he could pull it off, the first three would never see it coming. He'd only have the fourth to truly worry about. "I need a gun. And some practice."

"I'm so proud of you, Rico." Dom beamed at him like a parent.

"Let's hope Papà is too."

"I'd love to see the look on Andretti's face when he finds out."

Enrico would too. He knew Toni believed her father would win any upcoming conflict. But that faith in her father didn't make her right.

Though it also didn't make her wrong.

———◆———

He couldn't put it off any longer. Enrico strode down the front hall of his home and paused respectfully at the door to his father's study, tapping on it and waiting to be called in. When he heard his father's voice bidding him to enter, he took a deep breath. It wouldn't be a good idea to lose his temper. His father might be depressed, but he had no trouble accessing his anger when pushed—he'd proved that yesterday when they'd had breakfast at the Andrettis.

Enrico stepped inside the well-appointed room, a wall of windows looking out at the lake, his father and his desk at the far end of the room, a leather sofa and chairs grouped around a low table midway between the desk and the door. Books Enrico had handled many times lined the shelves around the room; the overall effect was of a library, but the goings-on in that room were anything but genteel.

His father looked up when Enrico entered, his drawn face softening with a weak smile. "Rico, how did things go with Antonella?"

"Well enough, Papà." Enrico took a chair in front of the desk. "Actually, I rather like her."

"I'm glad to hear that. I want you to be happy in this marriage."

How can I be happy without my son? Enrico almost snapped, but forced himself not to. "I don't understand how you can be so calm about all this. After what Andretti did, he deserves to die."

"He does, but..." Rinaldo's voice trailed off into a whisper.

"But what, Papà?"

"It is not possible."

"Anything is possible."

Rinaldo pinned him with a hard stare. "Let it go."

This time he couldn't help himself. "Let it *go*? How am I supposed to do that? If I marry her, I have to see Carlo Andretti over and over again, giving me that smug smile and rubbing my nose in the dirt. How am I supposed to *let that go*?"

"Rico, you must."

"I need a reason."

Rinaldo's face darkened. "Damn it, Rico, I'm your father. Your *capo*."

"And if I'm to be *capo* someday, I need to understand what's happening here. Why you've rolled over for Carlo Andretti. Why you stopped fighting."

Rinaldo looked down and passed a hand across his face. "I haven't wanted to tell you this, but you're right. It's time you knew."

Enrico leaned forward in his chair, his gut tightening. His father looked like he was about to deliver the worst news imaginable. But what could be worse than what had already befallen them?

Rinaldo opened a drawer in the desk and withdrew an envelope and handed it to Enrico. "This is from Carlo."

Enrico tipped the envelope and pulled out a series of photos. They'd been taken with a telephoto lens, and each one was of Enrico's uncle Leopoldo or his cousin Dom. The photos had obviously been taken during surveillance. And as if the message could be misinterpreted, each photo had a rifle sight drawn over it. A wave of heat flooded Enrico's face and chest. Pure unadulterated rage. Hadn't Carlo taken enough from them?

The photos shaking in his hands, Enrico looked up at his father. "We have to

34

crush him, Papà."

Rinaldo shook his head. "We can't."

"We *can*. You just have to try again."

"It's not that simple."

Enrico jumped to his feet and slapped the photos onto his father's desk. "What is wrong with you? It *is* that simple."

Rinaldo rose too and leaned over the desk. "It was my arrogance that got them all killed. We haven't the resources to fight Carlo Andretti. I will not risk any more Lucchesis. This is a fight we'll lose."

Dread chilled Enrico, almost making him shiver. "It's true, then."

"What?"

"We're broke."

Rinaldo looked away. "We might as well be."

"How did this happen?" Enrico asked, his voice raspy.

"You know that I've always held to the old ways." Enrico nodded; he agreed with his father's desire to keep the 'Ndrangheta out of drugs, prostitution, and pornography. "And you know that Carlo Andretti has been eager to embrace the new ones. That's partly why he was exiled from Calabria."

Enrico knew the tale—that Carlo had defied his father and gone too far in his tangle with another *capo*, bringing censure on the Andretti family. When Carlo killed Enrico's mother and brothers, that wasn't the first time he'd broken 'Ndrangheta law.

"What does all this have to do with us?"

"I took money from Lorenzo Andretti, in exchange for keeping an eye on Carlo."

A jolt of electricity arced through Enrico. "You work for Lorenzo Andretti?"

Rinaldo looked away. "You didn't grow up in Calabria. You never wanted for anything."

"But Lorenzo Andretti? How the fuck could you get involved with *him*?"

"Watch your language." Rinaldo fixed him with a hard stare before answering. "Lorenzo was very generous. He poured billions of *lire* into my hands. All as long as I kept Carlo in line. I think he did not want a repeat of what happened with Remo."

"The son he killed." Enrico remembered Papà telling them how hard a man Carlo's father was. Other children had the bogeyman; the children of the 'Ndrangheta heard tales of Lorenzo Andretti instead.

"There are those who admire Lorenzo."

"He's an animal."

"Animal or not, he's wealthy and powerful. Many men would want to be him."

Enrico wanted to spit. "Men who'd be happy to crawl in the mud."

"There are worse things."

"That's not what you said when I was a child."

"I was wrong."

Of everything that had happened, hearing those words from his father ranked among the worst. "You weren't wrong."

"I was foolish. I was arrogant. I got my family killed."

"Carlo did that."

Rinaldo shook his head. "It's my fault. My fault."

"I don't understand."

His father didn't answer for a long time. "Carlo and I were business partners at first. I laundered his money and we embarked on many projects together. But when he wanted to bring in a shipment of cocaine to Milan, I said no. He told me I could get fucked. So I went to Lorenzo, who agreed to help me sabotage the shipment. But things didn't go like I'd expected."

"What happened?"

"Lorenzo was supposed to dispose of the drugs. Instead, he sold them to the Albanians. Somehow Carlo found out, and that's when he came after me. When I asked Lorenzo for help, he turned on me. We had words over the drugs—Lorenzo *lied* to me, Rico—and he told me that if I wanted to do things my way, then I could—as long as I didn't expect any help."

Enrico sat back down in his chair, and his father followed suit. "And so you eventually kidnapped Dario."

"The war with Carlo was draining us." Rinaldo looked around ruefully. "I have always liked the best of everything. Too much." He ran his hands through hair that hadn't been graying two years ago. "When I had Dario, I thought Carlo would capitulate. I thought I could force him to negotiate."

"You took Carlo's boy. He should have given in. Any normal man would have."

"He's an Andretti. Like father, like son. Lorenzo killed one boy and sent away another. Carlo was willing to lose his son to my wrath instead of compromising. The Andrettis don't love their own blood."

But Toni wasn't cold. She wasn't that way at all. She was... different. Wasn't she?

Even so... "And now you want me to marry that jackal's daughter. How could you ever agree to this? Carlo killed our family. He broke 'Ndrangheta law."

"So did I, when I took Dario."

"But *you* didn't kill him."

"I still shouldn't have done it. I opened the door for Carlo to retaliate."

"*Merda!* Carlo has no honor, no respect. And he can't be trusted. I will have no part of that family."

"Rico, you have no choice."

Vaffanculo. He wanted to say it, but he held himself back, just barely. Instead he slammed a fist down on his father's desk. He wanted to punch something, someone. But Carlo Andretti wasn't there.

"It's done. There's no changing it," his father said.

Enrico's whole body itched with adrenaline. He needed some kind of release for it, so he bolted out of the chair and paced the length of the room, smacking his fist on the windowsills as he passed them. How could his father have done this? How could he have negotiated away any chance they might have had of crushing Carlo?

When he reached the end of the room, he inhaled deeply and counted to ten before exhaling. He had to get a grip. He had to *think*. There had to be some way out of this. What had his father missed?

"Can Don Battista help?" Enrico asked. Aside from being Enrico's godfather, Don Vittorio Battista was his father's best friend.

Rinaldo shook his head. "He's embroiled in his own fight right now with the Camorra. Besides, we don't have the right to vendetta anymore. If we fight, we lose everything."

An icy wash poured down Enrico's spine. *That can't be true. It can't.* "What do you mean, we don't have the right?"

"The only help Lorenzo was willing to give me was to mediate the *faida*—imagine it, Lorenzo Andretti, the great peacemaker!" Rinaldo's voice was bitter.

"Mediate?"

Rinaldo shook his head. "A war has been raging in Calabria among the *capi*. Between those who support the old codes and those who think they're passé. Many men have been killed, and profits for San Luca are down." All the clans tithed to San Luca, the birthplace of the 'Ndrangheta and home to the most powerful families, from whom the majority of the *cosche* had sprung. "Lorenzo and some other *capi* had the idea of forming a commission of sorts to resolve our disputes and end the bloodshed."

"How does it work?"

"The family heads convene and decide on a remedy for the dispute. Once the two sides agree, if one of them breaks the agreement, they face severe penalties, including persecution by the rest of the clans."

"What happens if we break the betrothal?"

"We lose half our holdings to Carlo. If we shed blood, we lose our lives."

Enrico felt sick. He'd never get out of the marriage to Antonella; he'd never see his son again—at least not on any regular basis. And he'd never get justice for his family. Unless... "Is there a contract?" When Rinaldo nodded, Enrico held out his hand and said, "May I see it?"

Rinaldo rummaged through the top drawer of his desk, then produced a document. Enrico scanned it, seeing his name and Antonella's, the terms of the betrothal, the terms of breaking it, and then a sentence that somewhat eased the turmoil in his gut. Some might call it hairsplitting; some might call it clever. But no one would argue that it wasn't bold. And many would applaud him for that boldness alone.

Though it still meant the loss of his son, a loss he wasn't prepared for. How would he bear not seeing Nico? How would he bear not getting to see his boy grow up? His throat clamped shut and he turned away from his father, hiding the tears that pricked at his eyes.

He took a deep breath. At least there was a way to achieve some kind of justice for his family. As long as Enrico married Antonella, he should be in the clear.

But that didn't mean Carlo would see it the same way. They needed leverage over him, something Carlo couldn't ignore. Antonella had said Carlo had been drained too, so he was probably still vulnerable. There had to be a way to hamstring him.

He'd give up his son, he'd marry Carlo's daughter, but he'd never let Carlo win.

He turned back and handed the contract to his father. "Papà, is there anything you can think of that might give us an advantage over Carlo?"

"I told you, we can't—"

"We're not going to fight him. Just hobble him."

Rinaldo thought for a moment. "There might be a possibility. Giacomo Parini is friends with Romano Marchesi, a banker who's under Carlo's thumb. The man came to me for help, but I turned him away."

"Can you contact him? We need to know everything we can about Carlo's dealings. I'm sure he's taken some chances."

Rinaldo met his eyes. "The leopard does not change his spots."

"But we must." Enrico would have preferred to charge ahead, to come at Carlo straight on. But in this case, stealth was called for. Stealth, patience, and cunning.

———————◆———————

Enrico spent the next morning with Dom, first scoping out where the killers lived, and then drawing up a plan for the order in which Enrico could go after them. Geographically, two of the targets lived close by each other, so logically, those would be the two Enrico would go after on the second day of their plan. Decision made, they spent several hours at a local gun range until Enrico was satisfied that he'd regained his excellent marksmanship.

Conducting the surveillance was the next step. Dom took the two men who lived close by each other; Enrico took the others. They'd need at least two weeks' worth of observation before drawing any conclusions.

Finished with the first part of his preparations, Enrico decided to swing by his old school and pick up Toni when she got out.

He arrived shortly after the students started pouring through the doors. Scanning the crowd, he searched for her face. When he found her, what he saw shot his blood pressure skyward. Four boys were standing around her, occasionally snatching at her clothes or hair. She clutched a book to her chest and tried to barrel past them, but they managed to block her way each time she attempted to escape. Enrico wasn't close enough to hear what they were saying, but he doubted they were giving her compliments.

Pushing through the throng of students reminded him of swimming against a strong current, but Enrico eventually made enough progress to get within earshot.

"There's an elephant who wants his trunk back," one of the boys said. He had dark brown, curly hair and red cheeks. The other boys laughed appreciatively.

Antonella said nothing, but her eyes glittered and the nose in question was red with impending tears. "Animals," she hissed.

The boys laughed harder. "Did you steal that thing from an anteater?" the same boy asked.

"*Basta!*" Enrico shouted. The boys' heads swiveled in his direction. So did Toni's, but she looked aghast instead of happy to see him.

The apparent ringleader, the boy with the curly hair, strutted toward Enrico. "What are you going to do about it?"

"Whatever I have to." He smacked his right fist into his left palm. Three against one—those were pretty good odds.

"Ooh," the boy said, raising his brows and his voice in an imitation of a frightened female. "I'm terrified!"

You should be. "Do you know who we are? Who she is? Who her father is?"

The boy hesitated, then shrugged. "No one's given a shit before."

"You want to bring all that wrath down on yourself?"

One of the other boys started to look uneasy. He grabbed the ringleader's sleeve. "Arturo, maybe we should go."

"Fuck this *stronzo*," Arturo said, motioning to Enrico with his chin.

No doubt the comment was meant to get Enrico upset. But nothing they said to him could make him any angrier than what they'd said to her.

Enrico pushed up the sleeves of his light jacket. "Call me a *stronzo* again."

The boy looked at what Enrico was doing and the calm way he was doing it, and Enrico heard the first quaver in his voice. "*Stronzo.*"

Enrico almost laughed. "You're as stupid as you are mean." With a lunge, he grabbed Arturo's shirtfront and hauled him close. "You have no idea who I am, yes?"

When the boy shook his head, Enrico gave him a cold smile.

"Rico, *per favore,*" Toni said. "Let him go."

"Why?"

"Don't make a scene."

She didn't understand the most basic thing about men, and especially boys: the only thing they respected was strength. Mercy, compassion—those didn't work on thugs like these.

Enrico shifted his gaze to the boy he held. Arturo needed to learn a lesson. When Enrico opened the left side of his jacket to reveal the Beretta in its shoulder holster, the boy's eyes widened. "You understand now? *I* give a shit. *I* care. Say another word to her or in any way disrespect her, and you'll find out how much I care."

"*Mi dispiace,*" Arturo said, stumbling over the words.

"Not to me, *idiota.* To her." Enrico spun the boy around. "On your knees and apologize."

The boy fell to his knees in front of Toni, while his friends started to back away. Enrico shook his head and clucked his tongue. "No, no, no. *All* of you. Now."

The other three boys joined their friend, and they all mumbled apologies to her. Toni stared at them stonily, her lips pressed together. "*Basta,*" she said, but she was looking at Enrico when she spoke.

The boys slinked away, and Enrico stepped forward. "I made the smallest scene I could," he said. "But it had to be done."

She shook her head. "You've only made it worse."

"I doubt that, Toni. They don't want to tangle with me." He tried to take her arm, but she wouldn't let him do so as they walked to his car.

"So you're going to follow me everywhere I go?" she asked. "Act as my bodyguard?"

He sighed. "Trust me."

"You think you can flash a gun and solve all my problems?" She stopped walking and looked up at him. "What if they tell someone? What if I'm questioned?

What if the *polizia* are called in?"

"I didn't hurt anyone. And they won't say a word."

She shook her head again. "You're so certain."

"They may be stupid, but they aren't suicidal."

"You would kill them over an insult?"

"*They* don't know what I'm capable of."

"You're as bad as my father. Terrifying people to get your way."

His face flamed. "I am *nothing* like your father."

"Are you sure?"

"Yes. I did that because I hated seeing you hurt. Not for any other reason." He touched her cheek. "What hurts you, Toni, hurts me."

"So this really *was* about you then." She gave him a wry smile.

He grinned in return. "You're twisting my words all around, and you know it."

"I'm not done being mad at you," she said, but she relaxed her shoulders and blew out a breath.

He brushed her hair back and kissed her. Heat flared through him at the contact, and he slipped his tongue into her mouth, making the kiss possessive, demanding. And making her press both hands into his chest to separate them. *Madonna*. It took all his willpower not to snatch her back against him. "Are you done now?" he asked.

"Am I done what?"

"Being mad at me."

She shuffled her feet and looked down, then she met his gaze and tapped him on the chest with the top edge of her book. "That wasn't fair."

"Who says I have to fight fair?"

"I do."

He mock-frowned at her. "Now you're taking all the fun out of it."

She laughed at his exaggerated expression. "I suppose we wouldn't want that."

"Definitely not."

They were just about to get into Enrico's car when Dario stepped in front of them. "Are you done making a spectacle of my sister?" he asked.

"Dario, it was nothing," Toni said.

"Does Papà know he's here? Does he know that you let Lucchesi kiss you?"

She said nothing, and Enrico jumped to her defense. "That was my doing."

"I'm sure it was. My sister isn't some *troia* you can paw in public."

Enrico boiled inside, but Dario was within his rights. "I won't do it again."

"No, you won't." Dario took Toni by the elbow and steered her toward his car. She looked over her shoulder at Enrico, but didn't protest. Was her brother's hold over her that strong?

Or did she care about Enrico so little?

CHAPTER 5

As Dario pulled out of the school parking lot, Antonella looked once again back at Enrico, this time turning her whole body. She raised a hand, as if to wave, but let it drop. Enrico just stared at her, clearly perplexed.

How could she ever explain the connection that she and Dario shared? He was her brother, her friend, her closest companion during childhood. Beyond that, they were twins. They'd had their own language growing up, a special code only they'd understood. It had driven Papà mad. And because Dario had refused for years to speak normal Italian—even though he understood it—their private language had infuriated their father even more.

No matter how Papà had raged at or threatened him, Dario had remained intransigent. He'd spoken to their parents only through Toni. She'd tried many times to get Dario to cave in to Papà, but he'd never yielded.

When they were around four years old, Dario had finally started to speak Italian. He'd never apologized or explained himself, and when Papà had smirked and said, "I knew you'd stop at last," Dario had refused to speak altogether for another week.

She'd never met a person as stubborn as her brother. Mules could go to him for lessons.

They drove in silence for some time, then Dario said, "Why didn't you come get me?"

"They wouldn't let me leave."

"How long has this been going on? I thought it had stopped."

"So did I."

When she ignored the question, he asked again. "How long?" His voice was gentle, soft.

She shook her head. "It *had* stopped. It started again today. I don't know why."

"I do."

She whirled to face him. "What?"

"I heard some whispers. About you and Lucchesi."

41

"What whispers?"

"That he took you to some place in Bellagio. That he kissed you."

Her cheeks burned. *Ilaria*. She was the only one Antonella had told.

But Ilaria wouldn't tell anyone; as a child of the 'Ndrangheta, she knew the importance of keeping secrets. Then Antonella realized—she'd told Ilaria in the girls' bathroom. They'd thought it was clear, but someone must have overheard.

Even so... "Why would that start the teasing again?"

He said nothing for a moment, just concentrated on the road. "Jealousy, I suspect." He glanced at her. "You know how girls are."

She did. They wouldn't necessarily cut you to your face, like the boys, but they could be even more vicious behind your back.

"My guess is it's Fiorella," he said. "She's dating Arturo."

Antonella shifted in her seat. "What does she have against me?"

"Toni, think about it."

Then it hit her, and a stone formed in her gut. Fiorella had dated Enrico briefly. But that was over two years ago. Could she seriously be holding a grudge?

Antonella knew the answer. The memory of Enrico's kiss, the delicious smell of him, the feel of his hard body molded to hers—yes, that was something a girl wouldn't forget, no matter how many years had passed.

The stone grew bigger. "What should I do about it?"

"Do nothing. And hope it goes away again." He snorted. "No doubt *that's* wishful thinking, though. Not after that stunt Lucchesi pulled."

Dario was right, and she herself had given Enrico grief about it. And yet... "He was just trying to help."

They were nearly home, but instead of continuing there, Dario took an abrupt turn into the mountains. "He's *always* trying to help. Big, heroic, Enrico Lucchesi."

Dario had to be thinking of the time Enrico had intervened when they were kids and a group of boys were taunting them in the schoolyard. And maybe he was also thinking about how he'd lost his finger. "Rico means well. He's a good person, if you'd let yourself see that." She said the words softly, rationally, as if she were trying to placate an angry lion. It was no use.

"So he's *Rico* now?"

Dario whipped the car over onto a gravel turnout and shoved his maimed right hand in her face. "How can you say he's a 'good person,' after what he did to me?"

A great sadness welled up in her chest. Her brother had been damaged—*Enrico* had been damaged—and she was to blame. "It's all *my* fault. Everything that happened to you. *I* planted the bugs. *I* started this."

He punched the center of the steering wheel, and the car horn emitted an angry blast. "It's *Enrico's* fault I lost my finger."

"He saved your *hand*." She paused. "What happened to you was terrible, but it wasn't Enrico's fault. It was mine."

"You didn't start this. Rinaldo Lucchesi did, when he betrayed Papà."

She wanted to shake him. "Will you listen to me? Papà never knows when to stop. He's so focused on how Nonno Lorenzo and Zio Benedetto wronged him, he can't see anything else. When he decided to sell cocaine, he was breaking 'Ndrangheta law, and Rinaldo was right to try to stop him."

Dario's brows rose. "You can't be serious. The laws are old; everyone sees it. How can we compete against the Russians, and the Albanians, and *Dio* knows who else, if they're raking in the cash and we're not?"

"Drugs are bad for everyone concerned. Including us. They ruin the places we live. Rinaldo Lucchesi is right."

"Only the weak are stupid enough to take them." He rolled down his window and spat. "Who *are* you? Did your last name already change?"

"I understand his point."

"That doesn't mean you have to take his side against Papà. That doesn't mean you have to marry his son."

Her vision blurred with tears. "I *need* to do this, Dario. I need to make things right. Before all the Andrettis end up dead. Before *you* end up dead."

Dario leaned toward her, one elbow on the steering wheel. "We can beat them. And if not, I can make you a young widow. I can get rid of Enrico Lucchesi."

A chill swept over her at the coldness of his tone. "Dario, no. *No.*" She closed her eyes, tears seeping out onto her cheeks. "I need to do this. If you ever loved me, you'll respect that."

"Why do you think I'm saying this?"

He slammed out of the car, making her flinch. After he'd paced for a while, she got out too. She leaned against her door, arms crossed. Dario marched violently back and forth, jaw rigid, shoulders held stiffly back, his whole body reflecting his feelings. She'd seen him like this many times before. There was no reasoning with him when he was in that state. She just had to wait.

After a time, he slowed, then swiveled toward her and didn't stop until he was close enough to touch her. He cupped her face in his hands and brushed the tears off her cheeks with his thumbs. "You're my sister, Toni." She stared into his eyes, so very like her own. He'd literally been beside her almost every step of their lives; she'd always tried to shield him from Papà, from a world Dario was too stubborn to bend for. She'd been his translator, his lifeline—no wonder he didn't like the thought of her leaving.

She opened her mouth to speak, but he shushed her. "I want you to be happy. You have always wanted that for me; I know this. If this is truly what you want, I'll respect your wishes."

"It is."

His eyes scanned her face. "The truth—is there any doubt in your heart?"

"Of course there is."

"You shouldn't marry him then."

"*No one* knows for certain."

Letting her go, he stalked over to a misshapen umbrella pine and punched its gnarled trunk.

"Dario!" When she saw the blood on his knuckles, she raced over and cradled his injured hand in hers. She flexed his fingers, watching him for signs of pain. He winced here and there, but didn't try to withdraw the hand. "*Idiota*," she murmured.

"You weren't listening to me."

"You have to hurt yourself to make your point?"

He said nothing for a long time. Then finally: "If you're ever unhappy, if you

DANA DELAMAR

ever want out of this marriage, say the word, and I'll free you."

She kissed his cheek. "*Mille grazie.*" When he said nothing, she added, "I know this is hard on you, having me leave. But I'll come visit. And you can visit me."

His face darkened. "I'll *never* step foot in that house again. Not after what they did to me."

She found the stump of his missing finger and stroked it. "Think of what Papà did to *them*," she whispered. "Think of that."

He released her. "I have. They still shouldn't have done it. Papà never would've gone so far if they hadn't taken me."

She let out a sigh. "Please try to find it in your heart to let it go, Dario. *Per favore.* For me."

"I don't forget, Toni. And I don't forgive."

He turned and got back in the car. She followed, her heart weeping for him, the way it always had. Her brother continually chose the hardest path. He was more like Papà than he'd ever believe, but she'd be wise to keep that to herself. Dario wouldn't thank her for the observation.

Perhaps, in time, Dario would come to accept Enrico. But such acceptance would be a long time coming, if ever.

———————◆———————

Now that he had the names and his plan with Dom in place, Enrico started his surveillance. His assignments were Luigi Gennaro and Leone Valentino. Because Gennaro lived in a relatively high-security apartment building in a fashionable section of Milan, Enrico concentrated on him first, even though he would be the last hit—the last hit and the most difficult one. Gennaro would be on alert by that time, and that alone would increase the danger and the complexity of the hit.

Enrico spent several days observing who entered and left Gennaro's apartment building on Viale Monza. The residents appeared to be mostly single and mostly up-and-comers, but some were older people and couples with university-age children, which gave Enrico an idea for how he might get inside without a key to the outer door.

But first he needed to figure out who the manager was and whether that person was easy to fool. He was in the midst of buzzing each apartment and asking for the manager when a burly man in his mid-thirties came up and pulled out his key to unlock the front door. Enrico barely gave him a glance, but something about the man made him take another look.

Enrico had obtained an old mug shot of Gennaro from a *carabinieri* officer on the Lucchesi payroll, and something about this man looked familiar. When he noticed Enrico studying him, the man's brows lowered, and he stepped close to Enrico, his face an ugly mask. "What are you looking at?" the man demanded.

It was *him.* Enrico's heart started pounding. "Nothing," he said and raised his hands up in the air, doing his best to make himself seem nonthreatening. He couldn't help checking for the tell-tale bulge of a gun under Gennaro's left armpit, and there it was. *Grazie a Dio*—he hadn't worn one himself today. The man frisked him with his eyes, and Enrico prayed that Gennaro hadn't noticed him do the same.

44

"What are you doing?" Gennaro asked.

"I lost my key to the front door."

"You tried Signor Agrioli?"

That must be the manager. "He's not in, and I can't remember who the off-hours manager is."

"Signora Passerini in 342."

"*Grazie.*"

Gennaro inserted his key in the lock to the outer door, and Enrico was about to let out a sigh of relief when the man turned back to look at him. "Which apartment is yours?"

Merda! Enrico spat out the last number he'd punched. "233." Gennaro lived on the fourth floor, in 406; the odds were that he didn't know the people on the second floor.

"So you're Dottor Tossetti's boy."

Sweat broke out on Enrico's forehead. That hadn't been the last name beside the number—he *thought*. Hadn't it been Laterza? Was the man testing him? He shook his head. "No, *signore*. My last name is Laterza."

Gennaro smiled. "Welcome to the building." He stuck out his hand. "I'm Luigi Gennaro."

Enrico shook the man's hand and pasted a smile on his face. "Riccardo Laterza."

Gennaro released his hand and opened up the door, ushering Enrico inside. As he passed in front of the man, Enrico's stomach tightened. What if Gennaro knew that he'd lied? Would he even feel the muzzle of the gun as it jabbed in his back, or would it all be over before any of it registered?

A wide stone staircase next to a tiny wire-cage elevator stood across the lobby from the outer vestibule. Enrico headed for the staircase, while Gennaro went for the elevator. "*Ciao!*" Enrico called over his shoulder and waved as he started up the stairs. Gennaro returned the wave as he waited for the old elevator to descend to the ground floor, its gears wheezing in protest.

To his dismay, Enrico discovered that the building featured a central atrium with a glass roof. The apartments ringed the elevator shaft, and the staircase landing branched on each floor to form a gallery of sorts, off which each apartment had a door.

Unfortunately, from the elevator, Gennaro would be able to see Enrico and where he went.

The whole layout was horrible for hitting someone. Not only would he be visible to anyone in the elevator, he'd be visible to everyone on the floor, should they open their doors. And he'd be visible to at least some of the inhabitants of the upper floors as well, if they too happened to venture out and look down.

Merda, merda, merda.

But first he had to avoid raising Gennaro's hackles. He took his time walking the stairs, but the elevator hadn't yet ascended past him as he reached the second floor. He approached 233 with trepidation, praying that Gennaro would pass him by before he reached it.

The elevator started clanking past, and Enrico willed himself to ignore it. To pretend he couldn't feel Gennaro's eyes on his back.

Enrico had just reached 233 when he risked a glance upward and saw the bottom of the elevator cage pass out of his sight. If he couldn't see Gennaro, Gennaro couldn't see him.

He waited a few seconds more, then raced back to the staircase and hurried down it, keeping his body pressed to the outer wall so he wouldn't be visible from the elevator as he descended.

The elevator came to a halt above as Enrico reached the ground floor, and he sprinted for the outer door and slammed outside, startling a young woman with a child as he barreled past them and down the street.

He dashed into a *gelateria* on the corner and caught his breath. That had been close, too bloody close.

What were the odds that he'd have ever shaken hands with one of the monsters who'd shot his family?

And now that Gennaro had seen him, he'd recognize him. That made a difficult job even harder.

But not impossible. He'd just have to be smarter.

Smarter than a trained assassin.

———◆———

What if he failed? What if he failed to kill Gennaro, Valentino, any of them? There were so many ways Enrico's plan could go wrong. Such as bumping into Gennaro during his surveillance. So many ways he could die.

He'd been putting off telling Veronica the truth—that he wasn't coming back any time soon. That he had to marry Antonella Andretti. But he owed Veronica the unvarnished truth. For once.

When he reached Cernobbio, he headed into town instead of going home. He parked near the main piazza and walked to the bank of payphones at one edge of it. He loaded the phone with coins and dialed Veronica's number in London. It was early evening now, and he should have called Antonella earlier, should have made plans with her. But he'd been putting off talking to her too. Ever since he'd learned that he was trapped, he couldn't face her. He liked her, yes, he was attracted to her, but he didn't want to lose his son by marrying her. He didn't want to give Nico up.

But he had to.

He listened to the phone ring, his finger hovering over the receiver's cradle, tempted to end the call before it began. But Veronica answered with a tentative hello, and now it was too late.

"We need to talk," he said.

"Rico, is everything okay?"

He almost blurted it out, but that would be cruel. "I just... I missed you. The two of you," he corrected himself. He didn't want to give her the wrong impression about his feelings.

"We missed you too," she said, and a quaver came into her voice. "When are you coming back?"

His throat constricted so painfully he could barely swallow. Ignoring the question, he said, "Is Nico awake? Can you put him on the line?"

"Of course he's up. The phone woke him." Nothing but irritation in her voice now. She smacked the phone onto a hard surface and left, muttering something he couldn't make out, but whose content he could guess.

A minute or so later, she came back on. "Here he is." Then to Nico: "It's Papà, baby. Say hi."

"Papà?"

The joy in Nico's voice brought tears to Enrico's eyes. "Papà is here, Nico."

"Papà! Papà!" Nico happily burbled at him for several minutes, his words a tumbling, babbling mess that resembled speech only in its cadence. When Nico ran out of steam, Veronica took the phone.

"He misses you so much, Rico. He goes to the window or the front door sometimes and then he turns back to me and he says 'Papà?' It breaks my heart."

A tear slipped down Enrico's cheek and he quickly wiped it away. "I wish I could be there."

"When, then?"

"I don't know."

"Last time you said a month."

His chest tightened. He had to tell her. "Veronica, I cannot get out of the marriage."

"Oh God," she said, her breath hitching. "You promised me, you said there was a chance—"

"I did not promise. I said I would try."

"Just come back here and marry me. There's nothing your father can do to stop you."

"My family is in a precarious financial position. I have to marry her."

"You're not some eighteenth-century duke. You don't have to marry for money."

"I will come as soon as I can. It will have to be at least six weeks. There is the wedding, then the honeymoon—"

"Stop it!" she shrieked, and Nico started wailing. "Stop talking like it's okay that you're abandoning us. Abandoning *me* with a child. Do you know how hard it is to take care of him by myself?"

"Veronica, I am sorry. I do not have any choice." He could hear his voice rising, and he took a deep breath. "Is your mum not helping? She always seemed to want to."

"She offers. But…"

"But?"

"What if something happens?"

"Veronica, what is going to happen? Sharon raised you and your brother. She can handle Nico for a few hours. Or even a few days." He heard Veronica's breathing—fast, rapid, shallow. She was worked up, far too worked up. "Have you been sleeping?" he asked.

"A little." Her voice broke. "I miss you so much. And every time I hear a noise, I think someone's breaking in—"

"Shh. You are safe. Nico is safe." He hummed a few bars of an Italian lullaby that he'd sung to her or to Nico when they hadn't been able to sleep.

She sniffed back tears several times, then she said, "I'm okay. I'm just so tired."

"I know." Suddenly he felt drained, as if he'd never move again. "Please, call your mum. She would love to help. You know she would."

"You're right." She sighed into the phone. "You *will* come back, won't you? You're not just telling me what I want to hear?"

"I will visit. I promise, Veronica."

"I'll hold you to that," she said before hanging up without a goodbye.

He stood there for a moment listening to the dial tone. What else did he expect? She was angry. She had every right to be.

Hers was another life Carlo had ruined. Nico's too. Enrico slammed the receiver back into its cradle. If he was going to have any hope of a normal life again, if he was ever going to see his son on a regular basis, Carlo Andretti had to be stopped.

Preferably dead.

CHAPTER 6

Four days had passed since the incident at school, and Enrico still hadn't called her. Should she call him?

Antonella paced around the room. She shouldn't have to call him, yes? He should be calling her. He'd been in the wrong, and it was time he made some effort... Though he *had* made an effort, hadn't he? He'd come to school to pick her up and he'd tried to help. Maybe he even had, despite her grumbling, since Arturo and his cronies had stayed away from her since then.

Bottom line: Enrico had made an effort, and she'd chided him for it. And then she'd left with Dario.

And she'd dared to accuse Enrico of sending mixed signals!

It was time to swallow her pride once again.

Sitting on the bed, she smoothed out her skirt and touched her hair, then laughed. It wasn't like Enrico would be able to see her. She picked up the handset and placed the call, her heart pounding. *Dio*, she should be over these foolish nerves. The formal engagement party was in a week and a half. And here she was, with her parched mouth, clammy palms, and skittering pulse at the thought of calling the man she would be marrying soon.

It wasn't normal.

Then again, nothing about the situation was. Sure, 'Ndrangheta families married off sons and daughters to cement alliances or settle feuds all the time. It was a common practice in Calabria.

But a strange one in the north. If they were in Calabria, her classmates would understand why she was getting married without having to be told. Here, she'd get only blank looks or cries of amazement. So she'd told no one other than Ilaria, whose father was part of the Andretti *cosca*. Ilaria understood, and Ilaria was her maid of honor by default.

And Ilaria would be her only classmate, her only friend, to see Antonella make the step into marriage, into adulthood.

The rest of her classmates... Well, they'd never understand it. Why she was marrying at sixteen with no baby on the way. To a boy who'd never taken any notice of her before.

There'd be some questions, questions she'd have no idea how to answer…

The ringing of the phone stopped and someone picked up the line. The maid. Again. Apparently Enrico and his father were deaf to the telephone. She asked for Enrico and ignored the knowing lilt in the maid's voice as she told Antonella to wait.

Dio mio, the maid must think her a fool with no pride—

"Yes?" Enrico snapped, his voice crisp and cutting.

"I hadn't heard from you, so I thought I'd better call. To make sure you were okay."

"I'm fine."

"You don't sound like it."

"I don't have time to play games with you. Or the patience."

He couldn't have shocked her more if he'd slapped her in the face. "I'm not playing games. You sound upset. I want to know why. And to help, if I can."

He let out a snort. "Remember how you didn't want my help? Well I don't want yours, either."

"Rico—"

"You can't help with this, Antonella."

"I don't even know what's wrong yet."

"Trust me. I need to work through this on my own." His voice seethed with irritation.

Was he grieving his family still? Had the upcoming wedding and the hoopla surrounding it opened old wounds?

"I know this has to be difficult. I keep thinking of our wedding as a happy occasion, but I know it might not be the same for you."

A frustrated growl filled the line. "You are the queen of understatement. The bloody queen."

"I—I'm sorry. This is all coming out wrong—"

"Just stop. Just stop and leave me alone. I don't need *you* trying to console me."

Tears filled her vision. She was hurt, yes, but so was he. Far more so. And *she* was the cause. She wanted to tell him, to just blurt it out, but that was impossible. Though she could do one thing. "I'll leave you alone then. But I wanted to thank you. You were right about Arturo. He hasn't bothered me." She paused, and when Enrico said nothing, she added, "*Mille grazie.*"

"I've got to go," he said and hung up the phone.

The droning of the dial tone unleashed the tears she'd been holding back, and she sobbed aloud.

The wedding hadn't even taken place, yet her marriage was already a disaster.

———◆———

Once she'd dried her tears, Antonella had called Ilaria and arranged to meet her in downtown Cernobbio.

The day was beautiful and bright, with a light breeze rustling the leaves of the

50

trees and kicking up waves that slapped the shoreline beside the promenade.

Antonella wore sunglasses to hide her swollen eyes, but Ilaria wasn't fooled. "Toni, what happened?" she asked as soon as they met.

Putting a hand over her mouth, Antonella shook her head. "It's Enrico. He's angry with me."

Ilaria frowned. "What for?"

"Things I can't change." She looked down at her feet, not wanting to meet Ilaria's eyes.

"What things?"

"My family. My father." She gestured around her with both hands. "This situation."

"He'll get over it."

Antonella pursed her lips and raised a brow. "That doesn't seem too likely."

"He's a *man*. They pout and stomp around for a while, then they eventually realize they're being idiots, and they stop. You just have to let them recognize it in their own time."

"I don't know if he'll ever get over this." She crossed her arms and stopped walking, gazing out at the rippling lake. "Maybe I'm a fool to hope that he'll ever look at me and not see the shadow of my father in the background."

"Toni, stop. Just stop and listen to me. Is Enrico Lucchesi more stubborn than Dario? Than your father?"

Antonella shrugged. "I don't know."

Ilaria chuckled. "You *do* know. It's not possible to be more stubborn than the men in your family. You've told me so a million times."

Ilaria had a good point. "You're right. I think."

"You just have to wait him out. Let him realize certain things. Let him come to you."

"Maybe I have been pushing too hard. I'd just—" She looked away and chewed at her bottom lip.

"You'd just what?"

Heat flooded her face. *Porca vacca*, why hadn't she kept her mouth shut? "I'd just like him to… find me desirable. Regardless."

"Oh sweetie. He's kissed you. He wouldn't have if he didn't."

Antonella took a deep breath. "I think that would be a stretch. He's kissed me three times. That doesn't mean much." She shook her head. "Not to a boy like Enrico."

"Give him some credit. Give *yourself* some credit, Toni. He kissed you. Not once. Not twice. But three times. *Real* kisses. If he didn't think you were attractive, why would he bother? Don't you think he'd behave like so many of them? Barely give you a glance and find a mistress the moment the marriage license was signed?"

"Maybe he was being polite."

"Is he being polite to you now?"

"Not at all."

"Well then. He's being honest. And that's better."

"And how is his yelling at me a good thing?"

"Because he's not hiding. He might be pushing you away or avoiding you, but he's not lying."

Ilaria pulled her inside a *gelateria*, and Antonella studied the flavors. "Maybe you're right."

"Of course I am. I've seen you deal with Dario and your father. You always manage to twist them around your fingers, and you have infinite patience with them. How is Enrico any different?"

I hurt him. But she could never tell Ilaria that. "It is different, and you know it. I know they love me; they have to. Enrico doesn't. And he doesn't have any reason to ever love me."

Ilaria hissed. "I really want to slap you right now. I know you've had a crush on him for ages, and *Dio* knows Enrico Lucchesi is something spectacular, but he's just a man."

Ilaria placed an order for pistachio gelato and nudged Antonella until she ordered the *nocciolato*, the combination of chocolate and hazelnuts that she could never resist. They collected their treats and went outside. Antonella took a spoonful, the cold gelato feeling delightful on her tongue. She resumed the conversation, said the thing she'd been reluctant to say in front of the boy at the counter.

"I want to be happy, Ilaria. I want *him* to be happy. I don't want the sort of marriage where we don't speak except about the kids. I don't want to sit home by myself every night while he's out... fornicating."

Ilaria laughed so hard she turned red. "*Fornicating*? You sound like Sister Maria."

Antonella blushed. "Well, I don't know what word to use."

"Yes, you do. Your father says it often enough."

"It's not polite."

"Or ladylike."

Antonella met Ilaria's dancing eyes and started chuckling. "No, it's not."

"Do you think," Ilaria asked, her voice deliberately proper, "that Enrico Lucchesi wants a *lady* in his bed?"

Antonella giggled. "I have no idea what he wants." She leaned closer and lowered her voice to a whisper. "But when we kissed the second time, he took my hand and put it on his *cazzo*. And it was hard."

Ilaria broke into a grin. "He doesn't want a lady then." A moment later, she sobered. "You need to be careful, Toni. Think what your father would do if he knew about that."

Antonella's stomach tightened. "You're right. But..."

"But what?"

"Do you think Rico expects me to know... *things*?"

"I'm sure he assumes you know the basics."

"But what if he thinks I should know how to please him?"

"You're supposed to be a virgin, so don't worry."

"Easy for you to say."

Ilaria shrugged. "I'm sure you'll learn whatever you need to know."

"How?" It wasn't like she could ask Mamma. As far as Antonella could tell, she and Dario had been immaculately conceived. Her parents never showed any sort of physical affection or interest in each other.

"I expect he'll tell you what he likes." Ilaria tossed her empty gelato cup in a rubbish bin. She motioned to Antonella's barely touched cup. "It's melting."

Antonella took another spoonful, the taste of hazelnuts and chocolate momentarily distracting her. "He's a very good kisser." She lowered her voice into a confidential tone. "I think he's had a lot of practice."

"Will you stop worrying?"

Although she dug her spoon into the cup again, Antonella's stomach was too knotted up to enjoy the treat. Without a word, she handed the cup to Ilaria, who shrugged again and started to finish it. "I don't want to disappoint him."

"You won't," Ilaria said around a mouthful of gelato.

Antonella stopped and sat on a bench along the promenade. Her throat was so tight she could barely mention what truly frightened her. "I know he's settling for me. That he's being forced. I'm afraid he's going to come to hate me as much as he hates my father."

Ilaria gently squeezed her shoulder. "It'll be fine. He's smart enough to know you're not to blame."

But I am, she wanted to say. She felt almost sick with dread. What if Enrico learned of what she'd done? He'd never forgive her. She had to keep it secret. But it would be so hard.

And wouldn't keeping secrets be a recipe for disaster? How could a marriage founded on lies ever be sound?

Ilaria gave her a little shake. "*Cara*, you have to stop worrying like this, or you'll make all your worst fears come true. Attitude is ninety-nine percent of everything. Isn't that what you always say?"

"I don't know what I'm talking about half the time." Though it was something her father had said to her again and again; at least he believed it to be true.

Ilaria laughed. "Who are you and what did you do with my friend? The Toni *I* know isn't afraid of anything. And she always gets her way—eventually."

"Enrico isn't my dad or my brother. He has this… *power* over me. It's hard to explain. I care what he thinks, and I worry about his opinion of me."

"You just don't feel secure with him. That's all."

That was it. Ilaria had pinpointed the very problem. "You're a genius," Antonella said and nudged Ilaria with her shoulder.

Ilaria tossed her dark curls over her shoulders and dusted off her hands. "My work here is done."

Antonella laughed. "No, it isn't. You have to help me figure out how I can feel more confident with him."

"Remember when he kissed you? And he made you touch him?"

"Yes," Antonella said, unsure of where this was going.

"How did he seem then?"

She thought back to the way he'd looked at her, the way he'd held her. "He was focused, intent."

"And how did you feel?"

She couldn't help smiling. "Beautiful."

"Did he seem false to you in any way?"

"No."

"Did he seem like he wanted to be anyplace else?"

"Just the opposite."

"Then trust *that*. Trust how *you* made *him* feel, how *he* made *you* feel. You can't fake that."

"But what about the rest of the time? He's shutting me out, and that's not a good thing. How can I get him to open up to me?"

"How do you get Dario to do that?"

"I wait him out."

"And now we circle back to what I said before." Ilaria gestured wide with her open hands. "Problem solved."

"I wait?"

"You wait."

"Hmm. Doesn't seem very… active."

"You wait for the right moment. Then you nudge. Not push."

"That *is* how I handle Dario and Papà."

"And Enrico Lucchesi is no different."

Maybe not. But getting to the heart of him, figuring out how he worked, what moved him, would be as tricky as defusing a bomb.

And possibly as dangerous.

———◆———

Enrico replayed his phone conversation with Antonella over and over in his head as he hiked through the hills of his family's estate. She'd been trying to be nice to him—to apologize—and he'd been rude. Mean, even. He was little better than those boys at her school. Just because he was in an intolerable situation didn't mean that he had the right to inflict his anger on her.

The more he reviewed his words, the more he cringed inside. What was wrong with him? He had so little self-control sometimes. He needed to keep his head, keep his cool, if he was going to avenge his family. He needed to play by the rules while circumventing them at the same time.

And one of the rules was that he had to be nice to his fiancée.

Besides that, he didn't like how he'd behaved. He was better than that. *Cristo*, did he want to turn out to be Carlo Andretti, a man who thought only of himself and his own selfish desires? A man so focused on hatred he couldn't think straight anymore? A man willing to hurt others again and again?

No. That was not who the Lucchesis were. That was not who Enrico was.

And Toni deserved his very best.

He owed her yet another apology. A big one.

Winding his way through dusty shrubbery and tall grasses, he headed from the untamed wilds of the hills back to the manicured perfection of the gardens surrounding the villa. It was time to swallow his pride and beg forgiveness.

Sweaty and disheveled, he beelined straight for the phone and dialed the Andrettis without pausing for so much as a glass of water.

When Antonella came to the phone, he plunged into what he wanted to say.

"Toni, please forgive me. I was in a terrible mood when you called. I had no right to speak to you like that. I'm sorry."

She said nothing, and he stumbled on, his heart lurching in his chest. "I know I don't deserve forgiveness, but please give me another chance."

Finally she spoke. "You do realize this is the third second chance you've asked for?"

Relief trickled over him. She didn't sound angry. Almost amused. "I do. Believe me, I do. I need to work on my temper. I'm trying."

"Try harder," she said with a chuckle.

"I promise." He blotted his sweaty forehead with the sleeve of his shirt. "Will you let me make it up to you? The *passeggiata* tonight, and then dinner?" Walking along the promenade together, him showing her off to the town, would make her happy.

"Let me ask Papà first." The phone clunked down on some surface and he waited for her to return, jingling the coins in his pockets and scuffling his shoe along the tiles in the kitchen. Nonna Drina, their cook and boss of the household staff, bustled away behind him, preparing him a snack. She pressed an icy glass of water into his hand and patted his cheek before going back to her chopping.

His mind whirled as the minutes dragged by. Where was Toni? What was taking so long? Was Carlo saying no? At least Toni didn't seem furious with him, though she had every right to be. Unfortunately, he couldn't explain about Nico.

Finally she came back on the line. "He said I could go. But you have to have me back by ten."

And just for that, he'd keep her until 10:01. "Pick you up at six?"

He could practically hear her smile. "I'll see you then."

Now all he had to do was be good to her, keep his cool, and hide any signs of negativity.

Her father was a bastard, but Antonella was a princess.

And Enrico needed to play the role of prince.

———◆———

Enrico waited for the wrought iron gates of the Andretti estate to open. They slowly yawned apart, and a shudder rippled down his spine as he drove through them. He'd come alone, unaccompanied by guards this time.

Surely Carlo could be trusted to follow through on the wedding at this point, given the terms of the contract. Carlo thought he had the upper hand; he could afford to be generous. Even magnanimous. Yes?

After following the circular drive up to the house, Enrico stopped the car at the base of the steps leading to the front entrance. To his surprise, there stood the man himself in an immaculate cream-colored jacket and linen trousers, smoking a cigar. Carlo descended the stairs, his pace unhurried, as if he were on a leisurely stroll.

Enrico got out of the Ferrari and met him, doing his best to keep a leash on his temper. "Signor Andretti," he said, deliberately being polite, but not using the "Don" that Carlo would expect. Carlo was no true *capo*, and Enrico would be damned if he'd treat him like one.

Carlo grinned and tapped ash from his cigar onto the gravel drive. "The pup bares its teeth again."

The taunt was designed to anger him, and it did its job perfectly. But he wouldn't give Carlo the satisfaction. "You are not my *capo, signore*."

This time Carlo laughed. He stared Enrico down, his gaze unwavering. "You still owe me respect, boy. As a member of our society."

It was true. And yet… Enrico met Carlo's gaze square on. "I have not been rude, *signore*. That is the best you can expect of me."

Carlo stepped a little closer, and Enrico steeled himself not to give ground, not to react. Not so much as a blink. Carlo's dark eyes narrowed, scrutinizing Enrico, no doubt studying him for weakness. "Treat my *daughter* rudely again, and you will owe me much more than politeness."

Enrico gave him a stiff nod. At least the man loved his daughter. "That won't happen again."

"I heard about what happened at the school," Carlo said. Enrico hid his surprise. "That's the only reason I'm letting this go. *Capisci?*" Carlo took a draw on his cigar and let out a stream of smoke, directing it away from Enrico. "I won't have my little girl hurt. Not by them, and not by *you*." Carlo punctuated that statement by jabbing a thick forefinger into Enrico's sternum.

"Understood."

"*Davvero?*" Carlo asked.

"My word is good."

"Your father's isn't."

A bolt of heat slammed into Enrico's chest and boiled up into his face. His hands balled into fists, and he dropped back onto his right foot so he could deliver a punch straight to that lying bastard's jaw.

Except that Andretti was telling the truth.

Enrico's father *had* lied to Carlo. He'd broken their deal. He'd double-crossed Andretti.

And didn't the truth sting?

Carlo's eyes dropped to Enrico's fists momentarily before coming back to his face. "Well?"

Antonella saved Enrico from having to respond. Her quick jog down the stairs caught their attention, and the way her eyes darted between them showed she hadn't missed the tension in the air. "*Ciao*, Papà," she said and lightly kissed Carlo on the cheek before closing a hand over Enrico's right fist and tugging him toward the Ferrari.

His cheeks still burning from having his father's shame shoved in his face, Enrico was all too glad to escort her to the car.

"Have her back by ten," Carlo called.

Not a minute before ten-oh-fucking-two. Enrico didn't acknowledge Carlo's words as he shut Antonella's door. He crossed to his own side and looked up just before getting in and caught a grin of triumph on Carlo's face.

Just you wait, Don *Andretti. I will soon have my vengeance.*

CHAPTER 7

"What was that all about?" Antonella asked as Enrico forced himself not to stomp the accelerator into the floor. He looked back in the rear view mirror at Carlo receding in the distance.

"Your father being his usual charming self," Enrico said. "Did you tell him what happened at your school?"

"No. Why?" Before he could answer, she said, "Did he disapprove?"

"He approved. He made quite clear that was the only reason he wasn't kicking my ass from here to Calabria for the way I spoke to you."

She clapped a hand over her mouth. "Oh no," she muttered.

"What?"

"Arturo had a huge black eye today and he was all scraped up. He said some guys had mugged him." She paused. "But that's not what happened, is it?"

"Doubt it."

"This is why I didn't want him to know."

"Apparently your brother doesn't share your scruples."

"He had no right—"

"He's your brother. He probably thinks I did his job. And he's not happy about it."

"You're right. He still shouldn't have told Papà."

Enrico downshifted as they headed up a hill toward town. "I hope this doesn't sound strange, but your brother is awfully attached to you." He tried to keep his voice light, but he was sure she heard his real question: How attached are you to him? He glanced at her, but her face was smooth and blank as stone.

"Dario and I have always had each other. Always. He would say we have a common enemy in Papà, but that's where he's wrong. Papà and I have always gotten along. Dario hasn't been so lucky."

"I'm starting to like your brother."

She gave him a sour look. "I know this is impossible, but could you please understand how I feel? I love my father. Just like you love yours."

But mine didn't kill most of your family. He exhaled slowly. "Okay. I get it."

He pulled into a car park near the promenade, where the townspeople were already strolling about, everyone enjoying this evening's *passeggiata*—whole families, young couples, old couples, groups of laughing kids racing past the rest, gravel crunching beneath everyone's feet.

Enrico remembered coming down here with his family, he, Primo, and Mario cutting up, pushing and shoving each other, telling jokes and laughing, until Papà would raise his voice and tell them to behave. Which they would do, for about ten minutes. Then it would start all over again and wouldn't end until—

His eyes misted over and he paused with his hand on the lever to open the car door. He hadn't cried for them. Not then. Not ever. Not even at the funeral. So why did the tears threaten to fall now?

"What is it?" Antonella asked and placed a hand on his arm.

He jerked away from her touch, then shook his head. *She* wasn't the enemy. "Nothing."

"It isn't nothing. What's bothering you?"

Taking a deep breath, he let his head fall back against the headrest, the leather of his seat creaking with the movement. "Can we just have fun?" He gestured around them. "I brought you here to apologize and show you a good time."

She stroked his cheek. "I want to know you, Rico."

A wave of longing strangled his throat. She'd hit upon the very thing he wanted most—someone to talk to, someone who understood. Someone who could know everything about him.

But she wasn't that person any more than Veronica was. Or his father. Or Dom.

He didn't have a single person in his life who knew the whole truth about him. They all knew only pieces.

And that was the way it had to be. No one could ever know all his secrets. No one but him.

He swallowed hard and stared at her for a long while before he trusted himself to speak. "I want that too," he said. And he meant it.

He just could never deliver on it. But he'd tell her what he could. "I was thinking about coming down here with my family for the *passeggiata*."

"Oh." Her eyes filled with tears and he had to look away. He felt like someone had scraped away every bit of his skin.

Her fingers stroked his hair, and he teetered on the brink of bolting from the car or sinking into her touch. Letting her in was dangerous, so dangerous.

And yet he didn't move. He let go of the door handle and closed his eyes. Neither of them said anything. She just stroked his hair and he let her, tears hovering beneath his eyelids.

He missed them so much. He missed his father too. The two of them lived in the same house, but almost never spoke. Sometimes Enrico got the sense that his father couldn't look at him and not see what was missing. *Who* was missing. Primo. Mario. Mamma.

A huge hole had opened up in their lives, and nothing could ever fill it.

He didn't know how long they sat there, but at some point he relaxed, almost as if he were in a trance. The tears left, the tightness in his throat and chest eased, and he was drifting, at peace.

He opened his eyes and turned his head to look at her. Toni smiled, as if sensing the change in him. "*Grazie,*" he said and took her hand and kissed it.

"Any time."

"Hungry?" he asked.

"Starving."

He looked out the windshield. It had grown dark, lights twinkling along the promenade now, the crowds of the *passeggiata* dwindling. "We missed it."

"We'll have plenty of others."

His chest warmed at the thought. He practically bounded out of the car and around to her side, opening the door and offering her a hand out.

This time, he didn't let go. He didn't want to. He twined his fingers through hers as they set out along the waterfront. It was shadowy beneath the trees now, and he had the sudden impulse to pull her down on a bench and kiss her.

But that could wait. She'd taken care of him; he ought to return the favor. She was hungry, and it was now his mission to provide her an excellent meal.

There was a new restaurant up ahead, one he'd never been to. She wouldn't have to worry about him having taken other girls there. He asked if she'd like to try it, and she agreed.

Dinner flew by in a breeze of jokes and teasing, the sort of light, flirty banter he'd have thought himself incapable of when they'd left her home and Carlo behind. Enrico hadn't felt this happy in a long time. And it was all because of the remarkable girl sitting across from him.

She brushed a thick wave of hair away from her eyes. "Why are you looking at me like that?" she asked.

"Like what?"

She blushed. "I don't know. You're just staring."

He reached across the table and took her hand. "You don't know how lovely you are, do you?"

"You've been with prettier girls, I'm sure." Her eyes stayed glued to their joined hands and her blush deepened.

"Look at me." He waited until she did. "Toni, you are the only girl I want to look at."

Her eyes glistened and her nose reddened. "You mean that?" she asked, her voice thick.

"I do." He squeezed her fingers and fished out his wallet, leaving the waiter a thick stack of *lire.* "Let me show you how much."

He escorted her outside, his hand on the small of her back. A cool breeze kicked up off the water, and he draped his jacket over her. When she nestled close to him as they walked, he slid an arm around her. She fit against him perfectly, her head resting easily on his shoulder. As soon as they reached the shadows of the trees, his heartbeat quickened and his eyes sought out a place for maximum privacy.

He soon spotted a bench set back from the path, so well sheltered by the trees that it was cast all in darkness. *Perfetto.*

He didn't say anything, just pulled her over to the bench and onto his lap. She let out a little huff of protest. "Rico, what—" she said, before he cut her off with his lips, this time letting himself go and kissing her fiercely. The way she was meant to be kissed.

Her mouth opened to his readily, and her hands wound into his hair, tugging him closer as she whimpered.

Ah *Dio*, she was hot in his hands, her lips and tongue working against his, her hips turning in his lap so that she nearly straddled him. He reached down between them and took her knee, breaking the kiss long enough to help her move so that she did in fact straddle him.

Her tight skirt had ridden up, exposing her upper thighs, and he placed his hands on her hips, pulling her up so that the mound of her *figa* was crushed against the bulge of his *cazzo*.

She pulled back. "We shouldn't," she whispered.

"I know," he said, then arched up against her, his *cazzo* straining against the cloth of his trousers. With his right hand, he reached between them and slid his fingers along her inner thigh, until they met the silky fabric of her panties.

She tensed. "Don't." He let out a groan of frustration.

"I won't do anything that won't leave you a virgin," he whispered.

She held him around the nape of his neck, the other hand tracing the light growth of stubble along his jaw. "No touching below the waist. Promise?"

He paused. He'd grown so used to Veronica, he'd forgotten how it was at the beginning. Especially for girls. He had to slow down, let her set the pace. "Promise." Besides, Carlo would have his balls just for holding her like this. But damn it, she was *his* fiancée.

Toni remained alert, her body as tight as a bow. His heart pounded in his chest as if he'd been running, and his mouth was dry. He had to be careful now. He didn't want to upset her. But he couldn't take her home just yet. Not without giving her a bit of pleasure to make up for all the pain he'd inflicted.

———◆———

Slowly, so slowly, Rico kissed Antonella again. She opened up for him, his tongue darting into her mouth. He smelled so good, like evergreens and citrus, with a spicy, masculine scent underneath that she could only think of as *his* scent. Rico's. She'd know it anywhere now, and she could never seem to get enough.

She broke off the kiss and nuzzled his wavy black hair, her fingers playing with the short strands at the base of his skull, feeling the strong tendons on either side of his spine. He was so hard everywhere against her—every muscle felt like marble, so very different from the softness of her own body, the softness she was used to. Just holding him was thrilling, new.

He slid his hands up her sides until he gripped her just below the breasts, his thumbs rubbing their undersides. Every place he touched felt like it had been dipped in fire, her whole body suddenly so sensitive it was almost overwhelming. She wanted more, but she had to keep her head. Rico had promised, but he was a man, and if she said yes, he probably wouldn't say no.

But just a little more, a very little more, that would be okay, wouldn't it? She slid closer to him, once again feeling his hardness between her legs, so tantalizing, but so forbidden. Ever so slightly, she rocked against him, the contact sending shivers along her spine and tightening all her limbs. Her hand trembled where it touched his jaw, and he twisted his neck and kissed the inside of her wrist, his eyes all the while locked on hers. She swore he was mesmerizing her somehow. But she didn't mind.

Watching her face, he traced the outside of her breasts, staying away from her most sensitive spots. She hadn't realized how good that light a caress could feel, and she had to stop from twisting her breasts into his palms, craving more of his touch, imagining what his fingers could do if he let himself go. If *she* let herself go.

And then he did something that was almost her undoing. He kissed a path along her jaw, down to her throat, where he lingered, licking her skin and sending sparks all through her. It felt like his mouth, his tongue, was everywhere on her body, even *there*, between her legs. When he bit down gently, she let out a deep moan that startled her, and she inadvertently flexed her hips against him, making both of them groan. A jolt of pleasure raced through her, and she wanted to do it again. Something was happening to her, something she liked, but was afraid of at the same time. If she started again, she might not stop.

She placed her hands on his chest and gently pushed. He looked up, puzzled. "This is... too much," she said, her voice shaky.

He smiled, a wicked, dazzling smile that she'd never seen before. "I think it's not enough."

"Oh Rico," she murmured. "What am I going to do with you?"

He kissed her cheek. "Everything. When you're ready."

"When we're married."

He mock-frowned at her, and she chuckled. "This was the last thing I expected to happen tonight."

"I've been thinking about it for a while now."

She wiggled off him and readjusted her clothing. "You have?"

He wagged a brow at her. "What else do you think comes to mind when a guy is with his girl in the dark?"

"I'm your girl?"

He nodded and rose, wincing a bit and having to adjust his clothing too.

She raised a hand to her mouth. "Did I hurt you?"

"No. I'm just a bit... uncomfortable."

Would he like it if she touched him? Would that help? She reached out, but he gently pushed her hand away. "Another time."

"Are you sure?"

A long moment passed before he spoke. "Yes."

———◆———

Enrico wanted to take Toni up on her offer so badly he was cursing himself, but now wasn't the time or place. They'd been lucky no one had happened by. Lingering longer would be unwise, and he didn't want to wreck the evening.

Besides, he'd promised to be a gentleman. If she touched him, *Dio* knew if he'd be able to keep that promise. Not that he'd ever force her. But he knew he could be damn persuasive. Veronica was a testament to that.

He picked up his jacket from where it had fallen and shook it out, then placed it across her shoulders again before steering them in the direction of the car park.

They'd just come out into the light when a man stopped on the path not far from them and lit a cigarette, the flame highlighting his features.

A shard of ice scraped down Enrico's back. The man was Guido Ripoli— he was sure of it. Dom had shown him several pictures. Ripoli was from Milan; what was he doing here? Had Carlo sent him to keep an eye on them? Had the man seen what he'd done with Toni?

"Rico?" Toni asked. He hadn't realized that he'd stopped and gone stiff until she spoke.

"Come on," he said and started walking, watching Ripoli closely, but he seemed to be unaware of them.

Or maybe he just wanted Enrico to think that.

Barely breathing, Enrico addressed the man as they drew near. "*Buona sera, signore,*" he said and nodded.

"*Buona sera,*" the man said with a dip of his chin, but no other sign of notice.

Still, every hair on Enrico's body stood at attention as they passed by. Given his own recent surveillance of this man's associates, a darker possibility occurred to him. Perhaps the man's presence meant something else entirely.

Perhaps Carlo had a job for his killers. A job close to home.

And if that was the case, Enrico had to change his plan. He'd wanted more time, to be sure he was ready. But now he'd have to speed things up and finish at least the first three hits in a little over a week. Something told him Carlo planned to strike at the engagement party, at a time when their guard would be down. But Carlo couldn't do that if his killers were dead.

Enrico had to act before Carlo did, or else all would be lost.

———◆———

Antonella floated into the house as if in a dream. Rico had called her his girl, and he'd given her an amazing present: her first taste of what things could be like between them once they were married.

Grinning to herself, she was about to take the stairs up to her room when she heard her father talking in low tones to someone whose voice sounded eerily familiar, and yet was strange.

She paused with one foot on the stairs, straining to listen. And then she heard it again. "*Sì*, Don Andretti," the man said to her father, his voice a guttural rasp.

Just like the voice of the man who'd so startled Enrico at the car park. It couldn't be. Could it? And if it was the same man, what did that mean?

She pivoted off the stair and slipped off her shoes before heading toward her father's study. When she reached the library, she paused, just one door away from her father's domain.

"You're bringing in Borelli, Valentino, and Gennaro?" the stranger asked.

"*Sì*. You all work so well together," her father said with a chuckle. "Any other questions?"

"Just where and when."

"It hasn't been settled exactly. I'll call."

"*Buona sera*, then, Don Andretti." The half-open door to her father's study swung wide, and Antonella slipped into the library and flattened herself against the near wall so the man wouldn't see her.

As he passed by, she snuck a glance at the back of him—same height and build as the man at the car park, looked like the same clothes and haircut. It had to be him.

What was going on? If this man worked for her father, why did Enrico know him?

And what did her father want this man to do?

Maybe she should just ask. She waited until the front door closed, then she stepped into the hall and went to her father's study. She tapped on the open door with her knuckles. "Papà?"

Her father looked up from the glass of whiskey he was pouring at the sideboard. "Come in, *dolcezza*." He finished pouring his glass and carried it over to his desk. Antonella followed, and he motioned to the shoes she was carrying by the straps. "So that's how you snuck up on me."

She laughed, playing it cool. "They were pinching my feet. Couldn't wait to get them off."

He glanced at the clock on his desk. "Ten fifteen," he said with a frown.

"We've been sitting out front for a while."

"Doing what?"

She blushed at his scrutiny. "Talking."

He raised a brow. "Toni."

"We kissed. A little."

He sat back in his chair, cradling the whiskey in his hands. "You like him?"

"I do."

"And he's treating you properly?"

It took everything she had not to fidget, though heat crept up her neck. "He is."

"You're blushing again. So either you're lying, or—"

"He's treating me with respect, Papà."

"He's a Lucchesi. I'm not sure they know what respect is."

"Enrico knows. He's not his father."

Her father took a sip of whiskey. "No, he's not. He's still got some fire in him."

"And you like that."

"I respect it."

She circled to the topic she wanted to discuss. "Who was that man I passed on my way in?" she asked. "I didn't recognize him."

"One of my men from Milan."

"Why was he here?"

"He's helping me with something I'm working on."

"What?" she asked, making the question as innocent as she could.

"Something that will make us rich."

"We're already rich."

"Richer then."

She leaned forward, feigning eagerness. "What is it?"

He pursed his lips and studied her. "It's a surprise."

Papà was rarely this cagey about his plans. Which meant he either didn't trust her or he didn't think she'd approve.

The last time he'd been like this, Enrico's family had been gunned down, and her brother had lost a finger.

What sort of scheme was her father planning now?

And what was Enrico's connection to it? Should she confess about Enrico recognizing the man earlier?

Or was Enrico the one who needed the warning?

With her father, it was so hard to tell. He could be devising some new way to make money, or he could be up to much, much worse.

Antonella's gut cramped. Without knowing more, how could she choose between Enrico and Papà?

CHAPTER 8

Despite his worries about Carlo's plans, Enrico couldn't stop thinking about Toni. *Dio mio*, had he ever been so crazy for a girl? Enrico forced himself to dress instead of attending to his swollen *cazzo*. He'd already done so twice since dropping Antonella off last night, but he couldn't stop his mind from drifting back to how she'd felt in his arms, the way she'd moaned when she'd rocked against him, the way she'd offered to touch him at the end. Her innocence was beguiling.

Not even Veronica had affected him this way. There was something about Toni. She wasn't the prettiest girl he'd dated, and yet he couldn't get her out of his mind. Maybe it was just because he knew he'd be marrying her soon.

Or maybe it had something to do with how she'd soothed his pain last night, the tenderness with which she'd looked after him. She cared about him in a way no one had in a long time.

Veronica wanted him, yes, but her feelings seemed... greedy, compared to Toni's. Toni didn't seem to want anything from him, other than that he treat her kindly. Something he'd done inconsistently, at best. He'd fix that from now on.

Tucking away his half-hard *cazzo*, he combed his wet hair and left his bedroom, heading downstairs to join his father at their dock.

They were meeting Romano Marchesi, the banker Giacomo Parini had told his father about, at Parini's store in Bellagio. Marchesi was understandably nervous; he worried that Carlo would find him out and kill him, so it had to look like they were meeting by chance, in case either party had been followed.

They took the boat across the lake, Enrico's father at the wheel, neither of them talking beyond the necessities—"You ready?" his father had asked when he'd appeared. And when Enrico had nodded, his father had said only, "Then cast us off."

The thump of waves against the hull, the splashing of their wake, the drone of the boat's motor, were the only sounds now, and Enrico's mind wandered back to what he'd been thinking in the car last night. About how Papà couldn't bear to look at him. It was true.

65

And it was horrible. He reached over and cut the engine back to idle. "What are you doing?" Rinaldo asked.

"I don't know. But I have to do it."

Rinaldo's brows came down low over his eyes. "You're not making sense."

Words lodged in Enrico's throat, painful words, and his heart beat in a staccato rhythm. "I miss them too."

Rinaldo stiffened and looked away. He cranked the throttle, and when Enrico tried to stop him, Rinaldo batted Enrico's hand away. "We're not talking about this," he said gruffly over the engine noise.

"Not now, or not ever?" Enrico shouted over the motor.

Rinaldo didn't answer, just kept his eyes trained on their destination.

Enrico lifted a hand to touch his father's shoulder, then let it drop to his side, his throat clamping shut. What did he expect? That two years would cure his father's grief? It certainly hadn't cured his own.

Neither of them said anything until they docked. Finally Rinaldo broke the silence. "I will talk when I am ready. Now is not the time."

It wasn't what he wanted, but it was a glimmer. Perhaps they'd someday be able to break through the ice that had formed between them.

He had to hope.

"With Marchesi, let me do the talking," Rinaldo said. "At least to start."

"*Sì.*" Enrico followed his father up the hill toward Parini's shop. "So what's our cover? Maybe I should get something for Toni."

Rinaldo stopped and gave him a look. "We're picking up her rings today."

Madonna. He'd forgotten he'd be presenting an engagement ring to Antonella in a little over a week. He hadn't even thought about it. Had been avoiding thinking about it. Thank goodness his father hadn't.

But how it must have hurt Papà to do so. What had he been thinking as he'd picked out a wedding set for the daughter of the man who'd killed his wife?

They'd never discussed it, but Enrico had privately vowed that no Andretti would ever wear Mamma's ring. Her beautiful ring with the enormous pink diamond that had been the talk of the lake. "Now there's a man who loves his wife," people would say when they saw it.

Mamma would say it was too much, truly, but Enrico could tell that she hadn't meant it, that inside she'd beamed at how much her husband had spent on her. Most people lived in homes that cost far less.

That ring hadn't been the one Papà had given her at their wedding; that one had been far more modest, what he could afford at the time.

The new one, the one he'd given her five years ago, that had been a ring a king would give his queen.

Perhaps the kind of ring Enrico would give Antonella someday. But it would never be that particular one. Not the one that had been drenched in Mamma's blood.

They reached the door of Parini Jewelers and stepped inside. The small shop was neat and clean, all dark woods and shining glass cases, the carpeting beneath their feet as plush as any in their villa. The walls were crammed with old masters, and Enrico could immediately see one of the connections between his father and

Parini—they had the same taste in art.

The man in question greeted them effusively, his balding head shining under the overhead lights. Enrico looked around, but no one else was in the shop. Marchesi apparently hadn't arrived yet. Well, all the better to make their meeting appear unplanned.

"Let me get the rings," Parini said and hurried into the back of the shop. He reappeared moments later, a small midnight blue velvet box in his hand. He opened it for them and set it on the counter.

"May I?" Enrico asked before touching them.

"Of course. They are yours."

Enrico took the rings from the box, conscious of Papà's eyes on his face. While not nearly as spectacular as his mother's ring, Enrico thought this set suitably impressive. A large emerald-cut diamond graced a delicate band with half a dozen more diamonds inset on each side. The wedding band likewise contained a half circle of inset diamonds. They would look beautiful on Toni's slender finger. "Stunning," he murmured.

"It should be enough to please Carlo," Papà said.

Enrico had been picturing only Toni's reaction, but Papà was right—the thing that mattered most was how Carlo felt. Too small a ring, and he'd be insulted.

"How much are they?" Enrico asked. Parini didn't answer the question, so Enrico directed a glance at his father, who shook his head. "Tell me," Enrico said.

"It's none of your concern."

Enrico shoved the rings back in the box and snapped it shut. "None of my concern? These are the rings I'm giving to *my* fiancée."

Papà raised a brow. "You didn't seem the slightest bit interested in the rings—or their necessity—until just now."

"How much?" Enrico demanded.

"More than the Ferrari you're driving."

Enrico was about to apply directly to Parini again, when the door to the shop swung open, the bell attached to the door giving a pleasant jingle.

A well-dressed man in his forties, with slicked back hair and a long thin nose, stepped inside. A look passed between Parini and his father. That must be Marchesi then.

The man glanced around the shop, as if checking for other patrons. Parini went to Marchesi and greeted him. The two of them conferred for a moment, then slowly made their way over to the counter where Enrico and Rinaldo stood.

Up close, Enrico could see that the man looked tired—dark purple half-moons cupped Marchesi's eyes, and lines of tension creased the man's forehead and bracketed his mouth.

"So you have decided to help me," Marchesi said, while facing Parini as if he were talking to the jeweler instead of Rinaldo.

"I think we can help each other," Rinaldo replied, also not looking directly at the man.

"How can *I* help *you*?" Marchesi asked, glancing at them from the side of his eye.

"Tell me about your situation with Carlo Andretti."

Marchesi's shoulders rose and his knuckles whitened where his hands clutched the glass case. "He is ruining me," Marchesi said, his voice low and desperate.

"How? I need specifics."

"Not in front of the boy."

"He stays. He's in this business too."

Parini made a show of pulling several rings from the case and setting them in front of Marchesi, who picked them up one at a time and examined them as he spoke. "The boy can keep his mouth shut?"

Enrico bristled, but let his father answer. "He's my son."

Marchesi said nothing for a moment, instead shaking his head and handing one of the rings back to Parini. He pointed to another in the case.

"Andretti runs a club, an exclusive club where gentlemen can…" Marchesi hesitated, then continued. "Can get certain needs met."

"A brothel."

Marchesi nodded. "I was photographed there without my knowledge. The photos were sent to me at the bank."

"And you don't want your wife to see them."

"I don't want *anyone* to see them. If they got out—" Marchesi stopped himself. "I'd be ruined."

Rinaldo shrugged. "Your marriage might be over, but surely you exaggerate."

Marchesi shook his head. "My tastes are… unusual."

"Ah," Rinaldo said, and Enrico wondered what his father was thinking. What could be so bad? Then Rinaldo said something that made Enrico blush. "Boys?"

"You don't need to know."

"No surprises. That's one of my conditions."

Marchesi set down the ring he'd been holding and braced himself against the case, his head hanging in defeat. "I like…" His voice warbled and he started over, turning a furious crimson. "I like women's clothing. To wear it when I'm having sex. With a woman," he added.

Enrico suppressed a laugh. Just picturing it, this man in a dress and wig—it was ridiculous.

"You're not a *finocchio*?" Rinaldo asked.

Marchesi shook his head emphatically. "No. But you see why I can't let this get out."

"*Sì.*" Rinaldo put his hands in his pockets and rocked back on his heels. "So, what is Carlo getting from you?"

"Money. Over two billion *lire* this year alone."

Rinaldo whistled. "You have that kind of spare cash?"

"Of course not. I've been borrowing from customer accounts. The investment accounts. I've been able to hide some of it with trading losses, but sooner or later…"

"What else?"

"I clean money for him. And he owns half my share in the bank."

"On paper?"

Marchesi shook his head. "It's still in my name. So are his accounts."

Rinaldo looked at Enrico and grinned. They had something. "Legally the assets are yours then."

"*Sì.* He told me what the government didn't know about, they couldn't tax."

"Clever," Rinaldo said. "But risky at the same time."

"How so?" Marchesi asked. "I wouldn't dare cross him."

"But *I* would." Rinaldo leaned forward as if to talk to Parini. "How badly do you want help?"

"I'm desperate."

"Enough to sell me your share of the bank—the part Carlo doesn't already own?"

Marchesi closed his eyes and swayed slightly. "Romano," Parini said, concern in his voice.

"I'm all right," Marchesi finally said and opened his eyes. "The bank, it has been in my family for over a century."

"From what you've told me, it is already in Carlo Andretti's hands."

Marchesi smacked a fist on the glass case, hard enough to rattle the rings inside and startle Parini. "You are no better than him," he hissed.

Rinaldo stiffened and Enrico grabbed his shoulder. He wanted to hit the man too, but even he could see the opportunity. "Papà," he whispered.

Rinaldo shook off Enrico's hand and addressed Marchesi. "I will let you live. I will also let you leave with your dignity and some money in your wallet. Carlo will not."

Marchesi let out a breath, his shoulders slumping. "I suppose that is the best I can hope for."

"You are lucky I need you. Not many men insult me and live."

Except Carlo, Enrico thought. But if they were able to pull this off, Carlo would suffer plenty. And that might be better than seeing him dead.

"I beg your forgiveness, Don Lucchesi," Marchesi whispered. "A broken man is sometimes foolish in his speech."

"I understand," Rinaldo said. "More than you know."

How were they going to manage this? They didn't have the money to buy Marchesi out. Enrico was dying to ask, but it would have to wait.

"Here is what I need from you," Rinaldo said to Marchesi. He outlined a plan that made Enrico smile.

Carlo's cleverness had led him straight into a trap of his own device.

———— ◆ ————

After discussing his suspicions about Ripoli and Carlo with Dom, Enrico turned his sights on Leone Valentino. Valentino had been the right-hand to Bruno Macri, the probable architect of the massacre. Livio had told him that Macri hadn't been seen since that night, so he was likely dead. But Leone Valentino was alive and well.

Enrico followed Valentino for six days, studying his routines. Every evening, around ten, the man had a cigarette in his car before going inside his flat in Milan and up to bed. His wife apparently didn't want him smoking in the house. They had a new baby; maybe that was why. When Enrico had learned these details, he'd hesitated. He'd be leaving a child without a father, a wife without a husband.

But Valentino had dealt his own cards. He'd taken money to kill a defenseless woman and a young boy. Primo may have been fair game, but the 'Ndrangheta codes were clear on this point: Mamma and Mario were not.

Men like Valentino didn't deserve to live.

Dom had given Enrico a throwaway gun. Now all he needed to be ready was the disguise of his youth. He kept himself clean shaven, his hair cropped close, his clothes those of a simple boy, not those fitting the son of a Mafia *capo*.

On the corner opposite Valentino's home, Enrico fiddled with the open pack of cigarettes in his left jacket pocket. He didn't smoke, but Valentino didn't know that. He checked his watch. Almost ten. His eyes glued to Valentino's door, Enrico took a breath to quell his nerves. His right hand found the loaded revolver in his jacket pocket. He'd carefully cleaned and oiled the gun the night before. He was ready.

And yet when Valentino's front door opened, Enrico nearly jumped out of his skin. *This is it.* His heart thumped in his chest. He pressed himself against the stone wall, trying to look casual as Valentino came down the walk, jingling the keys to his dark blue Alfa Romeo. He let himself inside and put down the window. Soon smoke drifted from the car.

Now, Enrico commanded himself. Yet his feet refused to move. Though the night was cool, sweat dripped down his back, his heart pounding as if he'd run a marathon. *Move, damn you. Move!*

He took a step, then another, his movements awkward, forced. Inhaling deeply, he conjured up the crime-scene photos—Mamma, Primo, and Mario covered in blood. This man was one of those responsible.

Fishing the pack of cigarettes from his pocket, Enrico tapped one out as he crossed the street and approached Valentino's car. When he was a few feet away, he said, "*Scusi.* Have a light?"

Valentino nodded and patted his jacket for his lighter. While the man was distracted, Enrico flicked the cigarette away with his left hand and pulled the revolver with his right and aimed it at the man's temple. There was no going back. Yet his finger refused to pull the trigger. Everything slowed to a crawl—the frown on Valentino's face, the scrunching of his brow, the flicker of surprise as he turned and saw the gun in the gleam of the streetlamps. The man's mouth formed a single word: "Who?" as his hands scrambled in his jacket, his expression hardening in an instant.

Now, damn you, now! Enrico's brain screamed at him as blood rushed in his ears. Finally his finger obeyed, the gunshot shattering the night.

Valentino's head snapped back and to the side, blood and gore spraying the passenger side of the car. The man slumped over. Enrico leaned inside, fired another shot into Valentino's head, then stuffed the gun in his pocket and walked quickly away.

His heart pumped wildly and he shivered inside. Enrico wanted to run, but he forced himself to keep moving at a steady, controlled pace. He walked two blocks, then he doubled over and was sick beside a tree. When he felt completely wrung out, he spat, then wiped his mouth on his sleeve. Even though the night was cool, beads of sweat dotted his forehead. A wave of heat ran through him, followed by a wave of cold, as if he had a fever. Taking a deep breath, he resumed walking, wiped down the gun, and tossed it into a sewer drain right before he reached the nondescript car he'd borrowed.

His hands trembled; his mouth tasted like ashes. He dropped the keys beside the Fiat, his heart slamming in his chest at the enormity of what he'd done. He'd taken a life. He'd committed murder, the most grievous of sins.

Picking up the keys, he got in the car and drove toward home. Dom had told him the first time would be hard; what he hadn't told him was that it would be excruciating. He was a killer now—a man who'd stepped out of the ordinary path, a man who'd chosen to live by violence. Enrico had never once in his life wanted to be that kind of man. He'd wanted a quiet life; he'd wanted to be an academic, or a banker, or an entrepreneur. He'd never wanted to be a killer. A Mafioso.

The plan had always been for Primo and Mario to follow in their father's footsteps. Enrico had been destined for something different—everyone could see that, even Papà.

And then Carlo Andretti had come along and changed everything. He'd ripped the lives from Primo, Mario, Mamma. Papà. And he'd ripped Enrico's life from him too.

Nothing had been the same since. And now that he'd killed Valentino, Enrico was committed to this deadly course.

When he reached a small church in the hills outside Como, he stopped. He needed to confess, to cleanse his soul.

The quiet church was empty but for an old *nonna* lighting candles and a young woman kneeling in the pews, praying fervently and crying.

He walked down the center aisle, his footsteps echoing as he made his way to the confessional. The sound seemed almost obscenely loud, and he tried to place his feet more carefully to muffle the noise. An old priest came forth and ushered him inside the booth. Enrico stepped in and sat, crossing himself and saying, "Bless me father, for I have sinned."

"What is troubling you, my son?"

The familiar question shook Enrico out of his shock. Prior to this, the worst thing he'd done was have premarital sex with Veronica. Murdering a man was something else altogether. He could not confess this. He could not ask for God's absolution. Not when he intended to do it again. Not when he would ask other men to do the same in the future.

"My son?" the priest said again.

"I shouldn't have come here. Forgive me, Father." Without waiting for a response, Enrico scrambled out of the confessional and ran out of the church without looking back.

Somewhere in that church, somewhere on that side street in Milan, he'd left the boy he'd been behind.

He'd taken the vows two years before, but it was only now that he felt like what he'd become: an 'Ndranghetista. A man of honor. A man who lived and died by his gun.

The life he'd always resisted was his now, fully, irrevocably. The *malavita*.

———◆———

It was nearly midnight when Enrico reached Cernobbio. He hadn't been able to talk to the priest at the church. But there was one person he could talk to about what had happened with Valentino. Dom.

He pressed the intercom button at the gate to Zio Poldi's villa. A guard answered and let him in. He drove through and up to the house, where Dom was waiting on the front steps to usher him inside. Dom took one look at Enrico's face and said, "You look like you could use a drink."

"I could. Several."

Dom and Enrico headed to Zio Poldi's study, and Dom poured them each three fingers of amber-colored whiskey while Enrico took a seat on a low sofa along one wall. Dom handed him a beautifully cut crystal tumbler, then sat in an overstuffed burgundy wingback chair across from Enrico, the leather creaking beneath him. "So you did it?" he asked softly.

Enrico nodded and took a sip of the whiskey, a sip that turned into a gulp. He took a deep breath before speaking. "I'm not sure I can do it again."

"It's not easy."

"No."

They sat in silence for several moments, Enrico's stomach churning as he relived Valentino's head snapping back, the smell of gunpowder and blood somehow still fresh in his nostrils. "I'm not sure I'm still human."

Dom leaned forward. "You've made your point with Carlo. You don't have to do the rest."

But Carlo could still do the job with three killers. Carlo could still have targets on Dom and Zio Poldi. Carlo could be planning anything.

Carlo needed a reminder that he wasn't invincible.

"I have to do this."

"Look, this shouldn't all fall on you. I can do the rest."

"If I'm to be *capo*, *I* need to do this. I need to prove to the men that I can lead them. That I'm not afraid."

Cradling his tumbler in his hands, Dom shook his head. "One is enough."

"It's not." Enrico took another drink, then set the whiskey on the table and raked his hands through his hair. His father wouldn't like him telling Dom, but he was going to do it anyway. "Carlo has you and your father in his sights."

"What?"

"He sent pictures to Papà. Surveillance photos of the two of you."

"That fucker," Dom said, his brows drawing down over his eyes.

"It gets worse." Enrico picked up the tumbler again and drained it, then held it out for Dom to refill.

Dom took it and rose, going over to the sideboard. "Worse how?" He refilled Enrico's glass and brought it back along with the decanter.

"Ripoli was following me last week."

"*Porca vacca*, Rico. Why didn't you tell me?"

"I didn't want to worry you."

"Does your father know?"

"Of course not. He'd skin me if he knew what I was doing. And he'd put a stop to it."

Dom gave him a sly look. "So what's the problem? I thought you wanted to quit."

Enrico stared at his whiskey, but no answers came from that quarter. "I do." He took a swallow. "And I don't." He rolled the tumbler back and forth in his hands, then set it down with a thunk. "I swore I would avenge them. I swore I would finish this."

"No one has to know it wasn't you."

"*I'll* know. *You'll* know." He took a deep breath. "This is my task to finish."

"*Cristo* and his cross."

Enrico gave him a hard stare. "I hope you don't think that was funny."

"I hope *you* don't think you have to be a martyr."

"I don't intend to die for this."

"That's what I wanted to hear." Dom held out his glass and inclined his head. "*Salute.*"

Leaning forward, Enrico tapped his glass against Dom's. "*Salute.*" He took a sip then set the glass aside. "Let's walk through the plan for tomorrow one more time."

———— • ————

"I still don't like you doing this on your own," Dom said. "It's too risky."

They were sitting in a borrowed car outside Cristiano Borelli's home in Milan. It was early evening, around six-thirty. Enrico would have preferred darkness, but Borelli liked to walk his dog around then, and he almost always took it into a nearby park, which would be the perfect place to hit him.

Enrico ignored Dom and screwed a silencer onto the Beretta. Yet another throwaway gun with the serial numbers filed off. He had no idea who'd done that work—maybe some young boy trying to impress his father and get into the society early. Or perhaps some new initiate. It couldn't be easy work.

Stop drifting, he chided himself.

"Rico," Dom said. "Look at me." He turned to Dom. "At least let me back you up."

"And have the men say one day that I needed a nursemaid when I avenged my brothers?"

"This is a difficult job. You have only twenty minutes—"

"I know."

"If you don't finish him by then, Ripoli will be in for the evening. And you can't wait until tomorrow."

"I *know*." And on top of that, he had a date with Toni tonight. In two and a half hours. It was nearly an hour back to Blevio. He was cutting it far too close.

But what choice did he have?

"Rico, if something happens to you—"

"Stop it, Dom. *Now*."

73

"Your father would never forgive me."

"*I* will never forgive you if you don't shut up." He exhaled slowly. "*I* need to do this. Not you."

"But I'd be acting on your orders."

"Not good enough. They see *my* face last."

"I'm a Lucchesi too."

"*Basta!*" Enrico snapped and sliced a hand under his own chin. A movement on the walkway across from them snagged his attention.

It was Cristiano Borelli, being towed down the walk by a large white bulldog. The dog was just out of the puppy stage and full of vigor, its knotty muscles straining under its short white coat as it yanked against its leash.

Borelli made a clicking noise at the dog, and it checked itself, settling into a bowlegged trot by its master's side.

Enrico let them get halfway down the block before he eased out of the car. He didn't quite close the door behind him. He held the gun down by his leg, the long silencer brushing against the outside of his right thigh.

Heart pulsing in his throat, Enrico followed Borelli, stopping whenever he stopped to let the dog piss on a bush or a clump of grass, each time making Enrico's adrenaline spike. As soon as the dog defecated, the walk would be over, and Enrico didn't want to shoot the man on this street. It was too public.

The man and dog stopped several more times before turning into the small, well-treed park, and although Enrico was relieved, his pulse sped up. He had to act now.

The dog sniffed at a bush, then squatted down. Borelli pulled out a cigarette and lighter.

Enrico advanced quickly. "Signor Borelli?" he said, feigning astonishment. "It's me, Giuseppe Riccardi's boy."

The man's brow wrinkled in confusion as he studied Enrico's face, missing the movement as Enrico raised the gun.

This is for them. Enrico squeezed the trigger, shooting Borelli in the chest, the muffled shot seeming loud in the silence.

The man fell to the dirt path, his hands clutched over the wound bubbling blood. The dog, finished with its business, growled, and Enrico stepped away from it, instead aiming his gun at the man's face. "*Scusi.* I misspoke. My father is Rinaldo Lucchesi." He waited for recognition to spread across Borelli's features. Then he pulled the trigger again.

The dog lunged and caught Enrico's left hand in its teeth. Pain lanced up his arm, and he brought down the gun butt across the dog's sensitive black nose. It let out a sharp whine and released his hand.

He'd seen Carlo discipline one of his Rottweilers that way. Who'd have known such knowledge would ever be so useful?

The dog sniffed at its owner's head and whined again before licking the man's cheek.

His hand throbbing, Enrico hurried back to the park's entrance, unscrewing the silencer and wiping down the gun with a handkerchief as he walked. He tossed the weapon deep into the bushes as he left the park, but retained the suppressor.

He had one more job to do that night.

When he got back to the car, Dom looked pointedly at his injured left hand. "The dog?" he asked as he put the car in gear and headed to their next destination.

"*Sì*." Enrico wiped the blood on his black trousers and inspected the wound. He'd probably need a tetanus shot, but he was able to flex his fingers. "Nothing serious."

"I should have been with you."

"You are."

"You sure you can—"

"*Sì*." Enrico cut him off with a glare. "It's barely a scratch. Just drive."

"Whatever you say, *il mio principe*."

Enrico's gut burned. Dom didn't have to like that Enrico would be *capo* someday, but he didn't have to be so free with the reminders. "You want to be more than an underboss?" Enrico asked.

"Of course."

"Then listen to me now. I'll make you *capo di società* if you stop complaining. This minute. And never call me that again."

Dom said nothing, and Enrico took his silence as acceptance. He stared out the window as they traveled through a rough neighborhood, graffiti freely evident on the facades of buildings long since boarded up. A stone sat in his stomach, heavy and hard, and he inhaled and exhaled, trying to dispel it. But the weight remained.

Twice now he'd sinned. Twice now he'd killed.

And he would do it at least twice more before the end of the next day.

CHAPTER 9

They sped down several streets, Dom silent beside him. Finally he said something. "I admire you, Rico."

Startled, Enrico turned to his cousin. "You do?"

"Our fathers, and I too, haven't done what we should have from the start. And here you are, still half a boy, and you're taking care of it."

"You're not that much older." Enrico took another throwaway gun from the glove box and attached the suppressor.

"At this point, three years is a world of difference."

"Well, if I finish it unscathed, it will be because of your help and *Dio*'s benevolence." Enrico paused. "I know I'm being foolish, taking this risk, but I cannot stand letting Carlo Andretti think he has bested us."

"Neither can I."

They pulled onto a quiet residential street, and Enrico's heart quickened. He really ought to have Dom's direct assistance with this one, but he had to do this alone, to atone for his two years of inaction. Two years they'd lain underground, unavenged. Two years they'd awaited justice.

Two years Carlo Andretti had gloated, had circled the Lucchesis like a shark.

No more. After tonight, Carlo would know that the game had changed.

Dom had observed Ripoli for about a week and a half. The man lived alone, but visited his ailing grandparents every day, arriving home at seven PM without fail. As long as Ripoli was sticking to his routine, all would be well. If Enrico failed to get him today, the odds of success plunged. And the odds of Enrico getting killed skyrocketed.

It was 6:56 as they glided down Ripoli's street. "He drives a silver Alfa 90," Dom said. "He usually parks it on your side."

Enrico scanned the parked cars, but didn't see a silver Alfa. A car pulled onto the road behind them, and Enrico strained to see what make it was in his side mirror. He didn't want to turn around and alert the driver. Finally he was sure. "He's behind us."

"I'll stop around the next corner. You'll have to approach on foot."

"Not a problem." He was squeezing the gun so hard he could feel his pulse in his fingers. He adjusted his grip and exhaled slowly.

Maybe he should have accepted Dom's help, but it was too late now. They were pulling to the curb out of Ripoli's sight, and it was either act now, or the moment would be lost.

Enrico slipped out of the car almost before it stopped moving, gun by his side, walking rapidly toward the silver Alfa that Ripoli was parallel parking.

While Ripoli was still distracted, his attention on not backing into the Fiat behind him, Enrico charged up to the driver's window and let loose a shot.

The glass shattered, but Ripoli seemed unhurt. He reacted instantly, reaching out and grabbing the long barrel of Enrico's gun. His vehicle rolled back into the Fiat, setting off the car's alarm.

"Lucchesi," the man grunted as he tried to wrest the gun from Enrico. Enrico's heart thrashed against his ribs, his breathing so fast and shallow his vision started to narrow. He was on the verge of panic. Any moment now he would be discovered, or Ripoli could gain control of the weapon.

They struggled, both grunting with the effort, when Enrico realized he had an advantage. He whipped his bent elbow forward, connecting with Ripoli's jaw and cheekbone.

It was enough to loosen the man's grip, and Enrico was able to twist the gun into Ripoli's face and pump two shots into him.

The man jerked as he died, the wound in his neck spraying Enrico with blood. But he'd done it. He'd killed three now.

One to go. If he managed to escape capture.

Doors to the surrounding apartment buildings were opening, people shouting about the alarm's racket, but no one seemed to have noticed yet what had happened between Enrico and Ripoli.

Enrico stuffed the gun in his jacket pocket and wiped his face on his sleeve and shoulder as he walked away, thankful that Dom had counseled him to wear dark clothes. He hurried to the corner where he'd left Dom.

No.

The car was gone. All he saw was an empty hole by the curb where Dom had been waiting.

Enrico's lungs spasmed, and he couldn't seem to catch his breath. He was just about to start running when he heard a car pull up beside him. It was Dom. He yanked the door open and scrambled into the vehicle as his cousin smoothly pulled away. "Where the hell were you?" Enrico shouted.

"*Polizia* passed by and were looking at me a little too much, so I pretended to drive off."

"We'd better ditch this car."

"And you'd better ditch those clothes. You stink of blood."

"I was too close. He grabbed the gun."

Dom let out a hiss. "You hurt?"

"No. I didn't have time to dump the gun though."

They heard the sing-song wail of sirens in the distance behind them. Ripoli's body had been discovered. No doubt the officer who'd been checking out Dom was putting two and two together. It was only a matter of time before an alert was issued for their car.

"Do we have any safe places nearby?" Enrico asked.

"I think so."

"You *think* so?"

Dom took a deep breath. "I'm a little lost, to be honest."

Merda. This just kept getting better. He should have convinced Livio to help. No one knew where they were, and until they found a safe haven where they could contact some of his father's men, they were on their own.

"Okay. Concentrate. Where's the closest location to us? Which direction from where we were?"

"East."

"Then head east." Enrico wiped down the gun with the handkerchief. "Pull over in that alley on the right."

Dom drove between a row of tall buildings, and Enrico tossed the gun into a reeking dumpster behind a restaurant, then dropped the silencer in another. When he got back in the car, he mopped his face and hair with the handkerchief. It came back red, and he stared at it, remembering the ruined mess of Ripoli's face after he'd pulled the trigger. He gagged, then pulled in air through his nose. He could not be sick, not on top of everything else. When he trusted himself not to vomit, he said, "Anything look familiar?"

"I'm not sure."

Enrico resisted the impulse to punch the dashboard. They were not going to fail. Not like this.

"What cross streets are we looking for?" he asked.

"Via Sangro and Via Crescenzago. It's an old warehouse. There should be a car there."

Enrico read off street names as they drove. When he said "Via Monfalcone," Dom slowed the car. "That sounds familiar." He advanced more carefully, studying the signs ahead. "Via Sangro. Got it."

They turned onto Via Crescenzago, and Enrico said a silent prayer of thanks. *Dio was* smiling on him, on this undertaking.

Within minutes, they'd reached the warehouse, and Dom tapped the horn. An unshaven middle-aged man Enrico didn't recognize came out and greeted Dom. He peered at Enrico and seemed to realize who he was, for he gave Enrico a deferential nod before motioning them inside.

A large sliding door opened in front of them, being pushed by another man Enrico didn't know. He'd been gone too long—as his father's son, as the future *capo*, he ought to know all of these men. Especially the ones at this warehouse, who were about to risk their lives and their freedom for him.

"What are their names?" he asked Dom as they drove inside.

"Tommaso is the one who met us. Filippo is the other."

Enrico greeted the men by name after he and Dom got out of the car. "We need a different vehicle. The *polizia* are looking for this one. I also need a change of clothes and a shower."

"Who'd you off?" Tommaso asked.

"Two of those who needed it."

Understanding animated the man's face and lit up his smile. "It's about time," he said and gave Enrico a quick bow.

Papà would be furious with him, but the men were applauding. The *cosca* had needed him to do this, no matter the cost.

"We don't have clothes or a shower here, but you can find both at an apartment on Via Mestre." Tommaso gave them the directions as he handed over a new set of keys to a nondescript Fiat with dirty white paint. "We'll take care of this one," he said, jerking his thumb at the car they'd left.

Enrico glanced at his watch. He had an hour and a half before his date with Antonella. He still might make it on time.

A car sped by outside, siren keening. "Third one," Filippo said.

"They're looking for us." Enrico's stomach knotted.

"They won't find you, not in that beast," Tommaso said.

Enrico motioned to the car they were leaving behind. "What will you do with it?"

"Change the plates and repaint it, of course." Tommaso motioned to several drums of paint and sprayers stacked in the corner. Filippo was already stepping into a special head-to-toe hooded suit that would keep him clean.

"You have my thanks," Enrico said.

"Remember us when you get back home. We'd like something else to do."

"I'll speak to my father about it."

The white Fiat stank of cigarettes, but Enrico breathed easier for the first time that night. This had been the most difficult test of his life so far, and somehow he'd passed.

But he almost hadn't. And the biggest challenge remained ahead of him: a trained killer on the alert.

———•———

Enrico was late, and he hadn't called. Antonella fidgeted with her dress and checked her watch again. Was something wrong? Did it have anything to do with that man from the car park?

Had Papà put his plan—whatever it was—in motion?

She paced the length of the ground floor corridor, her heels tapping on the marble, her anxiety rising with every step. She cast another glance at the door to her father's study, but it remained closed. He'd received several phone calls about an hour ago and had been closed up in there ever since, his voice low and urgent, occasionally rising to a shout.

Something had happened. Something that wasn't good. She just hoped it didn't involve Enrico.

Antonella was crossing back to the foyer when headlights flashed across the space and she heard the crunch of gravel under car tires. Rico!

She grabbed her handbag and a light jacket from the chair by the door and dashed outside. Enrico got out and greeted her with a peck on the cheek. He smelled of soap, and his hair looked a little damp.

"I was getting worried," she blurted.

"Sorry. I didn't sleep well last night. I took a nap and woke up late. I guess I should have called to let you know." He opened her door and waited for her to get in before closing it and crossing to his own side.

He'd needed a nap? He did look a bit tired. Perhaps he was falling ill. "You feel all right?" she asked when he got in.

"Of course," he said and smiled. But something seemed off. Maybe he'd been thinking about his family again.

"We don't have to do anything tonight, Rico. The party's tomorrow. I can wait until then to see you, if you need some time to yourself."

He didn't answer right away, just gripped the steering wheel without starting the car and stared straight ahead at nothing, as far as she could tell. Finally he shook his head. "I'm fine, Toni. Just a little tired, that's all."

"We could skip the movie. Just have dinner?"

"We'll see." He started the ignition and put the car into gear. As he drove, she noticed something odd—his jacket didn't fit. The sleeves rode up too far on his wrists as he turned the wheel, and he seemed to be straining the seams at the shoulders.

"Who cut that jacket for you?" she asked. "It's too small."

He gave her a sharp look that quickly turned sheepish. "You caught me."

"Caught you?"

"It was Primo's. I know it doesn't quite fit, but I wanted something of his."

Why couldn't she have kept her mouth shut? What on earth did she say to that? "I'm sorry," she murmured.

He said nothing, and the silence in the car grew, accreting mass bit by bit until she felt she was trying to draw solid matter into her lungs instead of air. "Rico, I thought we'd made progress—"

"We have." His tone was matter of fact. "But it's been a hard day."

She wanted to ask why but didn't dare. She wished they could start over in a different place and time, one where their families weren't at war.

But life would never be that easy for the two of them. Neither would marriage. In fact, it would be harder, because they'd have no respite from each other.

They needed to learn to communicate better. Though tonight probably wasn't the best time to raise that subject.

Or the subject of the man in the car park. But something was happening. She could feel it in her bones. "We need to talk."

He smacked the steering wheel with the flat of his hand. "Not now, Toni. I told you, it's been a hard day."

The bite in his voice made her shrink a little. But this couldn't wait. "Rico, I know."

"No, you *don't*." He pulled into a space in front of a small café she'd been to many times. He turned off the Ferrari and yanked the key from the ignition, then pounded a fist on his thigh. It landed with a meaty thud.

Her eyes were riveted to his face. He closed his own for a second, then blew out and opened them. "I can't talk right now. I just *can't*."

"It might help."

He turned to her, his face a study in agony. "They're dead. Nothing I say or do will ever bring them back."

"You shouldn't try to forget them."

He inhaled deeply. "I haven't. But maybe I should."

"Don't say that."

His voice rose. "What do you think I see every time I look at your father? I see *them*. I see them dead. And your father, all he wants is to shove that in my face. He doesn't want me to forget. You know why?"

She shook her head, afraid to say anything for fear he'd stop talking.

"He wants me to do something foolish. He wants me to break the contract."

"The contract?"

"You haven't seen it?"

"I don't know what you're talking about."

Rico let out a snort. "Of course not. My father didn't want me to know either. If one of us breaks the betrothal, our family loses half its holdings. If either side sheds blood, we lose everything." He stared at her, his breathing accelerated. "You see, don't you? Why your father keeps provoking us?"

Papà's words came back to her: *I'm working on a plan to make us rich.*

Was this what he'd meant?

"But he wants this marriage," she said lamely, realizing the stupidity of her words as she uttered them. He'd told her that so *she* wouldn't break it off. Papà had been acting strangely for a while now—accepting Enrico's insults to her, allowing her to go out with Enrico unescorted, even after she'd told him they'd kissed.

Things Papà never would have done before. Things he wouldn't do now without a good reason.

And that reason was money.

She felt like vomiting. She pressed a fist to her mouth, willing herself not to cry, her whole body going hot with embarrassment.

She meant less to Papà than money did, than power did. He didn't care if Enrico slept with her. He just cared about winning.

Enrico said nothing for a moment, then he brushed her cheek with his fingers. "Oh, Toni," he said, his voice so gentle that tears sprung to her eyes. "I shouldn't have told you."

She shook her head violently and forced herself to talk. "No," she said, her voice wavering. "I'm glad you did. I needed to know where I stood."

"He loves you. I know that much."

"It goes only so far with Papà." She closed her eyes while she said the rest. "I thought it was just Dario he didn't care for. But now I see how he's used me." Enrico would think she meant the marriage, but it went so much deeper. The bugs—Papà's big weapon. The ace up his sleeve. She'd given him that.

And he'd given her this. Second place—if that—in his heart, after the thrill of conquest. After the love of money.

Enrico slipped off his seatbelt and leaned toward her, cupping her cheek in his hand. "I wish I'd never said anything."

She almost agreed, but it was better to know. No matter how bitter the knowledge. Tears slipped down her cheeks, and it took everything she had not to sob aloud.

Enrico got out and came around to her side and opened the door. Leaning in, he undid her belt and pulled her into his arms. She went, as limp as a puppet whose strings had been cut, and burrowed her face in his shirt, not wanting him to see her. His hands stroked her back, and when some people walked by, he guided her away from the restaurant and onto a nearby bench.

She clung to him, sobbing silently, for she didn't know how long. Eventually the tears stopped. Papà was Papà. She shouldn't be surprised.

Enrico's stomach growled, and she remembered why they'd gone out. "You're hungry," she said. "Let's go in." She swiped at her face. She must look awful.

"Change of plans. I can get us a takeaway and we can go to the park."

She gave him a grateful smile. "Thanks."

He walked her back to the Ferrari, then went inside and came back out a short while later with a large bag that he put in the back seat. The smell of tomatoes and spices filled the car as they drove. "What did you order?"

"A few things. You get first pick. I like them all. I wasn't sure what you'd want."

They unloaded their picnic at a table in the park, and Antonella chose the chicken with artichoke hearts and penne. Enrico opened a bottle of wine. "No glasses," he said. "We'll have to share."

He handed the bottle to her and she took a swig, smiling at the novelty of the situation. Here she was in the dark, sitting with Enrico and sharing a meal and a bottle of wine.

And for once they weren't fighting. He sat beside her eating quietly, saying little, seemingly as lost in his thoughts as she was.

She picked at the food at first, but it was too good to waste, so she finally dug in, though Enrico finished well before she did. He grabbed a second meal and she laughed. "I'm a growing boy," he said.

"You're no boy, Rico."

"I suppose not." He was silent for a moment, then he said, "I guess I haven't been a boy for a while now."

"What do you mean?"

"This life forces you to grow up fast."

She set down her plastic fork. She knew what he really meant—losing his family had ended his boyhood. "You've taken the vows, yes?"

He nodded. "Right after their funerals."

"Your father should have given you some time—"

"Someone had to take Primo's place."

"That's all you are, then? A substitute for your older brother?" Her words came out sharper than she'd intended.

"And a poor one at that."

She hated the self-pity in his voice. "Stop underestimating yourself."

"It's how my father feels."

"He's said so?"

"No. But I can tell." He took a drink from the bottle and wiped his mouth.

"He was always closest to Primo and then to Mario. I was the one he didn't understand."

"Why?"

"I never wanted any part of this. I just wanted a normal life."

She said nothing for a few moments, rolling that idea around in her mind, savoring it. "I'm not sure either of us knows what that is."

"Well, it's not this. For the rest of our lives, we'll be wondering when the axe will fall, and how bad it will be when it does." He set the rest of his meal aside.

"It may not be that way. Once we marry, we should have peace."

He chuckled. "With *your* father? Seriously?"

She smiled. "Maybe that's a stretch. But at least the killing should stop."

"That would be something worth having."

When he handed her the bottle, she banged her hand into his, and he let out a little hiss of pain. "Sorry," she said and took his hand in hers to kiss it.

"Don't," he said and pulled it from her grasp, but not before she noticed that the skin was torn.

"What happened?" she asked and reached for his hand again. He resisted giving it to her at first, then he surrendered.

"A dog bit me."

"Why would it do that?"

"How should I know?"

He seemed defensive. Why? "Tell me how it happened."

"I was taking a walk. A man passed by with his dog, and it lunged at me and bit me."

"That's odd."

He shrugged. "Maybe it thought I was a threat."

"Dogs are good at reading people. They don't often attack for no reason."

"Maybe I was thinking about your father at the time."

She shouldn't find that funny, but she did. If she couldn't laugh, she'd have to cry. "You're ridiculously impossible."

He laughed and nodded. "I know. I have no idea how you'll ever put up with me." He reached over and brushed a few strands of hair from her face, then he leaned in and kissed her.

He tasted of the tomatoes and peppers in the chicken cacciatore he'd eaten. His familiar scent enveloped her, and she wound her arms around his neck and breathed him in. Rico. He pulled her close. How safe she felt in his embrace. How accepted.

Her heart swelled with emotion. Was this what love felt like? Not the painful longing she'd harbored for years, but this new one, this yearning to be in his arms, to be by his side, to hear him say her name and kiss her and hold her close. This desire to tell him everything, to have him know her more deeply than anyone else did.

Was love what she was feeling? He broke off the kiss and rested his forehead against hers, his breath washing against her face in warm puffs.

"Toni, I know I've been difficult. Even awful to you at times. I wish I could take it all back. I wish I could have treated you properly from the beginning." He paused and stroked her cheek. "I wish I hadn't been blind."

Her eyes welled up. "You're going to spoil me."

He laughed and kissed her. "I am. I'm going to spoil you rotten."

"Sounds like fun," she said. "In fact, I could use a little spoiling right now." She maneuvered herself onto his lap, gratified to feel that he was hard again. For her.

She rocked against him, and his breath caught. "I thought we shouldn't do this," he said.

"I'm not in the mood to care." Maybe it was the wine talking, but she couldn't give a damn what her father thought. What the church thought. What anyone thought. All that mattered was what *she* thought.

And she thought it was high time she was spoiled rotten.

CHAPTER 10

Toni felt so light, so delicate, in Enrico's arms, yet so alive, so vibrant. How had this scrap of a girl come to mean so much to him? She was who he wanted to be with tonight, here in the park. She was the one he wanted to pour his heart out to. Not Dom. Not his father. Not Livio.

Her. Toni.

He brushed the hair away from her neck and kissed the soft skin he'd revealed, drinking in her scent. She smelled like apricots and vanilla, a sweet medley he could almost taste on his tongue.

She shivered in his arms, twisting in his lap as he licked and nipped at the creamy column of her neck, his mouth traveling to the base of her throat where he nuzzled her, then licked her skin and blew across the moisture he left behind. She gasped and giggled and tried to pull away, but he held her in place.

"You can touch me," she whispered.

A thrill ran through him at the husky undertone in her voice. "Where?" he asked, his mouth going dry all at once.

"Anywhere."

He couldn't have been more surprised if she'd slapped him. What had happened to the girl who'd told him no the other night?

Her father had happened, that's what. She wasn't reacting out of love or lust. But out of anger.

And he couldn't let her. The boy he'd been two years ago might not have cared, but the man he was now did. "I think we'd better stick to the boundaries you already set."

Her brows came down. "You don't want to?"

"Oh, I want to. But you don't. Not really. Not yet."

"Don't tell me what I want."

He kissed her cheek. "Toni, you're angry."

"I am not."

"You're angry with *him*. And you're trying to use me to punish him."

Her mouth dropped open. "I'm not... using you."

"Be honest. With the both of us."

"I—I'm not—" Her voice cut off with a choking sound and she buried her head in his neck, breathing hard and sniffing loudly.

He said nothing, just stroked her back, her hair. Finally she mumbled something. "I couldn't hear that," he said.

She lifted her head and looked at him. "I guess you're not the only one who's difficult."

"We're a matched set." He reached for lightness, but the words came out weighted with emotion anyway. Something had changed between them, had been changing between them during the last two weeks, and the change was accelerating.

She'd become important to him. Someone who mattered. Someone he didn't want to hurt.

Someone he didn't want to lose.

She shifted off him and settled at his side again. "*Grazie*," she said.

"For what?"

"For knowing what I *really* want." Her voice grew tight. "For caring."

"I *do* care, Toni. Very much." He kissed her lightly, wanting more, but that was unwise. Not with how both of them were feeling.

"Rico, there's something I need to tell you."

Her tone put him on alert. "What?"

"That man at the car park. He was at our house when you dropped me off. Meeting with my father."

His gut tightened and his heart sped up. "Do you know why?"

"Papà wouldn't tell me." She twisted her hands together. "He said the man was helping him with a plan to make us richer."

Heat boiled up into Enrico's chest. He *knew* it. Carlo was planning something. He'd never intended for the wedding to come off. He'd never intended to let Enrico and his father live.

Enrico had to kill Gennaro. He couldn't fail.

And neither could their plan with Romano Marchesi. The banker had better live up to his end of the bargain. If he didn't, an ocean of blood would be spilled.

An ocean in which he and Toni would drown.

———◆———

Since Toni had liked it so much, Enrico had prevailed upon his father to throw the engagement party at the Villa del Balbianello instead of at their home. Besides, having the party there allowed Dario to attend without losing face and rubbed Carlo's nose in a harsh truth at the same time—he could never pull off the same coup. Carlo didn't have friends the way Rinaldo did. Carlo was all alone up here, in the north. Quite alone.

Signor Sporelli and the staff had worked well with the outside caterers; the loggia, where Enrico intended to present the ring, had been garlanded with white and pink flowers, and the interior of the house was likewise in bloom.

The whole affair was costing a fortune, Rinaldo reminded him. But money didn't matter when it came to Toni. She deserved the best, she deserved a perfect day, and Enrico was going to give it to her.

The guests—Carlo's family, including his father Lorenzo and his brother Benedetto, a few of Carlo's top men, the remnants of the Lucchesis, and Enrico's and Dom's godfather, Don Vittorio Battista—were now assembled in the loggia, looking at Enrico and Antonella expectantly, holding their glasses of prosecco in anticipation of the toast.

Enrico fiddled with the ring in his pocket and looked around at the mostly familiar faces. Most were smiling. Even so, more than one of these men would be happy to see him dead.

But he wasn't going to give them that satisfaction.

Toni stood beside him, radiant in a light, flowing sundress. She'd pulled her hair back off her face, and she couldn't stop smiling. He was so glad he'd chosen this place, that he'd insisted on having the party here. For her.

"When are we eating? I'm hungry!" a little boy said, and Enrico turned and saw that it was Taddeo, standing next to his grandfather.

Toni laughed. "In a minute, *caro*." She turned her attention to Enrico and raised a brow as if to say, "Well?"

His belly filled with butterflies, Enrico pulled out the ring and got down on one knee. "Antonella Andretti, will you be my wife?"

It wasn't the most romantic thing he could have said, judging by the look on her face, but he'd blurted out the first words he could think of. He should have rehearsed it, should have asked Dom for advice.

After what seemed like an eternity, Toni spoke. "Yes," she said, but the light had gone from her eyes. Why? He took her hand and slipped the ring on it. She smiled, but it was tremulous, as if she were about to burst into tears. Had his proposal been that bad?

"Happy wishes for the young couple!" Rinaldo called, raising his glass.

"*Salute!*" came the response from the attendees, and glasses clinked around them. A waiter pressed glasses into their hands and Enrico toasted her. That false smile stayed glued to her face like a mask as she tapped her glass against his, the crystal ringing with a beautiful chime.

They should be happy. *She* should be happy. But something wasn't right.

"You seem upset," he said in an undertone.

"It's nothing." But she couldn't look at him.

"You're not telling the truth."

"I'm fine, Rico. Just nervous."

Maybe that was it. But the lump sitting heavy in his gut wouldn't go away.

"Let's eat!" Taddeo piped up amid the outbreak of talk, and Enrico took her hand and led the way into the house.

An exquisitely decorated table awaited them in the villa's immense dining room. Light from the windows that faced out onto the gardens bathed the space and made the glasses and china sparkle. "You like it?" Enrico asked Toni.

"It's beautiful," she said. But her voice sounded flat. Damn it, he needed to talk to her and find out what the problem was. But it could be hours before he'd get a chance.

The meal passed in a blur of talk, Enrico's Zio Poldi, Dom, and Don Battista providing much of the light banter and joking that should mark such an occasion.

For once, Carlo wasn't gloating. In fact, he seemed to be stewing. He sullenly drew on a cigar and stared at Enrico. Or rather, at Enrico's injured left hand. Did he know?

As soon as the meal was over and the guests had pushed away from the table, patting their groaning bellies and pouring glasses of various cordials to sip as they wandered the property, Carlo approached Enrico and pulled him to one side.

"You think you're so clever," Carlo said. He motioned to Enrico's injured hand. "But you know nothing about dogs."

Merda! His heart racing, Enrico fought to keep his thoughts off his face. "What do you mean?"

"Dogs are loyal to their owners. You expected it to do nothing?"

"I don't know what you're talking about."

Carlo practically shoved his tumbler of whiskey in Enrico's face. "Don't insult us both. You killed Borelli. Like you killed Valentino and Ripoli."

"Prove it."

"The *polizia* could test your hands. The residue clings for a time."

"You would hide behind the *polizia*?"

Carlo's face went red right to the roots of his black hair. "I settle my own scores."

"And you expect any less from me?"

Carlo held Enrico's gaze for some minutes, then he said, "Is my daughter that undesirable?"

The question took him by surprise. "It's not that. You know it."

"Do I? That insult of a ring says otherwise."

"Insult? It's far more than most women get."

Carlo shook his head. "But it's not *the* ring. You're holding it back. Maybe there's another girl. One in England, perhaps?"

An icy knife lanced Enrico's gut. "Of course not." He summoned his anger. "Whether I want this marriage or not has nothing to do with your daughter, and everything to do with you and what you've done to my family." He spat at Carlo's feet and stalked away. Oh *Dio*, let him have been convincing.

If Carlo started digging, there was every possibility he'd unearth Nico.

———◆———

Antonella fought back tears as she hurried away from the others. She headed for the terrace where Enrico had tried to kiss her on their first date. It was private enough to give her a few moments to settle her nerves.

If that was possible.

Everything Enrico had said to her last night—had he meant any of it?

The ring was lovely, but it wasn't the one he *should* have given her. Though perhaps that was his father's doing, and who could blame the man? In any case, she'd expected too much.

She was looking at the ring when she heard a tread behind her. She looked over her shoulder, expecting Enrico, but saw Dario instead. He gestured at the ring. "That pig."

"I'm sure Enrico had no control over it. His father—"

Dario snorted. "Has he charmed every bit of sense out of your head? Are his kisses that special? He *insulted* you, and everyone knows it."

"It's a far more expensive ring than Papà gave Mamma."

Dario put his hands on his hips and glared at her. "Nothing I say is getting through to you."

"Stop it, please. Just—" She held up a hand, suddenly weary. "Just stop, Dario."

Her brother advanced until he was only centimeters from her. He tapped her on the side of the head. "*Think*, Toni, instead of living in a damn fairy tale. He is *never* going to love you."

She said nothing and turned her face away, not wanting Dario to see how close he was getting to her biggest fear.

He tapped her head again. "What will he think of you when he discovers your part in this?"

She went cold all over, as if she'd plunged into Lake Como in the middle of winter. "He's not going to find out."

"*I* think he should know."

She clutched at his shirtfront. "Don't you dare."

"It would be for your own good."

She couldn't keep the tears from forming. "I love him, Dario. Please."

He studied her face for several long moments, his own a stony mask. Then he closed his hands around hers. "I *should* tell him, but I'll let you do it. He'll take it so much better coming from you."

He dropped her hands and strode away, heading back up the hill to the house. He passed Enrico coming down. Enrico addressed him, and Dario said nothing, though he did turn his head to look back at her. For a long horrible moment she wondered if he'd tell Enrico, but Dario had never broken his word to her, and he didn't now. He might be the most difficult sibling in the history of the universe, but she could still count on him. He loved her—that was one thing she knew without a doubt. Maybe the only thing.

Concern etched Enrico's features as he drew near. "Why were you arguing?"

"He's upset about the ring."

"So is your father." He scanned her face. "And so are you."

"Rico, I'm fine. It's a lovely ring."

A shutter came down over his face. "You and I need to talk, now. But not here. I don't want anyone overhearing this." He took her arm and steered her farther down the hill to a gazebo wreathed in climbing roses. It was closed off on three sides and so would give them some privacy.

Her heart fluttering, she took a seat on the bench that ringed the interior, but he remained standing.

He crossed his arms and stared down at her. "My mother's ring shouldn't be available—and it *wouldn't* be available if it wasn't for your father. No Andretti will *ever* wear that ring."

A mix of emotions flooded her. "Is that how you'll always see me—an Andretti first?"

"Honestly, I don't know."

Her heart went from fluttering to frantically beating against her ribs. "I thought you were starting to—" She snapped her mouth shut. Saying those words was dangerous.

"To love you?"

She barely dared to nod, her breathing so fast and shallow she thought she might faint. And then she said something that made her wish she would. "I thought you were feeling the same way I was."

"*Cristo*, Toni. You always go right for the jugular." His voice was thick with emotion. What was he thinking? A muscle worked in his jaw and his eyes blazed.

"It's how I feel," she said. "I won't apologize for it."

When he turned his back to her, her anger flared, until she realized his shoulders were shaking. *Dio mio*. Rico was crying.

———◆———

Toni had just told him she loved him. He should be happy. He should be telling her the same. But Enrico couldn't. Another emotion had control of him, and he couldn't hold it back any longer.

He barely had time to turn around before the tears came. Hot, scalding tears. Mamma should be here on this day. Primo should be here. Mario should be here.

He'd tried to be happy, to forget. But Carlo Andretti—*he* was here. He was still alive. And he shouldn't be.

Toni came up behind him, slipped her arms around his waist, and hugged him close. "I'm sorry, Rico. I didn't mean to upset you."

He couldn't answer for a second. He sniffed tears back, then took a deep breath. "It's not you, Toni."

She let go and stepped in front of him, placing her hands on his crossed forearms. "Whatever it is, you can tell me."

"I miss them." That simple admission left his throat raw.

"Oh Rico." She wrapped her arms around him. He embraced her tightly, the tears flowing again, even harder, until his body was racked with sobs.

Dio, he was such a child, sobbing like that, but somehow Toni made him feel safe. Like she understood. Like she'd always be able to.

Finally he got a handle on himself. "I don't know what came over me," he said.

"It's natural. You told me you'd never cried for them. It's got to come out some time."

"Today wasn't the best choice."

She caressed his jaw. "I'm glad I was here for you. That you weren't alone."

A lump formed in his throat. "Me too," he managed, but it sounded strangled. He searched her face, her beautiful, beloved face, and said the words that rose up in his heart. "I love you, Toni."

Her eyes glistened. "You do?"

"I thought you already knew," he teased her.

She smiled. "I thought so, but I didn't dare believe I was right."

"Pretty gutsy to tell me first then."

Her smile broadened. "So you would have said it first if I'd said nothing?"

He shrugged. "Maybe."

With a shake of her head, she shot down that notion. "I doubt it."

"You're probably right." He chuckled.

She tapped the center of his chest. "You men are so afraid of how you feel. It's enough to drive a girl mad."

He raised a brow at her. "And *you* never do anything exasperating?"

"Never." Her eyes twinkled. "Ever."

He leaned down and kissed her, meaning to keep it light, but she felt so good, her breasts crushed up against him, and when her lush mouth opened to his, he couldn't ignore the invitation.

Spinning them around, he pinned her to the wall near the start of the wraparound bench, her back against a post. He slid a hand down to her buttocks and tilted her hips forward, but she wasn't tall enough to get good contact that way.

Didn't matter—he had plenty of other delights to enjoy. He kissed down her neck to her throat, then along her right collarbone. She writhed beneath his lips, soft moans catching in her throat, and she arched up, as if offering her breasts.

He started to push the strap off her left shoulder so he could bare her to his mouth, but something stopped him. He'd ruined Veronica's life by following his selfish desires. He couldn't do the same to Toni. If he failed, if his plan didn't work, if the marriage didn't go through, he didn't want her chances at happiness with someone else ruined.

He pulled back and stepped away from her, his *cazzo* practically screaming "*idiota!*" at him. But it was the right thing to do.

She looked up at him with dazed eyes. "Don't stop."

Was *Dio* testing him? Sure felt like it. "We should go back to the house."

"It's all right, Rico. We'll be married in two weeks."

"No. What if your father caught us? I won't give him an excuse to ruin this."

She nodded. "You're right."

He took her hand and kissed it. "Just so you know, this is killing me."

She rubbed a hand against him, making him groan. "I can tell."

"Evil girl. You'll pay for that later."

She winked at him. "I hope I do."

Where had *this* girl come from? He didn't know, but he liked her. "If that's a challenge, I'm taking it."

She wrapped her arms around his neck and gave him a lingering kiss. "Oh, it's definitely a challenge."

He pinched her butt and made her squeal with laughter, then chased her back up to the house, Carlo's icy stare for once not dampening his mood. He was in love with his bride-to-be, and *Dio* willing, he'd get to show her how much on their wedding night.

CHAPTER 11

Enrico and Dom had spent a couple hours after the engagement party strategizing about how to kill Luigi Gennaro. The man was certainly going to be on alert. On top of that, given Carlo's suspicions, it was entirely likely that Carlo had given the man some backup.

Though he'd conducted the other three hits in the early evening or under the cover of night, this one needed to be different. Gennaro would be more vigilant at night, would expect Enrico to use the darkness in his favor. So he'd have to take a bigger risk and wait for early morning.

He'd left the lake around three AM and headed for Milan. If Gennaro were trying to stay awake, he'd no doubt be about ready to nod off by four. Besides, as sunrise approached, it was only natural for a man to shake off his fears and relax.

But that would be a mistake.

Enrico had downed several cups of espresso—almost enough to make him jittery. After the mistakes he'd made with Borelli and Ripoli, he'd nearly lost his nerve. But he couldn't walk away now. Not when he was so close to his goal.

Not when Carlo knew it was him.

If he didn't finish this, he'd never be able to look Carlo in the eye again. And the odds were good that Carlo would take that sign of weakness as an invitation to roll right over him—to eliminate the last of the Lucchesis, marriage or no marriage.

After his encounter with Gennaro less than two weeks ago, Enrico had tested his entry plan on Signora Passerini and found that the old woman would let anyone in without much hassle—as the backup manager, she was used to being buzzed by owners who'd lost their keys or kids coming home without their parents.

He donned a pair of gloves, then pressed the button beside 342. It was a shame he had to wake her at this hour, but it was the safest way into the lobby. Even at this hour, enough partygoers were wandering by that he might draw attention if he tried anything else.

Halfway through his cover story—home from university, lost the key to the outside door, parents on vacation—Signora Passerini let him in. He stepped inside the vestibule and slipped out his gun, attaching the silencer as he headed for the stairs.

He bypassed the noisy wire-cage elevator and took the wide stone stairs at an easy jog—enough to raise his heart rate and dispel some nervous energy, but not enough to put him out of breath. He slowed when he reached the third floor, and ascended the rest slowly, careful not to make a sound.

The fourth floor was hushed as a tomb, yet the air felt charged, expectant, and Enrico's chest tightened. He hated everything about the atrium layout.

The setup was horrible for someone breaking into an apartment. If anyone heard anything, or happened to be coming or going, he'd be easily spotted. There was absolutely no way to conceal himself or minimize his exposure—other than through the time of day he chose.

Enrico and his brothers had all learned to pick locks as kids—a skill their father had deemed necessary for any Mafioso—and Enrico had given himself a refresher last night and the night before. He hurried to 406 and slipped his toolkit from his pocket, temporarily stowing the gun.

Gingerly inserting the tools in the lock, he manipulated them delicately, feeling the tumblers moving into place, wincing with each soft click. If Gennaro were still awake, he might hear. Finally the lock gave way. He stashed the tools and pulled his gun again, easing the door open.

After a few centimeters, the door stopped short. Gennaro had put a chain in place.

Fuck. Fortunately, he'd planned for such a thing, but it was just one more delay, one more opportunity to get caught. One more opportunity to let Gennaro know he was coming.

Stowing the gun again, he pulled out the cutters he'd brought. They weren't quite up to the task, but he hadn't wanted to deal with bulky—and obvious—bolt cutters. He had to snip the chain half a link at a time—two careful cuts, but the broken pieces fell to the marble floor with clinks that echoed.

His heart beating like a terrible drum, Enrico switched the cutters for the gun, and opened the door the rest of the way.

He was going in blind, with no idea of the layout. Gun drawn, he stepped into a narrow corridor and carefully closed the door behind him, not wanting some early bird to come nosing around.

Stopping, he listened, every cell on alert. Nothing.

In the dim light, he could see a living space ahead, an open doorway to his right, most likely the kitchen, then another opening beyond that where the corridor branched.

For a moment, he stood rooted to the spot, his breathing shallow, quick, almost on the verge of panic. Gennaro knew he was coming. He was going to get killed. He'd been a fool to think he could ever pull this off.

He forced himself to take a deep breath and blow it out. *Come on, Rico.* Shifting his weight to the balls of his feet, he crept down the hallway, doing a quick sweep of the kitchen when he reached it. Empty.

He peered into the living room, the shadows starting to lift as dawn approached, the sun's faint glow coming through the large windows that lined the far wall and the double glazed doors that led to the outside balcony. Nothing there either.

His pulse kicked into overdrive as he turned down the hallway. Three doors opened onto it, the first two ajar, the last one, the far one, closed. Most likely that was Gennaro's bedroom, and if Enrico were lucky, Gennaro would be asleep.

Enrico swept the first two rooms—one a small bath, the other a simple office—before continuing to the bedroom. He'd just about reached the door when his right foot made several loud pops as he stepped down.

As he looked for the cause—the floor was strewn with bubble wrap—he heard the unmistakable sound of a shotgun being racked. He dove for the floor as a blast opened up a half-meter wide hole in the bedroom door.

Without thinking, Enrico scrambled over to the hole and peered in. He could see Gennaro holding the shotgun, half-dressed, his hair mussed. The man had been sleeping perhaps, but his trick with the bubble wrap had worked.

Gennaro saw him and raised the heavy gun. It was now or never. Enrico stuck the Beretta through the door and shot Gennaro in the abdomen. The man fell to one knee, but managed to raise the gun, and Enrico rolled out of the way just before another blast took off the lower half of the door.

"Fuck you, Lucchesi!" the man shouted.

Gennaro had to reload now—he'd been overconfident in his choice of weapon. Enrico rolled back and took aim through the splintered remnants of the door, the scent of gunpowder thick in the air.

Gennaro was shoving two more shells in the gun, and had it loosely pointed in Enrico's direction. Any second he'd be ready to fire again. This one had to count.

Holding the Beretta in both hands, Enrico blew out and aimed, then squeezed the trigger.

The shot caught Gennaro in the throat instead of the face. Enrico must have tensed when he pulled the trigger. Gennaro pitched forward, clawing at his throat, and Enrico whipped open the door and stepped inside, advancing on Gennaro like an avenging angel.

A horrible sucking noise came from the man's throat, and blood poured down his chest. Gennaro let out a hoarse moan, his eyes widening with fear, and Enrico froze. But his brothers, his mother, had no doubt looked at this man with the same terror on their faces, and *he* hadn't stopped. Gennaro had shown them no mercy.

And neither should Enrico. *An eye for an eye.* He raised the Beretta and sighted on Gennaro's forehead. "Only scum kill women and children," he said before pulling the trigger.

The horrible sucking sound ceased, but Enrico's ears rang from the shotgun blasts. He stared at Gennaro for a moment, then he heard a commotion outside the apartment. He was trapped. Any second now, the *polizia* or *carabinieri* would arrive. And he refused to kill any of the innocent people outside.

There was only one way out. He ran to the living room and unlocked the double glazed doors, then stepped out onto the stone balcony. He'd considered coming in this way, but had deemed it impossible without bulky climbing equipment. No choice now.

When he reached the far end of the balcony, he saw the window beside it that opened onto the staircase. There'd be quite a drop from the window to the landing, but if he were careful, he'd be okay.

Lowering himself over the side of the railing, he kicked out the pane. Now came the hard part—getting through the window without plunging to the pavement below.

He swung one foot, then the other onto the narrow sill, then leaned forward and grabbed the window frame with his left hand. With a muttered prayer, he pushed off from the balcony and felt one terrifying moment when his center of gravity was against him, before his momentum pitched him forward and he was able to grasp the frame with his right hand. He teetered on the sill, almost falling through the window face-first, but stopped himself.

After he caught his breath, he eased into a crouch, then grabbed the sill and swore when remnants of the pane penetrated the gloves. Lowering himself over the edge, he hung suspended for a few seconds before dropping to the landing below. Shards of glass crunched beneath his shoes.

He'd made it. He almost laughed in relief, but there was no time for that. He scrambled down the stairs, the neighbors' angry shouts echoing in the stairwell behind him.

His breath coming fast, he raced down to the ground floor, then out through the entrance vestibule and onto the street. Sirens sing-songed close by—maybe a street away.

He bolted to his parked car and slipped inside just as the sirens grew louder and the blue and red lights strobed off the buildings around him.

Starting the car with a curse, he backed out slowly and drove off, praying that no one noticed him or the car's plate.

He drove several blocks, *polizia* and *carabinieri* vehicles streaking by in the opposite direction, his heart beating so hard he felt dizzy.

He needed a new car, immediately, so he headed to the warehouse where Tommaso and Filippo were. Hopefully they could bail him out once again.

He'd done it. He'd actually done it. And aside from a few cuts, he was uninjured. "*Grazie a Dio*," he murmured aloud.

Now all that remained was muzzling Carlo. Though if his father's plan failed and Enrico's loophole didn't hold water with the other bosses, he could be facing the wrath of the entire 'Ndrangheta. A wrath he'd never outrun.

———◆———

His father was already at the breakfast table when Enrico crept into the house. "Rico, is that you?" he called.

Merda. He looked a mess, and all he wanted was to crawl into bed. "Yes. I'm going to take a shower."

"Where have you been?"

Now he cared? "Out."

A chair creaked as his father left the table. Enrico wanted to bolt up the stairs, but he wouldn't be able to hide forever, so he turned to face his father coming out of the dining room holding a linen napkin in one hand. His eyes swept over

Enrico and he frowned. "Where have you been?" he repeated.

"Milan."

"Doing *what?*"

His father's sharp tone summoned Enrico's anger. Papà had done nothing for them. It had been up to Enrico to risk his life to avenge them. "Settling accounts *you* should have handled years ago."

Rinaldo's eyes widened, and his words came in a rush. "Tell me what you've done."

"I killed them. All four. The men Carlo paid."

"*Cristo,*" his father whispered. He reached Enrico in a few steps and took him by the shoulders. "You've killed us." He gave Enrico a hard shake. "You couldn't wait?"

"No. Carlo was sending them for us next."

"How do you know?"

Enrico relayed the story of seeing Guido Ripoli at the car park and how Antonella had confirmed his suspicions.

"So you started this after that? Why didn't you tell me?"

A million responses flitted through his head. "You told me you didn't *want* to talk." He stared at his father's angry face, then added, "And no, I didn't start this *after*. I started it before I knew. I started it after that breakfast at Carlo's house. There was no possible way I *couldn't* have started it."

"I thought you liked the girl."

"I do. I love her, even. But I couldn't let her father go unpunished."

"Your fucking temper, Rico. I told you it would get you killed. And now you've killed us both."

"I haven't."

His father stared at him open-mouthed. "You *saw* the contract. You know what it says."

"And I know what it *doesn't* say. Nothing in that contract forbids what I've done."

"Are you blind?"

"Are you? I memorized the important part. It says: 'Carlo Andretti and Rinaldo Lucchesi agree to lay down arms and forgo their right to vendetta.' You and Carlo are forbidden from violence; I am not, at least not until after the marriage."

Rinaldo said nothing for a moment. "You had better hope that's how Lorenzo Andretti and the other *capi* see it."

"My interpretation will hold."

"You've gambled our lives on *semantics.*"

"*Someone* had to."

The blow came quickly, a slap that made his ear ring and his cheek blaze. "You don't know what I've suffered. You don't know what it's like, what I was willing to do to keep you safe."

"I don't? You forget the sacrifice *I've* made."

His father's face hardened and his voice lowered to a hiss. "At least your child still breathes."

Those words hurt more than any slap. *Am I nothing to you?* He wanted to shout the question at his father's retreating back, but he feared the answer.

———◆———

Enrico and Rinaldo were hiding in Romano Marchesi's private bathroom, just off his office at the bank, waiting for Carlo to arrive. It was well after normal banking hours. Enrico leaned on the marble countertop while his father sat in an office chair they'd commandeered earlier for the purpose. They'd hardly spoken a word since their fight the previous morning, but that was just as well. They needed to maintain silence.

The plan was relatively simple—Marchesi needed to get Carlo on tape discussing the money laundering. Once the tape was made, Carlo would learn the truth—along with how the situation had changed.

Marchesi must have downed half a bottle of whiskey before they'd arrived. The man was still a little keyed up, but at the same time in that reckless mood alcohol could induce—the sort of false bravado that could ruin everything.

"You think he can keep it together?" Enrico whispered.

Rinaldo shrugged. "If he doesn't, we'll have to go with plan B."

"Which is?"

He patted the gun in the holster under his left armpit. "I shoot Carlo and take the consequences."

"No. *I'll* shoot Carlo."

"*You've* done enough."

Enrico didn't argue, but only because the outer door to Marchesi's office opened and they heard Carlo greeting the banker. As usual, Carlo got straight to the point. "I need another two hundred fifty thousand by close of business tomorrow."

Marchesi's chair scraped the tiles as he rose. "Two fifty? You think I'm made of money."

The scent of Carlo's cigar seeped into the bathroom. "Close to it."

"We have to discuss our arrangement," Marchesi said.

"There's nothing to discuss."

"I cannot continue to clean money for you, nor can I continue to give you money whenever you choose. The authorities—"

"Can suck my *cazzo*," Carlo said. "Everyone important is in my pocket already."

"The investment customers are getting suspicious. I'm posting loss after loss, but the market's on a tear, and they don't understand why they're losing money."

"Because you made mistakes."

"I can't say that for long and have them continue with me. Some of them have been saying they're going to move their accounts."

"Juggle the money."

"I can't do that forever. This bank isn't some slush fund you can raid when it suits you."

Carlo said nothing for a moment. Then: "Do you wish your private indiscretions to become very, very public?" After a pause, he added, "I know the editor of the *Corriere della Sera*. If it's not on the front page, it'll be on the second one."

"Don Andretti, I beg you. A bullet would be preferable."

Enrico looked at his father. What was Marchesi up to?

Rinaldo rose and drew his gun, motioning Enrico to do the same. Enrico turned the knob slowly and eased the door open a crack. He scanned the room from his vantage point—Carlo had come alone. No guard waited in the room with him, though that didn't mean there weren't guards outside.

At a nudge from his father, Enrico stepped out, and Carlo focused on him, then Rinaldo, Marchesi seemingly forgotten.

"What is this?" Carlo asked, his eyes flashing.

"Your comeuppance," Rinaldo said.

"You can't touch me."

Rinaldo gave Carlo a broad grin full of triumph. "I own this bank now. All its assets are under Lucchesi control."

Enrico had never seen Carlo Andretti at a loss for words. Until now. The man's hands flexed and his face reddened. He turned on Marchesi. "How is this possible?"

"They made me an offer."

"I will destroy you. I still have the photos."

Marchesi smiled, a private, bitter smile. He opened the top drawer of his desk and withdrew a gun. What was he doing? "You can't humiliate a dead man," the banker said and raised the gun to his temple.

"No!" Rinaldo shouted, and Enrico leapt forward, his left hand outstretched, but Marchesi pulled the trigger and the bullet did its job. The banker fell to the floor, his body twitching.

"Fuck," Rinaldo said.

"Your little plan is ruined." Carlo smirked at them.

Enrico shook his head. "Marchesi transferred ownership to us earlier today. And we have this." He picked up a handheld tape recorder that had been hidden behind a plant on Marchesi's desk and pressed the button to turn it off. "There's enough on this to land you in jail."

"You have nothing."

"Extortion, money laundering, bribery of public officials—it's all there."

"Marchesi was suicidal, babbling. It won't hold up in court."

"The extortion charges would."

Carlo shrugged. "So? It's a short sentence. And I have good lawyers."

"And how will you pay for them?" Rinaldo asked.

"With my money."

"It's our money now. Marchesi transferred all of his accounts to us."

"*Vaffanculo!*" Carlo shouted. "You're bluffing."

Rinaldo reached inside his jacket and tossed a copy of the contract on Marchesi's desk. "Signed this afternoon."

"You will return my money. Every last cent."

"What money? It was all in Signor Marchesi's name."

Carlo's face went from red to purple. "You won't live long before you regret this." He whipped around and stalked out of the office, slamming the door so hard the frosted glass rattled in its frame.

Enrico looked at his father, his heart pounding. Had they truly done it?

A genuine smile cracked Rinaldo's face. "That was almost as good as shooting him."

"Maybe better."

"Perhaps." Rinaldo holstered his gun and collected the contract from the desk. "We need to wipe down the things we've touched this evening and leave before Carlo takes it into his head to notify the *polizia*."

"Only a coward would do that."

"Or a snake, which Carlo certainly is."

They worked quickly, careful not to disturb Signor Marchesi's body. Enrico focused his efforts on Marchesi's private bath. There was no reason for either of them to have been in there. The rest of the office they didn't touch. They'd conducted business with the man—public and above-board business—earlier that afternoon. They were bound to have touched a few things. It would seem odd if they hadn't.

When they were in the car, Livio driving them back up to the lake, Enrico started asking the questions on his mind. "How did you pay Marchesi?"

"Pasquale d'Imperio agreed to invest in the bank. A loan to be repaid in five years' time. We will manage his fortune and wash his money, free of charge, until the debt is repaid, and give him a preferential rate after that."

"How did you arrange that? And how do you know you can trust this man?"

"He owes your *padrino* his life. Vittorio assures me that Pasquale can be trusted."

Enrico sat back. How quickly their fortunes had changed. "How are we going to run the bank without Marchesi?"

"You always said this was what you wanted to do."

"But I need the proper education—"

"You'll get it. And Franco will help. He can oversee that mouse Marchesi had as his right-hand."

Enrico's stomach rolled. He wasn't ready for any of this. "Even after I finish school, I don't see—"

"I do. You are smart, Rico. Capable and clever. I have faith in you. If you can keep your temper in check."

"I don't know."

Rinaldo rested a hand on Enrico's shoulder, the first time he'd touched him not in anger since the funeral. "You managed somehow to get to Carlo's men and survive. How hard can *this* be?"

Enrico's chest warmed at the words, and his stomach unknotted. It felt good to hear Rinaldo's simple declaration of faith. But he had one more worry on his mind. The biggest of all. "Carlo will be out for our blood."

"He must abide by the contract."

"Perhaps we should offer him a concession? A bit of the money back?"

Rinaldo shook his head. "Too dangerous."

No doubt that was true. "Would you really have shot him?"

Rinaldo held his gaze. "With pleasure."

They'd secured their future. They'd won. They'd outsmarted Carlo.

So why did Enrico feel they were in more danger than ever?

CHAPTER 12

Antonella had never seen her father so furious. He'd stormed into the house, slammed the door to his study, and spent the next hour barking commands into the phone. Something was brewing. Something bad.

When the furor had quieted, she knocked on his office door. "Papà?"

"Come in, Toni."

She found him seated at his desk, a full glass of scotch with the bottle beside it. He never drank that much.

"Is everything all right?" she asked.

He laughed and gestured to the bottle. "What do you think, *dolcezza*?"

"Can I help?"

"Not unless you can rid me of the Lucchesis."

This can't be good. "What do you mean?"

He took a healthy swallow from the glass; his hand was a little unsteady. "I hope you're not too attached to the boy."

Her blood turned to ice. "You can't be planning to kill them. The contract—"

"What do you know about it?"

"I know that neither side can shed blood. Or break the betrothal."

"The Lucchesi boy told you?"

She nodded. "And I know, Papà, what you were planning to do. With that man who was here from Milan."

He sat back in the chair, cradling the glass. "You know so much, *dolcezza*. And understand so little."

"Papà, you must stop this. Whatever you're thinking of doing, don't."

"Why? To spare that boy?"

"To spare *us*." Any pleas she made for Enrico would fall on deaf ears. "If you kill them, you kill us."

"My father won't kill another son."

"You're so sure?" She held his gaze. "Nonno Lorenzo didn't hesitate with Remo."

100

"He's already hesitated with me. That's why we're here. He could have killed me, but he exiled me instead."

"He's not the only one you have to worry about."

Her father shrugged. "The rest of the *capi* don't matter."

"Your father is but one man. And they are many."

"He's got enough of them under his thumb to make a difference. And when they learn what the Lucchesis have done, how they slithered around the contract, they'll side with me."

"What did they do?"

He eyed her for a moment before taking another swallow from his glass. "They stole from me, Toni. All of it. Everything we have."

Madonna. Had she told Enrico too much? "Enrico is involved?"

"He was there, at his father's side."

"How did they do it?"

"They found out about the bank somehow. Made a deal with Marchesi."

"Who's Marchesi?"

"Doesn't matter now. He's dead. The fucker sold me out."

She'd had nothing to do with it—they'd figured a way out on their own. But that didn't quiet her fears. "Do you think they have something more planned?"

"How the fuck should I know?" He rubbed a hand across his brow. "*Mi dispiace, dolcezza.* I shouldn't have spoken so harshly to you."

"It's all right. I know you're upset."

He took another swallow from his glass, and then he said, "The Lucchesi boy broke the contract."

Her belly cramped. "How?"

"He killed four of my men."

"How do you know?"

"The man who killed them was injured—twice. Whoever did it was bitten by a dog the day before the engagement party and was cut several times yesterday." He held her gaze. "The Lucchesi boy has wounds that match."

And Enrico had acted so strangely about the dog bite. "Why would he do this? Who were these men?"

"Who do you think?"

Her father's hit men. She swallowed hard. Enrico had recognized the man at the car park. And now she knew why. He'd been stalking the man, trying to figure out how to kill him.

"He's broken the contract," she whispered, unable to meet her father's eyes.

"So you see how he truly feels."

When he'd said he loved her, had Enrico lied? Had he looked in her eyes and kissed her and lied?

Or was her father trying to turn her against Enrico? He certainly had his reasons. "I don't believe you."

He fixed her with a level gaze. "Believe what you wish, *dolcezza.* The truth won't change."

———— ◆ ————

When Enrico picked Antonella up for their date the following day, she noticed a scrape on his cheek, and her father's words came back to her. *The man who killed them was injured—twice.* First Enrico had been bitten by a dog, and now this scrape?

She got in the car, her stomach unsettled, queasy. Could it just be a coincidence?

"You seem tired," Enrico said as he drove.

"What happened to your cheek?"

"Cut myself shaving."

"That's quite a cut."

"I slipped."

Her eyes fell to his hands on the wheel. Both were scraped and bandaged. "Did you hurt your hands at the same time?"

"Why the interrogation? I went for a hike and stepped on some loose stones and fell."

"You've become awfully clumsy all of a sudden." All she could think of now was how graceful he'd been, hopping in and out of the boat on their first date.

He pulled onto a side street and cut the engine. "Are you accusing me of something?"

"Should I?"

"Just say what's on your mind."

"My father's men. You killed them, didn't you?"

His eyes frosted over. "I got justice for my family."

For a long moment she forgot to breathe, and it seemed her heart ceased to beat. She'd made excuse after excuse, she'd opened her heart, for a boy who didn't want to marry her. A boy who didn't care about her at all. A clever boy who'd taken advantage of her feelings and tried to use them to drive a wedge between her and Papà. "I've been such a fool," she whispered. "I believed you when you said you loved me."

"I do love you."

"You broke the contract! You never wanted this marriage." Tears rose to her eyes and she dashed them away. It all made terrible sense now—he'd romanced her despite his true feelings, and those had leaked out often enough that she should have known better.

"It's true that I didn't want it—at first. But once I got to know you—"

"Enrico Lucchesi with Antonella Andretti, the ugliest girl at school? I was delusional." She opened the car door and scrambled out, her face flaming. That very first time he'd seen her, weeks ago at their breakfast, the look on his face then—*that* had been how he truly felt. He'd learned to cover it up, and she'd been fool enough to overlook every lapse. She'd done this to herself.

A car door slammed behind her and she sped up her steps toward home. "Toni!" Enrico called.

She made the rudest gesture she knew at him, but didn't say a word. She was done with Enrico Lucchesi. Done. But if she tried to put that into words, she'd cry. And she'd never cry in front of him again. She'd never let him know just how deeply he'd wounded her.

"Toni." Enrico took hold of her arm and swung her around. "Listen to me. I didn't break the contract."

"You killed those men!"

"The contract forbids our *fathers* from shedding blood. It says nothing about me doing so."

"You know what the contract *means*. You *know* it. Even if you think you're being clever, even if you get away with it, you were willing to risk our future for what you wanted most. And that *wasn't* me." Her voice broke in the most humiliating way, and she wrenched her arm free of his grasp.

Hunching her shoulders, she continued on her way. She'd trusted him, she'd given him her heart, and he'd given her what? A few kisses, a few false moments of happiness?

He caught up to her again. "Toni, *per favore*. I love you."

She whirled on him. "You love me? You don't know what the word means! You lied to me, Rico. You said you wanted this marriage. You never did. You led me on, you made me feel—" She choked on the next words, but forced them out anyway. "You made me feel *beautiful*. You made me feel *loved*. But it was all a lie."

"You *are* beautiful. And I do love you. I don't know how to prove it, but you just have to trust me."

"My father was right. The Lucchesis have no honor."

Enrico's face darkened. "I did what I had to. If our positions were reversed, wouldn't you have done the same?"

"*I* never would have said I loved you."

"That wasn't a lie. It wasn't." He looked so miserable, she almost believed him.

She crossed her arms. "I can't do this anymore. I just can't." She swore her heart hurt, actually physically hurt. She closed her eyes. "Take me home."

His voice, a hoarse whisper, almost undid her. "If that's what you want."

Without another word, without looking at him, she stalked back to the Ferrari and got inside. When they stopped in front of her house, she started to open the door, but Enrico grabbed her wrist.

"Toni, please. I beg you."

"How many second chances do you think I have in me?"

He frowned. "When you put it that way, I feel like a shit."

"That's because you are one." She yanked the door open and got out. Then she leaned back inside. "I hope you realize what you've done. Because maybe then you'll grow up. And no other girl will have to suffer like I have." She slammed the door and stormed into the house.

It didn't take her long to find Papà. He was walking in the garden out back, smoking a cigar. As soon as she saw him, she burst into tears. He took her in his arms and stroked her hair. "What's happened?"

"He did it, Papà. He killed them."

"He admitted it?"

She nodded, wiping at her tears. "He never cared about me. You were right."

"I am so sorry, *dolcezza*," he murmured, his touch comforting, his voice heavy with sorrow. "Did you tell him the marriage was off?"

"No. But I'm sure he can guess."

He stepped back from her and held her by the shoulders. "You will need to be strong for a while longer then."

"What do you mean?"

"I have a plan."

She narrowed her eyes at him. "What plan?"

"You just need to take the boy back. I'll handle the rest."

"Take him back? He *humiliated* me!"

"He won't ever be able to do so again."

A suspicion formed in her mind. "Why do you need me to take him back?"

"The wedding needs to go on. I need them vulnerable."

Dio knew Enrico had been horrible to her, but he'd had reason. And he never would have had that reason if she hadn't done her father's bidding in the first place. "Papà, no. I'm angry with him, but I don't want him dead."

"You want to marry him then? Because that's the alternative."

What if Enrico *did* care for her? What if he hadn't been lying about that?

Her father took a draw on his cigar. "You can't have it both ways. Do you want to marry him or not?"

So much hung on a simple yes or no. Just one word. She hesitated. How could she truly know Enrico's heart? There had to be a way. "I need a while."

"You don't have long. The wedding's in eleven days."

"But what about the contract? If you break it—"

"If all the Lucchesis are dead, who will complain?"

A movement at the edge of her vision caught her eye, and she turned toward it, making a show of thinking for her father's benefit. She saw it again. Enrico was peering at them from behind a hedge. The chrome of the gun in his hand glinted in the slanted evening sun, and her heart seized.

What was he doing here? If he'd been intending to kill them, why hadn't he done it?

"Give me a day to think."

"Of course, *dolcezza*."

She waited until her father went into the house, then she marched straight for Enrico's hiding place.

———◆———

If all the Lucchesis are dead, who will complain? Carlo's words reverberated in Enrico's ears. He raised the gun, but it shook and he dropped it back down.

Could he take Toni's father away from her? Could he condemn her to suffer the pain he'd suffered?

If he didn't, no one in his family would be safe. Even if killing Carlo cost him his own life, his father would be safe. Dom and Francesca would be safe. Nico would be safe. And Toni—Toni would find someone else. Someone who could put her first. The way *he* should have. A lump closed off his throat. He wished he could explain himself to her. He wished she could see the truth in his heart.

He wished he'd never hurt her.

But Carlo Andretti had to die. There was no other choice.

Enrico shifted position behind the bushes, getting ready to take aim again, and Toni's eyes locked on to his position. *Madonna.* Had she seen him?

She was hesitating over ending the engagement. Did that mean she wanted him back, or just that she didn't want him dead? Carlo seemed to be leaving the choice up to her. If she went through with the marriage, could Carlo be trusted to abide by her wishes? Or was he deceiving his own daughter too?

As soon as Carlo went inside, Toni beelined for Enrico's position. *Merda!* He froze. It had to be a coincidence. She couldn't have seen him...

She had. "Rico," she hissed as she neared him. "What are you doing here? With a gun?"

He slipped the weapon in his jacket pocket and stood up. He didn't want to lie to her, so he said nothing. She stared up at him, her eyes narrowed, her full lips pressed into a thin line. "You were going to shoot him. Weren't you?" When she put a hand over her mouth to cover her trembling lips, he looked away. "You were," she said, her voice cracking.

He couldn't look at her, couldn't stare that raw pain in the face. "What else am I supposed to do? You heard him."

"You didn't know that when you crept back here. You truly *don't* care about me. And here I was, wavering once again, actually considering taking you back."

He met her eyes. "If I *didn't* care, I would have shot him in front of you."

"So you'd spare me that. How generous."

"You think I haven't been agonizing over what his death would do to you? I've felt that pain. I still feel it. Every. Single. Day. I don't want that for you. I don't want to run the risk of your brother coming for me and then having to kill him. I don't. But what choice do I have?"

Her face blanched when he mentioned Dario. "You'd shoot Dario too?"

"If I had to."

The look she gave him was so full of loathing he wanted to crawl under a rock, where he belonged. "I'm sorry, Toni. It's the truth. You know they feel the same way."

"This has to *stop*. It has to. You say you love me. Then prove it. For me, for my sake, one of you has to be the better man. And it won't be my father."

"So it has to be me."

She nodded, her eyes fixed on his face. "Swear it, and I will know that you love me. Swear that you will keep the peace, that the *faida* dies with our marriage."

He wanted to say yes. But... "Your father can't be trusted to do the same. He could still intend to kill me and my family."

"He won't. Trust me, he won't."

"If I do as you ask, I'm putting my life, my father's life, the lives of my cousin and his family, in *your* hands, Toni. You are certain?"

She arched a brow and crossed her arms. "So how does it feel, being the one who has to trust?"

"Frightening."

And then she said something that surprised him to the core. "I am probably the biggest *idiota* who ever walked the planet, but I want to believe in you, Rico. I want to believe that your feelings for me are real."

Hope lit a spark in his chest. "They *are*." He paused. "They always will be."

"You will trust me, then? You will let my father live?"

He thought of Mamma, Primo, and Mario, who would never be fully avenged. He thought of Nico, who would be safe only if Enrico stayed a virtual stranger to his son.

Could he truly set aside his hatred of Carlo? Could he gamble with the future of everyone related to him by blood? Could he put his faith, his trust, in the slender girl who stood before him, a girl he'd betrayed and manipulated? A girl who still loved him, who still believed in him, despite everything he'd done?

"I put myself in your hands, Toni."

She took a faltering step forward, then another, and then she was in his arms. Where she belonged. She clasped him close, her body shaking. "I have never been so scared, Rico. I thought you were going to say no."

"I thought so too." He hugged her tight and spoke, wanting to lighten the mood. "But how could I deprive you of giving me my fourth—or is it fifth?—second chance?"

She chuckled and punched him in the side, hitting one of his many bruises from the attack on Gennaro. "Ouch."

She stepped back and wiped her eyes. "Are you trying to tell me I'm being a fool, trusting you?"

He shook his head. "You are one of the smartest people I know, Toni. And I'm honored that you are willing to trust in *me*."

"I will always give you a second chance, Rico. *Dio* help me."

He laughed. "You'll probably need that help. I don't know what I'm doing from minute to minute." He sobered and touched her cheek. "But I do know this. I love you, Antonella Andretti."

She gave him a wide smile, and he couldn't stop from kissing it off her lips. She molded her body to his, and every cell in his being responded. Every cell rejoiced. In eleven days, she'd be his.

In eleven days, if all went as planned, the *faida* would be over, and their families would know peace.

———————•———————

Carlo Andretti took a gulp of scotch and let it burn down his throat as he watched his daughter embrace Enrico Lucchesi. "*Dolcezza*, you are breaking my heart," Carlo murmured.

He'd counted on her going along with his plan. But if she had genuine feelings for the boy—well, he'd have to cut her out. He'd have to use her, unwittingly. He hated to do it. She might never forgive him, but she was a smart girl, and in time she'd see the wisdom of what he was going to do.

What he should have done long ago.

CHAPTER 13

Enrico sought out his father as soon as he arrived home. He found him standing in the solarium, gazing up at the stars through the glass panes.

"Papà, Carlo is planning to kill us at the wedding."

"I can't say I'm surprised."

Enrico explained what had happened with Toni, and how he'd overheard Carlo talking to her. "I trust her; I don't trust him. He knows we have him by the balls, and an animal like Carlo hates to lose."

"True."

"So, what do we do?"

"What do *you* think?" His father's tone was soft; he expected an actual answer. As if this were a test, and not real life.

He knew what he had to say. "Carlo won't give us peace."

Rinaldo nodded, but said nothing.

"We could try to come to an agreement."

His father still said nothing.

"Or we could kill him."

"Which do you prefer?"

The two possibilities chased each other through his mind. He didn't want to cause Toni pain, but there was the matter of avenging his family—and keeping safe those still alive.

If he chose his family, Toni suffered. If he chose her, his family might die.

This is what it meant to be *capo*. Making the hard choices. Deciding who lived and who died. Who cried and who cheered.

He'd never wanted the responsibility. But it would be his someday. And in this case, it was his now. Just as it had been when his father had wanted to cut off Dario's hand and Enrico had intervened. Though now the stakes were exponentially higher.

He was back to where he'd been in Toni's garden, just a short time ago. He'd let himself think she could negotiate a peace. What if she couldn't?

107

There had to be a third way.

"We set up men in positions around the church, and we go heavily armed. If Carlo draws on us, the decision is clear."

"You are letting him direct the play."

He looked away from his father's hard stare. He'd given the wrong answer. His father had negotiated the truce when he'd been forced to, and now he didn't have to bargain. He didn't have to play nice.

His father wanted Carlo dead.

Enrico wanted Carlo dead.

But every time he pictured how devastated Toni would be, his throat clamped shut. "I can't do that to her."

"No?"

"Not unless Carlo forces me."

Rinaldo studied him for a moment. "One day, your soft heart will get you killed."

"Then don't put me in charge. Choose Dom, when the time comes."

"*You* are my son. *You* will lead." His father stroked his mustache. "And you will learn."

"Papà, I know as long as Carlo lives, he's a threat. But I love Toni."

"A *capo* must always put the good of the *cosca* above everything else."

"But what about the old codes? You said we must abide by them, even though the others don't, even though they've grown rich while we have not. Following the codes isn't the best thing for our *cosca*."

"We have to be smarter, we have to find other ways than dealing in drugs. The bank is one. Those codes are key to the health of the 'Ndrangheta. We are becoming men concerned with greed at the expense of everything else. *That* will be the death of us."

"I promised Toni I'd trust her. I promised her I'd make peace."

Rinaldo's lips formed a thin line. "Then you've decided."

"I made her a vow. An 'Ndranghetista honors his word, you always said."

"And I still say it." He gave Enrico a curt nod and started to walk away.

"I know I'm not Primo."

His father hesitated for a moment, then he spoke without turning. "You will make a fine *capo* someday. When your heart is not so tender."

His throat squeezed shut. Would this be the closest they'd ever come to discussing their mutual sorrow? He tried to think of something to say, but words failed him. And then his father was gone.

He wished he'd been able to say what was in his heart, but he couldn't bear to have his father freeze him out again.

Someday they'd talk. But first they had to survive the wedding.

———◆———

On the morning of her wedding, and for the first time in her life, Antonella felt like a princess. Her ivory dress, with its pearl-encrusted bodice, lacey sleeves, voluminous skirt, and long train, had cost a fortune. Papà had paid the bill without complaint, even though he'd yet to see the result. Now it was time. She descended the staircase to the foyer, trailed by Mamma and Ilaria, who'd helped her do her hair and makeup.

Papà stood at the base of the stairs, looking elegant in a new gray suit he'd had made for the occasion. His face lit up when he saw her. "*Dolcezza*," he said and swept her into an embrace that ended with a kiss on each cheek. For once he seemed at a loss for words.

"*Mille grazie* for agreeing to end the *faida*, Papà. You've made me so happy."

A shadow crossed his eyes, and her pulse skittered. Her alarm must have shown on her face, for he smiled and touched her cheek. The shadow was gone. He offered her his arm. "We'd better be going."

She started to take it, but then she spotted Dario standing in the corner. He wasn't dressed for the ceremony. He'd been avoiding her since the engagement party, and she'd been so preoccupied, she'd let him stew. But enough was enough. "I need to speak to Dario first."

Her father frowned. "Fifteen minutes, or we'll be late."

Gathering her skirts, she gave Dario a hard look, then motioned with her head for him to follow her upstairs. She started without glancing back at him, and after a moment she heard his tread on the stairs behind her. When they reached his room, she held the door open, then followed him inside. Shutting it behind her, she pointed to his closet. "Change."

He crossed his arms. "You want me to applaud this marriage?"

"No. I want you to change."

He looked away, toward the window, as if she weren't there. "You know what it will be like for me. When you're gone," he added.

Her throat tightened. "It doesn't have to be that way." She touched him on the shoulder. "You just have to give in a little. That's all he wants."

"That is not *all* he wants. He wants me to lie at his feet and bask in his glow. Like the dogs."

"He wants your respect. And you refuse to give it."

His eyes met hers. "He's a tyrant."

"He's your father."

"Some father he is to us. He's bargained you away in marriage, and as for me, he wishes I didn't exist."

"You're his son. If you just humored him, things would be better."

Dario strode over to his closet and tore the new suit off its hangers and threw it on the bed. "You want me to change. You want me to put on this suit and smile at your husband and laugh at my father's jokes and be someone I'm not."

"I want you to be happy."

Dario laughed, and the sound was bitter. "I don't know what that is. I never have."

Merda. She searched for a good memory and found one. "Remember when Gioia had her puppies? And Papà let you have first pick?"

"He only did that because I'd fallen out of the tree the day before."

"And you'd broken your arm. And scared him half to death."

He looked at her. "He couldn't have cared less."

"He loves you, Dario. He just can't show it. He doesn't know how."

"He tells *you* all the time."

"Because I let him. You just push him away. You always have. He has his pride."

"And so do I."

It was her turn to cross her arms. "Is that what you'll take to your grave? Your pride?"

"Go to your wedding."

"I am not leaving without you."

"Go!"

He looked so hurt, so wounded, she opened her arms and folded them around him, even though he didn't move to embrace her. "I am not leaving you."

"Yes, you are." His voice was thick.

"I will always be with you."

One of his hands crept up and touched the back of her veil. "You will be his."

"This was always going to happen one day."

He said nothing for a long while, then finally: "I know."

"It doesn't mean I don't love you."

"You think he'll make you happy?"

"I do." She stepped back and looked at her brother's face. The anger was gone at least. "I'll be happier if you can be happy for me."

He started unbuttoning his shirt and motioned for her to turn around. "I'll do my best."

She gave him her back and sighed in relief. "You can manage Papà."

"I don't have your patience."

"Just don't fight him so much."

He said nothing for a moment. "Ilaria looks beautiful today."

She smiled. So her brother *had* noticed. "You think so?"

He chuckled. "I bet you've been looking at yourself so much you haven't given her a glance."

She'd let him think so. "Guilty." After a pause, she added, "You should ask her to dance."

"Maybe I will. You can turn around."

She did, and gave him an approving smile. The dark blue suit fit his coloring. She helped him finish up his tie and then stepped back. "Perfect."

He offered her his arm. "Shall we?"

They'd almost reached the foyer when she whispered, "Thank you."

"For what?"

"Being my brother." Tears blurred her vision. She'd miss him so much.

"I will always be with you," he said, echoing what she'd said upstairs. When they reached the bottom, Papà looked at the two of them and then checked his watch.

"Ten minutes. Did you sedate him?"

She couldn't help giggling, and when she looked over at Dario, he couldn't help himself either.

A weight left her chest, a weight she hadn't realized she'd been carrying. Her brother might just be fine without her after all.

———— ♦ ————

As they drew near to the church, Enrico's stomach tightened, his heart pounded, his breathing quickened. The next few minutes would determine so much of his future. If he had one at all. If Toni was in it. If Carlo lived or died.

Enrico could see why Carlo had chosen this church over so many others. It was isolated, surrounded on three sides by a large wooded estate, the other side on the fringes of a sleepy residential neighborhood. They should have insisted on the cathedral in the bustling heart of Como, where they'd be surrounded by people. Then again, the Lucchesis hadn't been planning for anything other than a wedding, not the way Carlo had. Here, early on a Saturday morning, the streets were silent.

A car with four guards preceded the one carrying Enrico, his father, and Livio. Dom, Francesca, Zio Poldi, and Zia Elma rode in the next car, followed by another with four more guards. Rinaldo had sent two sharpshooters ahead of them the evening before, with orders to take positions in the oaks opposite the church.

Yet still it seemed like the thinnest of protection.

Their entourage pulled into the car park surrounding the church. They came to a halt a few meters from the church steps, and the driver got out to open Enrico's door. As the man reached for the handle, he stiffened, then slumped against the car. Had he been shot?

Enrico pulled his gun, and his father did the same. Livio sprang from the front passenger seat, gun drawn, and crouched down beside the car on the side facing the church, since the shot had come from the opposite direction. "We need to get out," Rinaldo said.

"I can't open my door."

"Follow me." They scrambled out Rinaldo's side and joined Livio beside the car. The drivers of each car had been killed, trapping everyone in their party. Carlo stood at the top of the church steps, and his men had taken up shelter behind the hedge that fronted the church's car park. Bullets assaulted them, hitting their vehicles with hard metallic thunks. Zia Elma and Francesca were screaming behind them.

Yet Enrico heard no gunshots. Then he realized: They were using suppressors. As he had when he'd killed Carlo's men.

Enrico's gut turned to stone. He was going to kill Carlo Andretti if it was the last thing he ever did. He took aim at Carlo. His finger was squeezing the trigger when the church doors burst open. Toni rushed out and grabbed Carlo's arm, screaming "No!," her rage palpable in that one word. Enrico put the gun up, his stomach lurching.

He'd nearly shot the woman he loved.

Glancing to his left, he saw Livio take aim at them. Now it was Enrico's turn to shout.

He had to stop this before Toni was killed. Carlo was trying to wrestle her inside, but she was clawing at his face, slowing him down. "Cover me!" Enrico shouted at Livio and his father as he ran toward Toni and Carlo, gun drawn.

Heavy gunfire erupted from behind him, as his father's men joined Livio and Rinaldo in covering Enrico, and Carlo's men returned fire. Carlo thought he'd planned this well, and taking out the drivers first had been clever, but Carlo's men were trapped between the sharpshooters and the guards.

Even so, bullets pinged against the gravel crunching beneath Enrico's feet. Every step he took toward the church seemed like one he'd stolen. How could they possibly miss? His heart in his throat, waiting any second for a bullet to slice into him, Enrico raced up the dozen stone steps and lunged at Carlo, who'd nearly succeeded in shoving Toni back inside, out of the line of fire. Now was his chance. He shoved his gun against Carlo's neck, just below his left ear. Carlo froze.

"No!" Toni screamed again, this time at Enrico. The anguish in her voice made him hesitate. He could end it all, right here, right now. He could avenge his family, he could keep Nico and everyone he loved safe. All it would take was one little squeeze of the trigger. His hand tightened on the gun. Every cell in his body screamed at him to do it, that it was the safest course.

But he couldn't drown out the sound of Toni's voice, her pleas for her father, her commands that he stop. Her tears.

He pressed the gun harder against Carlo's neck, for the first time realizing that the gunfire had stopped. "You have a choice to make, Don Andretti," Enrico said, his voice low and hard. "Come to terms with us or die."

"*Porco Dio!*" Carlo swore, the blasphemy even more jarring since they stood in the doorway to the church.

"Which is it?" Enrico asked, jabbing Carlo with the muzzle.

"Fucking Lucchesi," Carlo muttered. "I should have gunned you down when you and your father came to the house for breakfast."

"But you didn't, and here we are."

"Papà, you have no choice," Toni said.

"Fine." Carlo's reply was so clipped, Enrico wasn't sure he'd heard it at first.

"Where can we talk?" Enrico asked Toni.

"I'll get the priest." She darted inside while Enrico kept the gun pressed to Carlo's neck.

"Call off your men, and let us collect the dead," Enrico said. So far, there were no sirens. Perhaps they'd gotten lucky and no one had noticed.

Or perhaps someone had and didn't dare interfere in 'Ndrangheta business.

Carlo barked commands at the men behind the hedge, and they rose up, at least a half dozen of them. They holstered their guns and gathered their fallen comrades and loaded them into the trunks of their cars, as Rinaldo's men did the same. Somehow, they'd lost only the four drivers. Several of their guards were bleeding, but since they were all moving, none of the wounds appeared life-threatening.

Still no sirens. It was a miracle.

Toni reappeared, the priest at her side. His eyes widened when he saw Enrico's gun. "What is the meaning of this?" he asked, then he glanced around, taking in the wounded guards milling about the cars, and stopped asking questions. "Follow me," he said, and Enrico beckoned his father forward before stepping into the church. He moved the gun down to Carlo's ribs, keeping it out of view, but making sure with a jab that Carlo knew it was still there and still lethal.

The pews were filled with relatives and friends on both sides, all of them turning in their seats to look at their little group. Enrico caught a glimpse of his godfather, Don Battista, and Lorenzo and Benedetto Andretti, Carlo's father and older brother, rising from their seats before he had to turn left and follow the priest and Toni into a small office stuffed with a desk, three chairs and a sofa.

Rinaldo, Dom, and Zio Poldi crowded in, followed by Don Battista and Benedetto and Lorenzo Andretti. Carlo shook his head when his brother and father entered. "I don't want you here," he said.

"We came to offer our assistance," Lorenzo said. "Since all of you have your blood up."

It was true, and yet, adding more Andrettis to the mix was the last thing Enrico wanted. "I agree with Carlo. We don't need outsiders to settle this."

Lorenzo's gaze swept over them all, coming to rest on Enrico. "I believe my son has proved he cannot be trusted."

"And how will your presence change matters?"

Lorenzo gave him a sly smile. "I have some expertise when it comes to making peace."

"Only by killing your enemies," Carlo said.

"Or removing them from my sight," Lorenzo said. Enrico realized he was referring to Carlo's exile from Calabria.

Carlo's hands balled into fists. "You're right. We *are* enemies. And I don't need more of them in this room."

"We'll leave you then," Lorenzo said. "Surrounded by Lucchesis."

After they left, Rinaldo gave Don Battista, Dom, and Zio Poldi a look. "Enrico and I can handle this."

Don Battista walked over to Enrico, put a hand on his shoulder, and leaned in for a confidential word. "You don't have to go through with this marriage. I can arrange another bride, one from a strong family. A true alliance."

Had Don Battista made such an offer a month ago, Enrico would have considered it. But not now. "I love Toni."

"You are certain?"

"My feelings for her are about all I am certain of."

Don Battista patted his shoulder and wished him luck, the same way Livio had almost a month ago. "*In bocca al lupo.*" *In the mouth of the wolf.*

As he replied, Enrico couldn't help glancing at Carlo. "*Crepi il lupo.*" *May the wolf die.*

When the four of them were alone, Carlo gave a pointed look at Enrico's gun. "Can we have a civilized discussion?"

"With you?"

"Rico," Toni said.

He pocketed the gun, and they arranged the seating so that Carlo faced Rinaldo, Enrico, and Toni on the sofa. A coffee table stacked with books on the great artists provided a buffer zone.

For several long moments, no one spoke. Carlo pulled out a cigar and lit up, then rose and grabbed the ashtray from the priest's desk. After he'd taken several drags, he broke the silence. "Four kills in three days," Carlo said, his eyes on Enrico. "I underestimated you."

"I did what had to be done."

Carlo turned to Rinaldo. "You broke the contract."

Rinaldo stroked his mustache and shook his head, unable to keep a smile from curving his lips. "I did nothing. That was my son's doing."

Carlo's eyes snapped back to Enrico. "You acted without your father's consent?"

Enrico stared at him, enjoying the surprise on Carlo's face. "My father gave up his right to vendetta. *I* never did. Read the contract carefully."

"Do you mean to refuse my daughter after all?"

"I intend to marry her, as agreed."

"Why should I allow it?"

Enrico leaned forward. "Because I have proved myself worthy of her." He continued while Carlo digested what he'd said. "What sort of man would you wish for her, *signore*? A man who would provide for her and keep her safe, or a man who bows his head and accepts what others *give* him?"

After a long silence, Carlo nodded. "I respect that. However, the four you killed were good men, and hard to replace."

Enrico's blood boiled. The gall of this man, complaining about losing his pet assassins. He was about to retort when he realized Carlo was deliberately baiting him. So he'd do the same. "Consider keeping your life as payment for theirs."

Carlo's body went rigid, his eyes narrowing. Seconds ticked by, and all Enrico could hear was the rush of blood in his ears. Finally Carlo spoke. "You are young, and so I will let that pass."

Enrico suppressed a smile. He needed Carlo to agree to the wedding. Time to offer a concession. "In the spirit of peace, and to cement our alliance, we can move five hundred million *lire* into an account bearing your name." He glanced briefly at his father, but he registered no objection.

Carlo huffed with laughter. "A wedding present?"

"Call it what you like."

Taking another draw on the cigar, Carlo asked, "And what do you want in exchange?"

"Toni. And no more trouble."

"My peace cannot be purchased so cheaply."

Enrico looked at his father, who said, "You will remain a preferred customer at the bank and will pay half the normal rate for any services rendered, provided you abide by the old codes." That was quite a price break on the money laundering; Carlo had better appreciate it.

"If I don't?"

"Then you'll receive no discount, but also no interference."

"You are too generous." Carlo's tone belied his words. "You insult me with this pathetic offer."

Enrico smacked a fist on the table beside him, and the potted plant on it jumped. "There *will* be peace between us. Even though it is far from what you deserve."

"Rico, *per favore*," Toni said.

Carlo turned to her. "*Dolcezza*, we are discussing business."

"And it affects me." She took Enrico's hand, pulling it into her lap. Her fingers were cold, and they shook a little, but her voice did not. "Papà, you promised me we'd hold to the agreement. That is what I expect, and what I wish. Take the offer. Make me happy."

Carlo said nothing until he'd taken another long draw and then exhaled a stream of smoke. "Make it a billion *lire*, and we have a deal."

Enrico looked at his father, who shook his head. "I can offer no more."

A muscle ticked in Carlo's jaw. "I can take no less."

"Are you trying to sell me?" Toni asked, her voice honed to a keen edge.

"*Dolcezza*, that money is mine."

They were never going to agree. Why should they? Enrico jumped to his feet. "You've been planning this ambush for weeks. Your man, Ripoli, followed Toni and me, and then he met with you that same night so you could settle the details. You are nothing but a snake. And I can't trust a snake, much less make a deal with one."

"*I'm* a snake? You're the one who broke the contract!"

Toni rose and spread her arms. "*Basta!*" she shouted. After a moment where she glared at both of them in turn, she said, "Papà, we need to talk in private. Now."

Enrico looked at her in alarm, but her face revealed nothing. She merely motioned him and his father out the door.

What was she going to do? And would it help or only make things worse?

———— • ————

Antonella's heart was beating so fast, she could barely keep from shaking as Enrico and his father left the room. She'd thought she'd gotten a handle on her anger, but it had only grown during their discussion, and she could hold it in no longer. "You promised me you weren't going to kill them."

"*Dolcezza*—"

"You tried to turn my wedding into a slaughter! You fired on women. Francesca is *pregnant*. Have you *no* shame?"

"Rinaldo Lucchesi betrayed me, and the boy broke the contract." Carlo pounded a fist on the table, upsetting the stack of books and making the ashtray rattle. "Rinaldo and I had a deal. A partnership. He can't be my father's lapdog and be loyal to me."

"I'm so stupid."

"Why do you say that?"

"Because I *believed* you. After everything you've done, I still trusted you to keep your word. But that's all changed."

He stared at her, stunned. "What are you saying?"

"You've put blood on my hands. These people came here for my wedding.

You've used me. *Again*. I'm your daughter, not a strategy."

"Toni—"

"No, no, no. You don't get to talk. You get to listen. For once." She paced over to the window, her stomach so knotted she thought she was going to vomit. Enrico had nearly been killed. His entire family had nearly been slaughtered. He'd put his faith in her, and she'd failed.

"Twenty years from now, when I look at pictures of this day, what do you think I'll remember?" She looked at her father, but he remained mute. "I'll remember that you betrayed me. I put my trust in you, and you tore it to bits." Her throat tightened and tears pricked her eyes. She struggled to get the words out; they were horrible words, but they were true, and they needed to be said. "You don't care about me. You never have. And I have to live with that."

He set his cigar in the ashtray and joined her at the window. When he tried to put an arm around her shoulders, she shrugged him off. He looked so wounded, she almost felt sorry for him. But he'd more than earned her scorn.

"*Dolcezza*, I did all this for you. For your future."

"You did it for *you*. Like everything else you do. The rest of us, the rest of the world, we don't matter. *You* are the center of the universe."

"That money is all I have to keep the Lucchesis from controlling everything."

"Rinaldo is hardly a despot."

"I will not have the likes of Rinaldo Lucchesi telling me how to conduct my business."

"Maybe someone should."

"Watch your tone."

"I will not." She was angering him, but she didn't care. "Let's talk about how you've managed the business. Two years ago, you started a very expensive war, almost bankrupted us, and nearly got my brother killed. And now you've lost all our money. For the second time."

His face turned red. "*You* betrayed me to that boy. You told him about Ripoli! If you hadn't—"

"And you *lied* to me. When you accepted the truce, you did it only to rebuild our finances. You were *always* going to kill them." She was shaking so hard inside she felt as if she had a fever. "Rico was right. You are a snake."

His face darkened from red to purple. "You are my daughter. You cannot speak to me like this."

"Someone has to. You are in no position to fight the Lucchesis, and yet you would rather destroy our *cosca* than admit that."

He studied her for a long time, saying nothing. When he spoke, his voice cracked. "So even you, my own daughter, are turning against me?"

"How can I ever forgive you?"

In a hoarse voice, he said, "*Dolcezza*, I was this close to defeating the Lucchesis two years ago, but I gave that up when they sent your brother's finger to us, and I saw the look on your face."

"But you *didn't* give that up. That's my point."

"I got Dario back for you."

"You make it sound like he's my pet."

Her father shrugged. "I know he means a lot to you. Maybe someday he'll amount to something, but I don't have much hope."

"Dario is smarter than you give him credit for."

"He's also stubborn, defiant, and impossible."

"Like father, like son."

He snorted in amusement. Then he said, "You have to understand. With the Lucchesis gone, we'd own Milan and the lake. My father and brother are always planning something, and I know they will want what we have. We must be strong enough to defeat them."

She took his hand, and he squeezed her fingers in his. When he said nothing more, she spoke. "You're right. We *do* need to be strong. But something has to change. We are isolated here. We need friends. Alliances. If the bugs have told you nothing else, you should know that."

"The bugs also told me I can never trust Rinaldo again."

"Can you trust me?"

"Of course."

"Prove it, then. Swear to me that you will not act against them. That you will accept a binding alliance with the Lucchesis."

"*Dolcezza*, you are asking me to let Rinaldo Lucchesi be my master."

"You used me to trick them. Not once, but twice. You used me to plant the bugs."

"I was involving you. I thought you wanted to be part of the business."

"You killed a defenseless woman and a child because of those bugs. You stained *my* hands with their blood. You call yourself a man of honor. Where's the *honor* in what you've done?"

He said nothing, and she pressed the point home. "You are a wild dog without a master, attacking sheep and children. Someday someone will put a bullet in you. And you'll deserve it."

He rubbed a hand over his mouth and stared out the window at the woods across the roadway. "This is what you think of me?"

She hated to say it, but it had to be said. "Yes."

He looked at her, his eyes bleak. "I have only ever wanted to make you happy. If this is what you want, I'll do it."

She needed to make sure he meant it this time. "This is what you *owe* me for today, for all the times you've lied to me. Swear to me that you will honor the truce. Swear to me and keep your word, or I will sever all ties to you."

He studied her face, and she did her best to show him nothing but stone; she wanted to console him, to wipe his sadness away, but he'd take that as a capitulation. "I remember the day I first held you. You were so tiny, so fragile. I swore then I would always protect you. You hold my heart in your hands, Toni."

Her eyes filled with tears. "You've forced me to this, Papà. You've forced me to question my love for you." She waited a moment, then she whispered, "Swear it. Swear you will keep the peace with the Lucchesis."

"I swear." He touched his chest over his heart, and her throat clamped shut. She hugged and kissed him, then called Enrico and his father back.

She took Enrico's hand, her heart pounding. He'd been so angry when he'd left the room. Was he clear-headed enough now to see past it? "Do you and your father agree to a lasting peace? A lasting alliance?"

"Does Carlo?" He looked at her father, who nodded. "And you will take the rest of our terms?" Enrico asked.

"As long as you stay out of my business, I agree to all of it. You have my word."

Enrico squeezed her hand and shook his head. "I do not see how I can believe him."

She pulled Enrico's head down to her level and whispered in his ear. "Remember what I said in the garden? That one of you has to be the better man?" He nodded. "He is afraid I no longer love him. I did that for you. Now do this for me."

He pulled back, and as he searched her face, her pulse quickened. She'd begged him to trust her once, and she'd failed him. What if he wasn't willing to do so again?

Finally he spoke. "*Cara,* I accept."

Finally, they'd have peace.

And soon she and Enrico would produce a child that would forever join the Andrettis and Lucchesis by blood.

———————◆———————

The wedding ceremony passed by Enrico in a blur. He barely remembered saying his vows; all he could remember was how, even though he'd already seen her in the dress, Toni had still taken his breath away when she'd come down the aisle. The greatest feeling of pride had washed over him at the moment she'd said her vows. This beautiful, wonderful creature was officially his wife. His to love and to honor for all the days of his life.

He was the luckiest man alive. Even if he'd nearly been killed at his own wedding. Even if he'd had to carry a picture of his son in his pocket. The son who couldn't be—but should have been—with him today. The son he could never let Toni discover.

After their meeting in the priest's office, Carlo had been subdued, but Enrico should have known it wouldn't last. Immediately after Enrico and Toni had exchanged their vows, Carlo had embraced her, astonishing Enrico by openly weeping as he'd kissed his daughter on both cheeks. As soon as she'd been enveloped in her mother's embrace, Carlo had turned to Enrico, the joy on his face gone, the glitter in his eyes now one of malice. His voice a snake's hiss, Carlo had clapped him on the shoulder and leaned in so only Enrico could hear. "If you ever hurt Toni or let harm come to her, I will make you suffer. And then I will strangle you until the light leaves your eyes."

It had been on Enrico's lips to frighten Carlo, to remind him of what he'd done to his men, to remind him that Toni was now in his care. He'd never harm her of course, but Carlo wouldn't believe that.

However, giving Carlo any cause for alarm would merely fan the *faida* back to life. So he'd said the other thing that was in his heart, the thing that was true: "She is my most precious charge. We will always agree on that."

Carlo's snarl had softened then and he'd looked at Enrico with something akin to respect. Perhaps even approval.

And now it was time for Enrico and Toni's first dance as man and wife. She smiled up at him as the opening notes of "Quando Un Amore Se Ne Va" started. She placed one hand on his shoulder and he clasped her lightly at the waist, thankful that Mamma had made all her boys take dancing lessons. He'd never be a professional, but he wouldn't embarrass Toni as they waltzed around the floor.

"I love you," he whispered as they finished their first turn.

"I know," she said, her tone teasing, light, making his throat tighten. Just weeks ago, she'd never have been able to take that tone with him, to be that carefree about her feelings and his. To flirt.

"You *know*?" He failed to make his face even remotely stern. "Perhaps I'll have to put you over my knee later."

Her cheeks turned the prettiest shade of pink. "And what will I be wearing when you do such a monstrous thing?" Her tongue darted across her bottom lip, which she caught between her teeth as she gazed up for his reaction.

He nearly swallowed his own tongue. Where had *that* come from? His bride was full of surprises. "That depends on how naughty you intend to be."

Her eyes sparkled. "Very, very naughty."

"Then nothing at all."

"Promise?"

Dio, she was killing him. They had the dinner and the party to get through, then bidding everyone good night, and then their trip to Venice—it'd be a lifetime before he got her in bed. "I promise that if we talk about it anymore, I'll have to spank you here and now."

She giggled, the pink of her cheeks deepening to red. "You wouldn't."

"Are you testing me?"

She wiggled her brows. "Perhaps."

A laugh rumbled out of him. As much as he'd love to see the shock on her face if he gave her a swat after their dance, it would have to wait. He bent close to her ear. "Minx." He nipped at her earlobe. "I love you when you're like this."

"And I love you always," she said.

His heart did a funny little flip in his chest. Aside from when Nico had been born, he'd never been happier. And to think he'd first dismissed her. What an idiot he'd been. Fortunately, he'd have the rest of his life to make it up to her. Even though their wedding day had started off rocky—to say the least—he'd make sure it ended well. Very well.

CHAPTER 14

When the wedding guests had finally had their fill of fine food, wine, dancing, laughing, and shouting *"Bacio, bacio!"*—Rico's cue to kiss her—the two of them were able to slip out of the reception and drive to Venice for their honeymoon. They arrived around ten at night.

Antonella found the ancient city enchanting as they traveled by gondola along the Grand Canal, lights from the *palazzi* that lined it spilling across the water. The gentle rocking of the boat and the splashing of the waves almost lulled her to sleep. It had been a long day. And yet, when Enrico took her hand and kissed it, a sudden awareness swept her fatigue away. Soon they'd be in their hotel room. Alone.

She didn't know whether she was more excited or more terrified. It was hard to tell. Enrico slung an arm around her, and she shivered. He'd touched her more than this before; why *now* was it affecting her so much?

Because there was nothing to stop him. No boundaries, no rules, no barriers.

Anything could happen.

She took a deep breath to calm her nerves. All the fears she'd poured out to Ilaria weeks ago came roaring back. What if she disappointed him?

"You're awfully quiet," he said.

"Just thinking."

He chuckled. "Worrying?"

She nodded, and he squeezed her hand. "Stop," he whispered, his lips brushing her ear. "I'll take care of you." He kissed her cheek, the contact lingering, gentle. When he smoothed her hair away from her neck, the touch of his fingers made goose bumps rise along her forearms. "Relax, *cara*, and leave everything up to me."

The gondolier steered them over to a magnificent palazzo right on the Grand Canal: the Hotel Bauer, where they'd be staying for the next two weeks.

Enrico helped her out of the gondola and escorted her inside. Her heart was beating so fast she could barely register their surroundings, beyond their sheer opulence.

But nothing prepared her for the gorgeous honeymoon suite they were taken to. The outer door opened into a foyer with mirrors on each wall. An ice bucket with a bottle of prosecco sat on the table in the center. The bellman explained that each mirror had a room behind it. Two were closets, one was a powder room, and the mirrored door straight ahead led to the main living area of their suite, a long, dark-paneled room filled with elegant overstuffed furniture. A tray of fruit and sweets sat on the coffee table. Two large windows looked out on the Grand Canal and the Basilica di Santa Maria della Salute opposite the hotel.

To their left was the door to the private areas of the suite. First they reached an oversized bath, all in the finest marble. Though it far outshone anything Toni had seen before, she barely took a look before the bellman led them to the room that made her heart beat even faster: the bedroom.

Its walls were covered in a dark red damask paper that almost made the large space seem small. A vast bed took up one wall, and floor-to-ceiling windows another. Her eyes skipped over the bed, and she turned to see what was on the wall behind them. What she saw took her breath away and made her cheeks flame: an immense mirror that gave an unobstructed view of the bed. There really was only one reason for a mirror that large, and it wasn't to provide a way to check one's outfit.

Another walk-in closet, where their bags were already waiting, completed the room. But she could barely tear her eyes from that mirror.

And Enrico certainly noticed. He placed a large, warm hand on the nape of her neck and kept it there while he tipped the bellman and asked a question or two. She couldn't even hear what Enrico was saying. All she could focus on was the touch of his hand and the swooping, fluttering feeling in her belly.

When the bellman left, Enrico squeezed her neck gently, and she nearly jumped, which made him laugh. "You need some prosecco, I think."

She swallowed, aware that her mouth was suddenly dry. He stepped in front of her and pulled her close. "*Cara*, I promise you, there's nothing to be afraid of. I will go slow. And we won't do anything you don't want."

His voice was so reassuring she leaned against him. "You know, you were right."

"About what?"

"That we should wait. I don't know what I was thinking before."

"You were angry, upset. Not thinking clearly."

"Even at our engagement party?"

He laughed. "You sound like you weren't there. I know it was a roller coaster for me, and I don't think it was any different for you."

How well he understood her. She looked up at him. "Pour me a glass? And I think I saw a tray of sweets in the living room."

"I'll be back in a second." He left her alone in the bedroom, and she took a good look at it this time, her eyes finally coming to rest on her reflection in the mirror.

She looked flushed, happy, and wide-eyed. She ran a hand across her hair, then smoothed her dress—the same blue one she'd worn on her first date with Enrico—and looked around for some place to sit. There was a single chair in the corner, but no place for two other than the bed. Maybe she should have followed him.

But it was too late. He came in the door bearing the tray, the bottle of prosecco, and two crystal glasses. He set them on the dresser below the mirror. He shed his jacket and tie, then he worked on the bottle, carefully pointing it away from her and anything breakable while he untwisted the wire cage holding the cork in place. He eased it off with his thumb, the bottle giving off a pop as the cork came free, but no bubbles escaped.

"I'm impressed," she said.

He grinned. "Opening a bottle of prosecco without spilling is the *least* of my talents."

That pulled a laugh from her and she let it out gladly, grateful to have an outlet for the nervous energy roiling inside her.

He poured them each a glass, the bubbles fizzing up in the straw-colored wine. He brought his glass to hers.

"To us, and a long happy future together."

"To us," she repeated and touched her glass to his, the crystal ringing beautifully. The prosecco fizzed and bubbled over her tongue. It was probably her third or fourth glass that day, but she didn't think she'd actually tasted it until now, with Enrico's eyes upon her face, his gaze hot and smoky.

He was looking at her the way she'd always wanted a man to—as if she were a tasty morsel he wanted to feast upon.

As if she were the most desirable woman in the world.

He set his half-empty glass on the dresser, then picked up the tray and carried it to the bed. He placed it in the center, and lay down beside it.

When she made no move to join him, he beckoned her with one finger. "Come here."

She walked slowly to the bed, her heart suddenly in her throat again. She perched on the edge, her hands holding the glass in her lap, her body turned away from him, as if she were about to bolt from the room, which she half felt like doing.

"Toni, we're just going to share these. Nothing else. Until you're comfortable."

She took another sip of the prosecco and turned to look at him.

"Go ahead, lie down." He cleared a place on the tray for her glass.

Gingerly, as if the bed were made of eggshells, she straightened out until she was on her side facing him. He held up a strawberry that had been dipped in chocolate. She went to take it from him, but he shook his head. "Open your mouth."

She did as she was told, and he brought the berry to her lips, running the chocolate across them before allowing her to bite into the treat. The rich dark chocolate and the sweet taste of the strawberry filled her mouth. She chewed slowly, watching his face all the while.

His eyes lasered in on her lips and stayed there. They really were one of her best features, weren't they?

When she finished, he offered her a hazelnut-chocolate praline, one of her favorites. Again, he watched her eat, his eyes glued to her mouth.

She finally giggled, breaking the hush that had fallen between them.

"What's so funny?" he asked, clearly amused.

"You. You won't stop staring at me."

"There's nothing else I'd rather look at." His eyes roamed over her face for a moment, before meeting her gaze. "You don't have any idea how much I've looked forward to this moment. To finally be alone with you, as husband and wife."

"And you have no idea how uncomfortable *I* am."

He grinned. "Oh, I think I do. It's pretty clear from the way you've been acting since we arrived."

She looked down at the beautifully embroidered gold duvet that covered the bed. "I don't want to disappoint you."

"That's not possible." He placed a hand over hers, then grabbed the tray and moved it to the nightstand behind him. When he turned back to her and took her in his arms, his lips descending on hers, she was ready. Ready at last.

Her mouth opened to the gentle stroking of his velvety tongue. He plunged inside, his kiss turning greedy, fevered, and a groan escaped him, sending a thrill through her. *She* was exciting him. Her. Antonella Andretti. Antonella *Lucchesi* now. Enrico's wife. *His.*

He brought a hand up and pressed his fingers into her hair, directing her movements, controlling the kiss, and she reveled in how firmly he possessed her, how decisively he took the lead. He rolled her onto her back and kissed along her jaw, to her neck. His lips and tongue caressed her sensitive skin, sending sparks along her veins, making her breasts more sensitive and heat pool in her belly. She wanted him to keep touching her, to keep going, to never stop.

His hand moved down her body, first skimming a breast, then descending to her hip and squeezing her flank. "You feel so good," he murmured, and she became aware of his hard *cazzo* pressing into her belly.

She knew the mechanics, where things went. She also knew that it would hurt. He grabbed the fabric of her dress, started to bunch it up to her hips, his fingers searching for the hem around her thighs, and she grabbed his wrist. "Don't." He stopped moving and looked at her. "I mean, can we slow down?"

He smiled and kissed her. "What happened to the naughty girl I danced with at the wedding?"

"I think maybe I had too much prosecco." She didn't loosen her hold on his wrist, and he didn't let go of her skirt.

He cocked a brow. "Maybe you need more now."

She swallowed hard, summoned her voice from her strangled throat, and said what was scaring her. "How much is it going to hurt? Do you know?"

He let go of her dress and brought his hand up to caress her cheek. "Oh *cara*, I should've realized." He traced the line of her brows, the high ridges of her cheekbones, the length of her nose. He seemed to be lost in thought.

"It's that bad?" she asked.

"No, not really."

"How do you know? How many girls have there been?" She hated herself for asking, but it was obvious—he had experience she lacked, experience he'd hinted at.

He glanced at her, then away, before sitting up. She missed his heat and the feel of his hard body pressed to hers, and she sat up, touching his shoulder. "Please tell me."

"You're not going to like what I have to say."

Her pulse quickened and her stomach clenched. "Why?"

He drew a circle on the duvet with his index finger and took a deep breath. "There was a girl. *One* girl. While I was in England." He looked up at her. "I was upset about the betrothal. I was furious with my father about how he chose to end the *faida*. I didn't understand. And on top of it, I didn't know you. I hated the idea of having my wife chosen for me. Of having my whole *life* chosen for me." His fingers curled into a fist. "So I chose the one thing I could."

She sucked in a breath, pain hitting her fast in the chest, like a stab wound. He'd broken the contract even before he'd arrived in Italy. Was she destined to be one of those wives Ilaria had talked about, the ones who stayed home, virtually untouched except to have children, while their husbands kept mistresses or chased other women? Did Enrico plan to keep this girl, to bring her here? She opened her mouth to speak, but no words would come.

He must have read what was on her face because he touched her cheek again and spoke urgently. "I'm putting this all wrong. It's over with her. It was a mistake. We weren't well-suited." His thumb smoothed along her cheekbone, his fingers cradled her jaw. "She wasn't *you*."

She could hardly think what to say, but finally words came. "Were you ever going to tell me?"

"I'm telling you now."

"Only because I asked."

His thumb stopped stroking her face, and he looked at her for a long moment. "You shouldn't ask questions if you don't want the answers. You asked, I answered. Would you rather I lied?"

"No. I want us to be honest with each other."

He said nothing for a few seconds, then he pulled her close until she was nestled against his shoulder, his arms wrapped around her. "That's what I want too." He rubbed a hand up and down her back. "So I will tell you a little more. This girl, she *was* special to me. We had something… important. Something I will never forget. But I knew when I came back here that it was over. I'm not the sort of man who makes vows and doesn't keep them." He stroked her hair. "If I was, I never would have come back. I'd have run away, as far and as fast as I could."

"Are you in love with her?"

"I thought she was beautiful, but I never loved her."

"You said she was special."

"She was."

"But?"

"She wasn't right for me. She wasn't who I was meant to be with." He kissed the top of her head. "That person is you."

"How can you know that?"

"I just do. I feel it. Ever since that day at the promenade, when we were in the car and I was upset and you were just… *there* for me, I knew. You cared about me. You understood." His voice grew thick. "I have felt so alone these last two years.

But with you, that's gone." He pulled back to look at her. "That's how I knew."

Her eyes welled. He wouldn't have felt so alone if it hadn't been for her. If she hadn't planted the bugs. If she hadn't helped her father. Her throat ached with the need to tell Enrico the truth. But if she did, would he ever forgive her? "I'm sorry for everything that happened to you—"

He cut her off with a finger on the lips. "Stop. We need to let the past be the past. We—you and I—*we* have a future together. Whatever happened before, whatever our fathers did, we have to set that aside. Or we're never going to be happy together." A shadow flickered across his face, and she wanted to ask what it was. She wanted to tell him everything.

But he was right. Sometimes the past needed to stay in the past. If he could do it, so could she. They'd both made mistakes, though she couldn't help thinking hers were more severe. But she'd been a child then. Papà had made it seem like a game. She hadn't known what would come of it. Even Papà couldn't have guessed. "Okay then," she said.

Rico tipped her chin up and kissed her, softly this time, his tongue stroking her gently. When she answered his strokes with flicks of her own, he gave that little groan again, low in his throat, the one that all her senses thrilled to. He pushed her back on the bed, kissing her urgently, his hands going to the zipper at the nape of her neck. "Wait," she said. "The curtains."

He chuckled. "I suppose leaving them open would be too wicked, even for me." He rose and closed them, while she lay back, staring up at him, admiring the graceful lines of his body.

Rico truly was a beautiful man, from his black wavy hair to his broad shoulders and narrow hips. Every bit of him was perfect, as if he'd sprung fully formed from Michelangelo's marble. As if *Dio* had made him for her, as if he'd read her mind and created the man of her dreams.

He turned and caught her staring, a devilish smile lighting his face. "Satisfied?" he asked, motioning to the drapes, but she was sure he meant something else entirely.

"Yes." Her mouth had gone dry again, and she seemed a little short of breath. This was really happening.

His hands went to one of his cufflinks. "Let's play a game," he said. "For every item I take off, you take something off too. And if you don't, I put you over my knee."

She smiled. What had she been thinking, teasing him like that at the wedding? She truly had been drunk, that had to be the explanation. She sat up and removed an earring and set it on the nightstand as he set the cufflink beside it. He started on the other, and she removed her other earring. So far, so good.

He unbuttoned his cuffs, then started on his shirt. She waited until he had his shirt off before taking off her bracelet. He smiled at that and tossed his shirt onto the floor. He toed off a shoe, and she followed suit, removing the other as he did.

She'd never seen him without a shirt, and she found the rippling of the muscles in his well-defined torso and arms entrancing. She wanted to run her fingers all over his skin, to feel the hardness of his body with no barriers between them.

To her surprise, he had a tattoo on his right bicep. It appeared to be new.

"What's that?" she asked and pointed to it.

He shook his head. "Later." He pulled off a sock, and she removed her necklace. He took off the other and she removed a ring from her right hand. He let out a sigh. "I should've excluded jewelry."

"But you didn't," she teased. "Not my fault."

He grinned and moved his hands to his belt buckle. She bunched up the skirt of her dress and pulled off the keepsake garter she was still wearing around her thigh. "I wish I'd taken that off with my teeth," he said.

When the image of him doing just that flashed through her mind, her skin flared with heat. She had to take a breath before carefully removing her pantyhose as he dropped his trousers to the floor.

Hooking his thumbs in the waistband of his boxers, he gave her a mock pout. "How is it that I'm nearly naked, and you're still almost dressed?"

"You didn't think this through. Again, not my fault."

He pushed off his trunks as she raised her hands to the nape of her neck to unzip her dress. When his *cazzo* was revealed, springing up unrestrained and unobstructed, she let out a little sound of surprise. That was supposed to... fit inside her?

When she continued to hesitate, he stepped forward with a grin. "You stopped. Which means I win."

"You surprised me."

He motioned her to turn around and his hands went to the zipper at the back of her neck. As he slid it down, baring her skin to his gaze, he whispered against her neck, "You've been to museums. You had to have seen pictures."

She shook her head. "You seem much larger. Too large."

He rubbed the part in question against her lower back and buttocks. The feel of it—steel encased in velvet—made her arch her back. She had the sudden desire to know what it would feel like inside her.

His hands descended to the clasp of her bra and she moved to stop him. "Toni," he said, his voice low, his tone firm. "I told you what you would be wearing when I put you across my knee. Do you remember?"

"Nothing." The word almost stuck in her throat, and she lowered her hands, letting him finish unhooking the bra, letting it fall away to join her dress on the carpet. He hooked his thumbs at the top of her panties on either side and dropped kisses along her shoulders and the nape of her neck as he pushed the last vestige of her clothing to the floor. Except for her wedding and engagement rings, she was completely naked.

"*Bellissima*," he murmured against the skin of her right shoulder, his hand squeezing the soft flesh of her hip. "*Troppo bella*."

She turned around, resisting the urge to cover herself, but tried to press herself against him as another form of cover. He wouldn't let her, instead stepping back and holding her at arm's length. "No fair," he said. "You saw me. Now I get to see you." His eyes swept over her, top to bottom, lingering on her breasts and the place between her legs before coming back to her face.

He walked over to the bed and sat on the edge of it, then patted his lap. "On your belly."

"You're not really...?"

"A deal's a deal."

Blushing furiously, she lay down across his knees. He caressed her bottom for a moment, then brought his hand down in a hard smack. "Ow!" she said and started to rise.

He put an arm over her back to hold her in place. "That didn't hurt."

"It stings." He was right, but she didn't want to concede the point.

He rubbed the area he'd hit, which tingled under his touch and felt deliciously warm. Just when she was relaxing, he smacked her again on the other cheek.

"Hey!" she protested.

"I didn't say I was going to stop."

"I thought it was over."

"It might be. If you stay still." His hand caressed the spot he'd smacked, which she was sure must look as red as her cheeks felt. They reddened further as she pictured what he must be seeing, which part of her he was staring at.

His hand moved lower, until it played along the crease of her buttocks where they met her thighs. Some strange impulse urged her to spread her legs, to let his fingers go where they seemed to want. Would he touch her *figa*? She parted her legs ever so slightly, and he didn't disappoint her.

She stiffened when his fingers made contact with that tender flesh, and he stopped until she relaxed, then he started again. His hand moved deftly, drawing from her new sensations that made her moan. She'd touched herself before, in secret, even though it was a sin. But his fingers felt so different, so much larger, so out of her control. What he was doing felt more wonderful, more exciting than her own private explorations.

When he stopped, she let out a moan of frustration that made him laugh. "Ready for more?" he asked, as he helped her off his lap until she stood in front of him.

"Please."

His eyes descended to her breasts, making them ache for his touch. When his hands and mouth followed her silent desires, she let out a moan that shocked her. She was turning into some brazen *troia*, wasn't she?

He seemed not to notice the change in her, seemed to think it unremarkable. Maybe how she was feeling was normal. Natural. Right. It certainly felt that way.

She wanted him closer and stepped up to the bed, cradling his head in her arms, delighting in the waves of electricity arcing through her, sending unfamiliar sensations to every cell in her body. She was on fire, she ached, she yearned. She wanted him inside her.

"Rico," she said. "I'm ready. Just please... be gentle."

"Of course." He looked up at her, his face solemn. "It'll hurt, a little, that can't be helped, but I promise you'll enjoy it."

He made room for her on the bed and then moved over her, his hands and his mouth caressing her everywhere, making her want, making her need.

And when the time came, he was true to his word. The pleasure far outweighed the momentary pain, and as he moved above her, inside her, whispering how much he loved her, she felt the most incredible bliss, the most incredible happiness. He was hers, she was his. And nothing could ever change that.

———— ◆ ————

After they'd caught their breath, Rico settled down beside Antonella, and she got a good look at the tattoo on his arm. It was all in black, a circle of roses around three words done in a swirling script: *Quattro in tre.* She traced a finger over it. "Four in three?" she asked.

He frowned and scrubbed a hand over his face. "I'm tired, Toni."

Her stomach tightened in an unpleasant way. "What aren't you telling me?"

With a sigh, he rolled onto his side, facing her, the tattoo hidden now by the sheets. "It has to do with my family."

"Oh." But judging by the crispness of the ink, the tattoo was new. "I know what the three is. But not the four."

He traced a finger along the edge of her face, his eyes following its path, not meeting her own. "The four refers to the men who killed them. The three is the number of days it took me to kill those men."

She'd known that he'd done it, but it didn't seem real until just now. "So you got a tattoo to commemorate the occasion?"

His hand stilled and his eyes locked on to hers. "The tattoo is so I never forget."

"You said we needed to put the past aside."

"And I mean that."

"But—"

"But that doesn't mean I'll forget it."

She searched his face, saw his strength and his sadness. "You still want to see my father dead, don't you?"

He leaned forward and pressed a kiss to her lips. "I promised you, *cara.* I will not kill him."

"You're evading the question."

A wistful smile curved up the corners of his mouth. "Don't ask questions you don't want the answers to."

He was right. She didn't want to hear him say it, not really.

She touched his jaw, felt the light scratch of his stubble against the pads of her fingers. "The past is the past," she whispered.

"I'm glad we agree, *bellissima.*" His mouth descended on hers and he rolled her onto her back, surprising her with the ferocity of his kiss. He nipped down along her neck, his tongue soothing the bites, and one of his hands stole between her legs, drawing a moan from her.

This passion, this love—*this* was their future.

———— ◆ ————

Antonella took a long shower afterward, surprised by the twinges of soreness in her legs and lower back, but overall she felt wonderful. Floaty. She put on one of the fluffy hotel robes, luxuriating in its plushness. When she came back to the room, Rico was asleep, and she pulled the bed linens over him. Then she set about straightening up. There were clothes everywhere. She gathered them up and set them on the dresser.

Rico's jacket had fallen off the back of the chair in the corner, and she picked it up, surprised by its weight. She patted the pockets and realized—the weight was from a gun. Curious, she pulled it out, and a photo fluttered to the carpet. She picked it up and could hardly process what she saw: Rico, a lovely blonde-haired girl beside him, and an infant in his arms. Judging from the blue blanket, it was a boy. He was kissing the child on the cheek as the girl looked on, a broad smile on her face. That must be her, and the baby must be... his.

She sat down hard in the chair and stared at the photo. *This* was why he hadn't wanted to marry her. *This* was why he'd been so angry.

Her throat clamped shut as she looked at the picture. Oh *Dio*, what Rico was giving up for her. It wasn't fair. It wasn't right.

But it was done.

She pressed a hand over her mouth, struggling to keep from crying. He'd told her he didn't love this girl, and she believed him. But surely he loved his son? What could possibly induce him to walk away?

She looked over at him, fast asleep, his breathing light and even. What could make him leave his child? But what other choice did he have? If he'd tried to stay in England, her father and the whole of the 'Ndrangheta would have hunted him down for breaking the contract, for turning his back on his vows to the society.

"Oh Papà, what have you done?" It was bad enough that Rico had lost his mother and his brothers. Now he'd also lost a son.

Unless he did mean to go back. Had he told her the truth?

She searched her heart, replayed everything he'd said, and all she could conclude was that he'd meant every word. If he'd lied to her, he was very, very good at it. And he had, in his own way, tried to tell her the truth. He'd hinted at the child, however obliquely. His son was the "important" thing he had with this girl. That was why she was special to him.

Rico stirred in the bed, and she stuffed the gun and photo back into his pocket. She wiped her eyes and took a deep breath. He'd said they needed to let go of the past. She hadn't told him all of her secrets either, and that was for the best. If he ever knew what she'd done, if his son ever came to light, there would be horrible repercussions. Neither one of them would ever find peace. Their families would make sure of that.

She rose and went to turn off the light on his side of the bed. When she reached for the switch, his hand snaked out from under the covers and grabbed her wrist, making her gasp. He immediately let go, his eyes wide open. "Sorry," he said. "You startled me."

"Likewise." He patted the mattress beside him, and she sat down, leaning forward to brush a hand across his short hair. "I love you, Rico," she said, her voice thick with emotion.

He took her hand in his. "And I love you." He kissed her palm. "Is something wrong? You sound like you've been crying."

She couldn't stop herself from asking. "Are you *truly* certain about this marriage? That it's what you want?"

His brow furrowed. "Of course. You're not still worrying about the tattoo, are you?"

"I just feel…" She hesitated. "You've given up so much to be with me."

He said nothing for a long moment. Was she imagining it, or were his eyes welling up with tears? But when he spoke, his voice was even, steady. Controlled. Maybe too controlled. "I may have given some things up, but I've gained so much." He kissed her palm again and drew her down against his chest. "Now please stop fretting, or you'll ruin our honeymoon."

She lay sprawled across him for a long time, until a bulge at her belly alerted her to the fact that he wanted her again. She palmed him, and he grinned at her. "You're insatiable," she said.

"You make me that way."

A lightness filled her chest. She shrugged out of the robe and kissed him. If that was the case, if he could set aside everything he'd lost, she'd make sure he never regretted his choice.

———◆———

After an enjoyable shower together, Enrico tucked Toni into bed. She was almost asleep on her feet, but he felt energized after his nap. He prowled around the suite in a robe, went into the living room and flicked the TV on, then almost as quickly flicked it off.

Pacing back to their bedroom, he peeked in on her. The lamp on his side of the bed was still on, casting a dim glow over Toni. She looked so beautiful, with her black hair spilling across the pillow, her dark lashes fanning over her cheeks, her lush mouth looking swollen from his kisses.

Damn him, he wanted her all over again. But she needed her sleep, and he was content to watch over her. He sat down in the chair in the corner and leaned back, stretching out his legs. She'd tidied up while he'd been asleep. His eyes roved over the clothes she'd carefully folded and stacked on the dresser, and with a start, he noticed his jacket on top of them. *Cristo*, what if she'd looked in the pocket?

He jumped up and grabbed his coat. No doubt she'd realized there was a gun in there, but had she dug any further? His eyes glued to her sleeping figure, he rooted around the pocket and found the photo with his fingers. Still where he'd left it.

He let out a breath he'd been holding and withdrew the picture. He should have left it at home, he should have hidden it, but he'd wanted Nico with him on this day. He hadn't wanted to forget about his son.

But when he'd told Toni that they needed to let go of the past, he'd meant it. He'd realized as they'd spoken that it was the only way he could ever find any sort of happiness.

He took the photo out to the living room and found the crystal ashtray sitting on the coffee table, a box of hotel matches sitting beside it. He took one last look at his son, then pressed his lips to the paper. "I love you, Nico," he whispered. Then he set the photo in the ashtray and struck a match.

He loved his son; he always would. And he'd do his best to see him whenever possible. But Toni must never know; Carlo must never know. Nico was too precious to risk.

He dropped the match on top of the picture, his vision blurring with tears as it curled up and blackened in the flame, slowly reducing to ash. A tear traveled down his cheek and he wiped it away, sniffing back the rest.

He started when Toni's hand clasped his shoulder. How much had she seen? He looked up at her, his heart beating fast, and saw a pain there that mirrored his own. "Was that..." She paused and cleared her throat. "Was that your family?"

He nodded, his throat so tight he couldn't speak. It was true—Nico was his blood. Even if Toni meant his mother and brothers, it wasn't a lie to let her think he grieved for his family.

"*Mi dispiace*," she whispered and pulled him close.

He held her tightly for a moment, then swallowed down his tears. "You're my family now," he whispered.

"And you're mine." She kissed him softly. "And someday we'll have children too." She ran a finger across his lips, her own trembling. "I know we can't replace everything you've lost, but we can try to make something new."

The pain in his chest eased. "Thank you for understanding."

She said nothing for a moment. Then she smiled. "I'm going to spend the rest of my life making you happy."

"Me too."

She placed a finger against his lips and shook her head. "This is one time where I get the last word."

He grinned. "I don't think so."

"I *do* think so." She arched a brow. "Am I going to have to put you over my knee?"

He shook his head and pulled her down onto his lap. "Let's play a game."

"But all I'm wearing is this robe."

His grin widened. "Then we both win."

EPILOGUE

Carlo Andretti took his scotch and his cigar outside and sat on the rear terrace of his home, looking out at the moonlit lake. He pulled his coat a little closer and gazed up at the stars, the same stars that shone down on Venice, where his daughter was. Lucchesi had better be treating her right. No one would make Toni unhappy and live. He'd made that promise to her the day she was born, and that was one promise he'd always keep.

Taking a sip of the scotch, he let its mellow fire soothe the ache in his throat. He'd hurt his little girl today.

He missed Toni already. The house seemed empty without her. Romola and Dario were there of course, but he had little to say to them, and they even less to say in return.

After a long drag on the cigar, he watched the smoke he exhaled dissipate into the cool night air. The day had been difficult, more difficult than he'd anticipated. He'd let loose his rage at the Lucchesis, he'd tried to show Rinaldo and Enrico that they hadn't beaten him. But he hadn't won.

And he'd nearly lost his daughter's love in the process.

What he'd said to her was true: from the minute she'd been born, she'd had his heart locked in her tiny baby fist.

People said he was cold. People said he was a murderer. But no one had realized he could love too. Not even him. He'd thought his father had stripped that emotion from him, but Toni had brought it back.

He'd do anything for his Toni. Even sacrifice his pride.

Besides, he needed to rebuild his war chest. She had been right; he'd let his arrogance get in the way of his decision-making, let his pride dictate his actions. Now was the time to wait. Rinaldo was weak, Enrico was young, and soon Andretti blood would flow through the Lucchesi *cosca*. He'd convince Toni to tell him the Lucchesis' secrets, and in time the north would be his.

The *faida* wasn't over. Not truly. Not while the Lucchesis drew breath. It had merely been tamped down, its coals still glowing beneath a thin layer of ash.

AUTHOR'S NOTE

Due to the high level of secrecy maintained by the 'Ndrangheta (the Calabrian Mafia) and the relative scarcity of former members turned state's witnesses, there are few resources detailing the inner workings of the society. Therefore, I have used artistic license in portraying certain aspects of the 'Ndrangheta.

Additionally, to make this series easier to read for American readers, I have used the term *cosca* rather than *'ndrine* to indicate an individual crime family. I have also greatly simplified the organization of individual crime families and have chosen to name crime families after their *capo*'s blood family; in real life, a *cosca*'s name may consist of a region or place, or a hyphenated combination of the names of the two or three primary blood families that control the *cosca*.

In Italy, women typically don't take their husband's last name; for simplicity's sake, I have chosen to reflect the traditional American practice of taking the husband's last name upon marriage.

At the time *Malavita* takes place (May–June 1984), one US dollar was worth approximately 1,696 Italian *lire*. Therefore, it took 1.696 billion *lire* to equal one million US dollars. Since one 1984 US dollar is worth roughly 2.28 US dollars in 2013, one million dollars in 1984 is the equivalent of 2.28 million dollars today.

Please note that where actual businesses or locations are mentioned, such as the Villa del Balbianello, no real-life Mafia connection is alleged or intended, past or present. These businesses and locations are used in a strictly fictional sense.

All persons mentioned in this series are fictional; no resemblance to actual people, living or dead, is intended. The family names used in this series were deliberately chosen not to reflect names of actual crime families.

ABOUT THE AUTHOR

Dana Delamar is the author of erotic romance, LGBTQ romance, and the "Blood and Honor" Mafia romance series, which is set in Italy among the Calabrian Mafia. Her first book, *Revenge*, received 4 stars from *RT Book Reviews*, was a Top Pick at The Romance Reviews, and was a double-finalist for Best First Book and Best Romantic Suspense in the 2013 Booksellers Best Awards.

Her second book, *Retribution*, received 4 stars from *RT Book Reviews* and was a semi-finalist in the Kindle Book Review's 2013 Best Indie Book Awards. Her book *Malavita* was a quarter-finalist in the 2014 Amazon Breakthrough Novel Awards, and her book *Redemption* was a finalist in the 2014 Maggie Awards and a semi-finalist in the Kindle Book Review's 2014 Best Kindle Book Awards. *Her Two Men in London* (co-authored with Kristine Cayne) was a Top 5 Finalist in the Romance category of the 2019 Kindle Book Review Awards.

Dana is also an editor with over thirty years of editing experience in both fiction and nonfiction and has worked with everyone from newbie writers to experienced pros. The books she's edited have won numerous awards and critical acclaim, including two Top Picks from *RT Book Reviews*.

danadelamar.com

MORE BY THIS AUTHOR

Thank you for reading *Malavita*. I hope I have entertained you.

Writing a book is a rather crazy endeavor, similar to trying to put together a thousand-piece puzzle with no picture to guide you. When I started this series, it was going to be only one book. Then two. Then four. Now it's grown to five with more books in the "Blood and Honor" world on the way. I hope you're having as much fun as I am on this journey.

If you enjoyed *Malavita*, please consider writing a review to help others learn about the book. Every recommendation truly helps, and I appreciate anyone who takes the time to share their love of books and reading with others. (And feel free to friend me on Goodreads—I love seeing what everyone is reading!)

To hear about my new releases, you can sign up for my VIP Readers List at danadelamar.com.

Malavita is the prequel to the "Blood and Honor" Mafia romance series. Because the leads of *Malavita* are teens, *Malavita* is more of a sexual slow burn than the rest of the series, which is definitely a hard R, so be forewarned.

Keep reading for a special preview of the next book in the series, *Revenge*, which picks up the story of Enrico Lucchesi as an adult and the continuing feud with the Andrettis.

A SPECIAL PREVIEW OF *REVENGE*
(Blood and Honor, Book 1)

**Double-finalist (Romantic Suspense and Best First Book)
in the 2013 Booksellers' Best Awards!**

**A woman on the run. A damaged Mafia don.
A rival bent on revenge...**

Kate Andretti is married to the Mob—but doesn't know it. When her husband uproots them to Italy, Kate leaves everything she knows behind. Alone in a foreign land, she finds herself locked in a battle for her life against a husband and a family that will "silence" her if she will not do as they wish. When her husband tries to kill her, she accepts the protection offered by a wealthy businessman with Mafia ties. He's not a mobster, he claims. Or is he?

Enrico Lucchesi never wanted to be a Mafia don, and now he's caught in the middle of a blood feud with the Andretti family—a conflict that had been on hold during his marriage to his beloved late wife, Antonella Andretti. His decision to help Kate Andretti sparks the feud between the families back to life. When Enrico is betrayed by someone in his own family, the two of them must sort out enemies from friends—and rely on each other or die alone. The only problem? Enrico cannot reveal his identity to Kate, or she'll bolt from his protection, and he'll be duty-bound to kill her to safeguard his family's secret.

Attacks from without and within push them both to the breaking point, and soon Enrico is forced to choose between protecting the only world he knows and saving the woman he loves.

---•---

Twenty-eight years ago
Cernobbio, Lake Como, Italy

As his assassins set the trap, Carlo Andretti leaned forward, his nose nearly touching the window. *Vengeance is mine. Just like the Lord above.* His pulse quickened, his mouth went dry, his body itched to be in on the action. To aim a gun. To pull a trigger.

The Lucchesi family's driver and their bodyguard waited outside the restaurant in a large black Mercedes, smoke from their cigarettes floating out the open windows. *Idiots. Anyone could get the drop on them.* These *were the men Lucchesi trusted with his family?*

Bruno, the man Carlo used for all his dirty work, snuck up behind the car, followed by one of his assistants. The two men dispatched the guard and driver without effort, slitting their throats in tandem, the strike perfectly timed.

Sipping an espresso in a room across the street, Carlo watched his men melt back into the dark. It wouldn't be long now until they attacked their true prey. He savored the hot bitter brew he swallowed. Rinaldo Lucchesi, the *capo* of the Lucchesi family, had interfered in Carlo's business for the last time. He thought he could come up north, into Carlo's territory, and impose his principles and his will.

Rinaldo and his ridiculous, short-sighted philosophy would be the ruin of the 'Ndrangheta. Carlo was not going to let Lucchesi expose their bellies to the sharp teeth of Cosa Nostra or the Russians. Lucchesi might be suicidal, but Carlo most assuredly was not. He had a family to look out for, a child he adored. He couldn't let Lucchesi destroy her future, and he couldn't let him destroy the future of all the 'Ndrangheta.

Taking Carlo's son hostage to force him to capitulate was where Lucchesi had miscalculated. He'd taken the wrong child. In a contest between Dario and Antonella, Toni won every time. Had Lucchesi taken Toni.... Carlo's gut quivered. Everyone would know his weakness then. He'd make any sacrifice for his tigress, his cunning little she-wolf. The child of his heart. The child who *was* his heart.

If Toni knew he was risking her twin brother's life this way, she'd be appalled. But if his plan worked, he'd have the boy, his vengeance, and the way clear in the north. Milan and the lake would be his alone. And once their riches were his, nothing could stop him from pushing his father and his brother off their perch, high at the top of the 'Ndrangheta. They'd censured him once, they'd exiled him up north, thinking that would keep him weak, that their lapdog Lucchesi would be able to muzzle him. They were about to learn otherwise.

The front door to the restaurant swung open, its glass catching the light of a streetlamp, and the Lucchesi woman and two of her children strolled out, the boys flanking her on either side. Rinaldo and their middle boy, Enrico, were not with them. Unease wormed through Carlo's belly. *Where are they?* He glanced around and saw nothing out of the ordinary, but the nighttime shadows could be both

137

friend and foe.

The woman and her boys had almost reached the Mercedes when they stopped short, the woman placing a restraining hand on the shoulder of her youngest child. The eldest son, Primo, nearly a man now, the one who was supposed to be *capo* someday, pulled his gun and looked in the passenger side front window. No doubt he saw the bodies, because he shouted, "Go back!"

It was too late.

Bruno and his four men charged toward the family, opening fire. Primo whirled around to meet them, but bullets slammed into his chest before he could get off a shot.

Carlo felt an odd sort of admiration as the boy fell, blood blanketing his once-white shirt. Primo had tried to defend his family like a good man of honor. But the boy had been ruined, his mind tainted by his father's notions.

None of Rinaldo's line would survive the night. It was fitting that Lucchesi's heir died first.

The woman and the youngest boy, Mario, sought cover by the car. Apparently they crawled inside, since Bruno whipped his arm overhead, signaling the men to surround the Mercedes. The hit men didn't hesitate, spraying the car with bullets. The percussive blasts of gunfire beat a joyful staccato in Carlo's chest. How well he remembered the wild buck of a gun in his hands, the acrid smell of gunpowder, the coppery tang of blood in the air, the ringing in his ears in the wake of a kill. But he was *capo* now, and he had to be protected for the good of the family. Still, he missed the old days when he had administered justice firsthand.

Mario attempted to flee through the far door onto the street. One of the shooters fired into him, not stopping until the boy's body grew still, his head and shoulders hanging out the back door. It was a shame about this boy as well; he was a fighter.

After slapping in a fresh clip, Bruno leaned in the car and fired a final bullet, presumably finishing off the woman. Then he walked over to Primo and shot him in the head.

Three down. Just two more to go, and his vengeance would be complete.

Except no one charged out of the restaurant. No more guards. And no more Lucchesis.

Where the hell are they? This was supposed to be a rout, a decisive victory. A definitive end to the feud. And Carlo was supposed to be the victor.

Setting his cup on the sill, he rose, peering out the window, looking up and down the street as he pushed the curtains wide. With a deafening roar in his ears, the horrible truth sprang upon him, sending his stomach plunging to the floor, the espresso threatening to come back up. *Rinaldo and Enrico weren't there and never had been.* No self-respecting man of honor could stand by while his family was slaughtered.

Carlo watched, fists curled, as Bruno and his men left the scene. They'd reconvene at the house, where it was safe to talk. Already, sirens keened in the distance, though no one had interfered during the shooting. That didn't mean there weren't witnesses, but he wasn't concerned. Only someone exceedingly foolhardy would testify against the 'Ndrangheta.

Waiting for Bruno in his study, Carlo clipped the end off a cigar and lit it, inhaling in sharp, short puffs. *Who had fucked up?*

Bruno knocked on the door, then entered. Bruno's suit strained across his shoulders, but somehow there was a new smallness to him, a hunched quality that made Carlo's face go hot. Along with gunpowder and fine cologne, Bruno smelled of guilt.

"Why should I let you live?"

The man looked at the floor, his hands jammed in his jacket pockets, his dark hair, usually carefully slicked back, now half falling in his face, hiding his eyes. "Our informant told us the entire family would be there. It was the youngest boy's birthday."

"Where are Rinaldo and Enrico?"

"At home, I assume." Bruno glanced up. "Trying to eliminate them there would be suicide."

Carlo wanted to rage at the man, but a fuckup, even a monumental one, shouldn't rattle him. He was *capo*; he was in charge. The men looked to him in a crisis, and if he faltered, he would be lost. *They* would be lost. "Hands on the desk."

Fear flashed through Bruno's eyes. "Both hands?"

"When did you become deaf?" Bruno probably thought he was going to take a few fingers, maybe one of the hands. Maybe he even feared that Carlo would take both. Smiling, Carlo picked up the cigar cutter.

Bruno swallowed, but he didn't beg. Good for Bruno.

On the other hand, he'd fucked up. Bad for Bruno.

Carlo couldn't suffer such incompetence unchecked; it was bad for business, it was bad for discipline, and it was bad for morale. A little fear liberally applied kept the men content.

But worst of all, Bruno had cost him probably the only opportunity he'd ever have to get rid of the Lucchesis with minimal bloodshed. Now the long bloody war between the families would continue. Carlo would lose many more men. Someone had to pay for that mistake.

The man's eyes followed the cigar cutter as Carlo returned it to his jacket pocket. Bruno let out a short quivering breath when the tiny guillotine disappeared. Carlo gave him a smile, a distraction. Before the man could react, Carlo pulled a gun from the same pocket and shot him in the face. Blood and brain matter and bits of bone sprayed out the back of the man's head, then he slumped to the floor. Seeing the pool of blood spreading from the body, Carlo let out a sigh. He should have taken Bruno outside. He'd liked that carpet.

Hell, he'd liked Bruno too, but there was no place for sentiment in this business. A *capo* had to hold his love close; the fewer vulnerabilities he had, the better. Loving Toni the way he did was all the risk he could afford.

Placing the gun on the desk, he sat down and picked up the cigar, taking a long drag. He let the aromatic smoke fill his lungs, let it bring him calm. After a while, he smiled.

It is so much sweeter this way. He picked up the phone, punching in a number he knew well. Rinaldo answered after a few rings. "There's something I must tell you," Carlo said.

"Carlo? Are you ready to be reasonable now and end this trouble between us?"

Laughter bubbled up from his gut. "Oh, I'm ending this, but not how you think."

"What do you mean?"

"Tell me, Rinaldo, did you hear the sirens earlier?"

Lucchesi's voice shook with urgency. "What did you do?"

"I've taken what you love most in this world. Your wife and sons. Shot down in the street outside Marinucci's. Only one boy left. It'd be a pity to lose him too."

The howl of rage, of anguish, that came down the line stirred something greedy in the pit of his belly. When the howling stopped and the cursing started, Carlo broke in. "I will not be trifled with, Lucchesi. And I will never be reasonable." He hung up, and when the phone rang, he pulled the cord from the back to silence it.

Picking up the cigar, he took another drag. Sometimes life was very, very good.

There was no need to send other men after Lucchesi. He'd made his point, and every other boss who thought about crossing him would think twice and repent such scheming.

He'd sent a clear, unambiguous message: Carlo Andretti would bow to no one. Even if he had to leave his own boy to Rinaldo Lucchesi's doubtful mercy.

———— ◆ ————

Present day
Rome, Italy

This time, the end of Enrico Lucchesi's world arrived in a beautifully wrapped box. The package, covered in a fine, silvery foil paper with a crisp white satin bow, arrived early that morning at Enrico's hotel suite in Rome. There was no card, no return address. Enrico's pulse rate kicked upward. In his line of work, nothing good ever came from an anonymous delivery.

Ruggero Vela, his senior bodyguard, eyed the package on the wooden writing desk as if it were ticking. When Enrico touched the box, Ruggero nudged his hand away. "Let me, Don Lucchesi." Enrico bowed his head and stepped back, watching his guard slice into the wrapping. Ruggero's hand was steady, his cuts deliberate.

Inside was an ornately carved wooden box that looked oddly familiar. Enrico had seen it somewhere, but he couldn't place it. Ruggero put his hand on the latch, then looked up at him. "Perhaps you should stand farther away." Never an order from his guard, always a suggestion. But one he'd be a fool to ignore.

Enrico stepped over to the far wall by the sofa and crossed his arms. How incongruous. He and his men were dealing with a possible bomb while the vacationers and business people in the suites surrounding them enjoyed a full five stars of luxury. What was it like to almost never know fear, to live every day with the comforting certainty that another one was coming? The only certainty he'd ever had was that any day could be his last.

His heart jumped in his chest. How was it that this situation never became routine? The sick expectation, the sense he'd finally meet his death today, his skin going clammy, his stomach twisting, his mouth dry, his skin practically twitching from anticipation of a fatal stab from a knife or the punch of a bullet. Or in this case, the tearing of shrapnel from an explosion.

He frowned when Antonio Legato, his newest bodyguard, stepped in front to shield him from a potential blast. He never should have endangered the boy this way. A familiar litany filled Enrico's head: *Will he be just one more dead body you walk away from? Just one more unfortunate mistake? Just one more eventually forgotten casualty in your quest to outlive Carlo Andretti?*

Ruggero eased open the latch, then edged the lid up, its metal hinges creaking. The stern lines of his face deepened as he stared at the contents. He ran a hand through his dark curly hair.

Enrico uncrossed his arms and took a step forward. "What is it?"

The guard let the lid fall completely open, then stepped away from the box, shaking his head. "You'd best see for yourself, *signore.*"

Enrico crossed the room and looked into the box. As he registered the contents, his stomach flipped like a dying fish. Nestled within white tissue paper, a falcon stared up at him, its gray and white feathers limp, its round dark eye filmed over. A black cord cut into its neck, strangling the bird. The raptor's open beak suggested it was giving a last angry cry at the injustice of its death.

He looked up at Ruggero, their eyes locking. A falcon was featured on the Lucchesi coat of arms. The message was obvious.

As he lowered the lid, Enrico's fingers lingered over the etched surface. A pattern of vines and flowers danced around the edge, and a boar-hunting scene occupied the center. Where had he seen this box before?

And then it came to him. It was the box Carlo Andretti stored his cigars in, the one he'd offered to Enrico on several occasions when he'd been in Carlo's study. And if he had any doubt about who was sending this message, the timing of it couldn't be ignored.

"It's from Andretti," he said to Ruggero. He drew in then let out a deep breath, seeking calm. Andretti wanted him dead. That was nothing new.

"You aren't surprised."

"Do you remember what day it is? What happened exactly a year ago?" Enrico fought to keep his voice steady, yet still he detected a catch.

Ruggero thought for a moment, then understanding dawned on his face. "Your wife. I'm sorry, I forgot."

"Carlo didn't forget. He still blames me."

"He thinks you can cure cancer?"

"I don't know what he thinks. Only that I didn't do enough." *And maybe I didn't.*

Ruggero motioned to the box. "What do we do about this?"

"For now, nothing."

The guard's brow creased. "You are virtually undefended with only me and Antonio. We should call in more men before leaving the city."

"We leave today, as planned. Just us three." He'd be damned if he'd let Carlo pick the tune he danced to. He'd seen what fear had done to his father, what mistakes it had caused him to make. What a bleak future it led to.

"Don Lucchesi, that's suicide," Antonio said.

A muscle in Ruggero's jaw jumped and he pinned the boy with his eyes, not looking back to Enrico until Antonio lowered his eyes and mumbled, "Forgive me, *signore.*"

Ruggero took a breath then said, "With respect, *capo*, Andretti knows where you are. He could have men waiting for us outside."

Enrico shook his head. "Carlo likes to play with his food before he eats it."

"So, you are the mouse?" Ruggero asked.

Enrico scrubbed a hand through his hair. "He thinks he'll see me cower and run. But I am no mouse."

"At least let me call in reinforcements for when we arrive in Milan."

Enrico nodded. "There's no sense being completely foolish." As he watched his guard make the call, he rubbed his stomach, a queasy feeling growing, like he'd just eaten a pound of pancetta. He hoped he wasn't leading them into a trap. A giant, man-sized mousetrap.

———◆———

"Carlo is a dead man," Enrico muttered to himself as he strode through the crowd in the hotel lobby hours later, his empty stomach knotted, drawn up tight under his chest. His eyes swept the area, noting the details of his surroundings, the placement of people and weapons—at least those he knew about. His guards were good; in fact, Ruggero was one of the best. But no one was perfect.

"What did you say, Don Lucchesi?" Antonio asked as he matched Enrico's pace.

"Andretti is dead."

"So you've decided then?" asked Ruggero, on his right.

Enrico heard the anticipation in Ruggero's voice and wondered again if there wasn't a touch of the sociopath to him. Enrico hated killing, though it was sometimes necessary. But Ruggero seemed perfectly suited to his line of work.

"Don't get excited yet. I decided the moment I saw what was in the box. Now all that remains is the when."

"Soon, I hope," Ruggero said.

Enrico gave him a tight smile. "Soon enough." If only Antonella hadn't made him promise not to harm her father, he'd have given the order long ago. He owed his mother and Primo and Mario justice. But he'd promised his wife that he'd keep the peace between their families, that he'd honor the truce that had been sealed by their marriage. Those twenty-six years of peace were over now—undone by her death. At least Andretti seemed to think so.

Perhaps Enrico had been naïve to think that Carlo would honor his daughter's memory by keeping the peace she'd helped broker. He should have known better.

A vulture would never be anything but a vulture. Andretti had never had a scrap of honor and never would. The man was a bottom feeder, a scum, a leech on society—

Enrico's attention was caught by a large, heavyset man in a sharply tailored suit standing to the left of the lobby doors. Massimo Veltroni, Carlo's man. Veltroni's black eyes snapped to his, the intent in them clear. A chill ran through Enrico, that sick anticipation rising again, his skin prickling with awareness. Damn it—he'd been stupid, stupid, stupid. And now it was going to cost them dearly. *Per favore, Dio, spare Antonio. He's too young.*

He tapped both guards on the shoulders and they followed his gaze, closing ranks in front of Enrico, automatically shielding their *capo* from danger.

Enrico's hand fell down to grip the Glock 9mm in his jacket pocket. As *capo*, he rarely carried a weapon, but Ruggero had insisted after seeing the dead falcon. Now he appreciated his guard's caution.

He couldn't tear his eyes off Veltroni. The image of a cobra looking to strike came to Enrico's mind. The man reached into his suit jacket, a tight smile on his face.

Enrico tensed, and Antonio and Ruggero pulled their weapons, Ruggero's movements so fluid and practiced they made Antonio look like a clumsy amateur. Which he almost was. Antonio had his gun out and ready mere seconds after Ruggero did. But seconds counted. Seconds meant the difference between alive and dead. Enrico heard women shriek at the sight of the guns, and then the scuffle of feet as people scrambled to get away from them. But he didn't look behind him; eyes on the threat, always. That was the rule. Distractions meant death.

When Veltroni saw the guns, he broke into laughter, a genuinely mirthful smile creasing his features this time. Enrico was puzzled. There was nothing funny about the situation. Not in the slightest.

Veltroni slowly withdrew his empty hand from his coat, his fingers in the shape of a gun. He pointed at Enrico and pretended to take a shot, even blowing off smoke from the end of his thick forefinger. Reaching up, he tipped the brim of his fedora to Enrico. Then he turned and ambled out the door.

"Fuck," Antonio said, his voice hushed.

Fuck was right. They'd almost walked into a trap, and Enrico's pride had led them there.

Antonio and Ruggero put up their guns and Enrico released his grip on the Glock. Glancing around them, they hurried outside to the car waiting to take them to the private airstrip.

This day had started off bad, and it was quickly going straight to hell.

———◆———

Kate Andretti snuck out of bed, careful not to disturb her sleeping husband. She looked down at him, his wavy, sandy brown hair scrunched up by the pillow, his tanned face slack and innocent as he snored. She hated sneaking off to take her birth control pills, but Vince couldn't understand why she didn't want to get pregnant now. There was no sense bringing a child into a marriage that was less than stable.

But she had hope. Three months ago, Vince had told her about a job at the Lucchesi Home for Children. Even though the work was glorified data entry, she'd taken it. She was happy computerizing the orphanage's records and helping out with the kids.

And she was happy that Vince had actually listened to her when she'd said she needed to work, that she needed to make friends. Maybe he'd finally understood—at least in part—her reasons for waiting. But still she hid the pills from him. Just in case.

Easing the bathroom door shut behind her, Kate crouched down and pulled a box of tampons out from under the sink. Vince would never think to look in that box. For a big tough guy from New Jersey, he was bizarrely squeamish about her "woman things." Fishing around the bottom of the box, her fingers connected with the packet of pills.

Every day, she pulled that box out. Every day she hated the necessity of doing so. Vince was under a lot of stress—he'd been working long days and sometimes nights in his uncle's business—but that didn't give him a free pass to yell at her. He'd always begged forgiveness later, so she'd let it go. To a degree. But something told her to stay cautious. To wait.

She stared at the pill packet in her hand. How had she'd gotten to this point? Lying to her husband. Lying to herself. Hiding things and hoping their marriage would survive somehow.

This sucks. It just does. I want to trust him, I want him to trust me.

But what about the spots on his jacket last night, the reek of gunpowder all over him?

Maybe he'd just splashed wine or something on the jacket. And he often went target shooting; she'd gone with him many times and had proved herself an excellent shot. The first time she'd pumped a full clip into the two kill zones on a target, Vince had looked at her with more than a little admiration.

But what if it wasn't wine? What if it was… blood?

Dread coiled in her belly. Something wasn't right. She'd known it ever since she'd met Vince's uncle, Carlo Andretti. Her immediate impression had been favorable; Carlo was relatively handsome for a man in his sixties, with thick silvery hair swept back from his hawk-like nose and dark eyes brimming with intelligence. He'd kept himself trim, his waist showing only the slightest paunch, despite his love of cigars and fine scotch. His grasp of English was nearly impeccable, though his accent was a war between British and Italian inflections.

Carlo had seemed charming enough until they were actually introduced. His keen eyes had flicked over her in a lightning-quick inventory that had made her think he wanted to see her wearing much less. She'd told herself she was imagining things, but when Carlo took her hand, his index finger had snaked across the back of hers, not once, but three times. Then he'd smiled at her, and she'd barely suppressed a shudder, feeling like a small and tender animal who'd been sighted, and the wolf was licking its chops.

That was when she started wondering about Carlo. Who he really was, what his business really was. Why he thought he owned her. Why he thought he owned Vince. Why everyone around him jumped when he spoke.

Supposedly Vince was acting as a liaison with Carlo's import/export operations in the United States. More or less the same job he'd had in New York, except that now he was handling matters from the Italian side. He'd told Kate it was a promotion of sorts, a tryout to see if he could handle additional responsibilities in the organization.

Was any of that true? Something about Carlo screamed "Mafia." Was it his swagger, the way he seemed to view everything around him as his property? Or was it just her dislike of the man that was coloring her viewpoint?

Vince couldn't be Mafia too, could he?

The day they'd met, at her cousin Terri's party in Jersey, Vince had played airplane and ball with Terri's kids for hours. Her heart had melted at the sheer joy on his face, and then it had turned to absolute mush when he'd asked her out, after saying that he'd cleared it with Terri, because he thought it important that her family approve of him.

Could a Mafioso be that tender?

Kate shook the memory away and pushed a pill through the foil backing on the packet. Taking a swig of water, she swallowed it. She loved him, her tough guy with the soft heart. But something had happened to him in Italy, something that had changed him.

The bathroom door swung open. Vince blinked, scrubbing a hand through his rumpled hair, his handsome face creased from the pillow. Then he squinted at her hand. "What's that?"

Kate flushed, her heart hammering, and closed her hand around the packet. "Nothing, honey."

"Give it." He held out his hand.

She cursed under her breath. *Why hadn't she put the packet away first?* "It's just some pills."

"I'm not gonna ask again."

That tone, too familiar of late, raised her hackles. "Fine." She slapped the packet into his open palm. He held it up to the lights above the mirror so he could read it. After a moment, his face went dark.

"Birth control? You're on fucking *birth control?*" His anger seemed to expand in the small space, echoing off the marble tiles on the walls and floor.

Kate forced herself not to cringe. "Look, I told you. We've only been here six months. It's just too soon."

"So you fucking *lie?* You told me you'd stopped these." He tossed the packet in the toilet and flushed it. "I've been fucking you for *nothing.*"

Kate's jaw dropped open. It was time to whip out her NYC-girl attitude. Never mind that she'd been raised upstate. "Piss. Off. What do you mean you've been fucking me for *nothing?* Supposedly you love me, right?"

"I been trying to make a baby with you. And you been lying to me."

She snorted. "I'm not the only one of us who's lying."

His hazel eyes bore into hers. "What're you saying?"

"You reeked of guns when you came home last night. And what was all over your jacket?"

He hesitated, just the barest millisecond, but she caught it. "I went shooting with the boys. And I dropped my fork in some sauce at dinner, got it all over my jacket."

Funny how when he said it, it sounded like the lie it was. She was about to call him on it when he grabbed her by the shoulders and shook her, his eyes darkening. "*You're* the fucking liar. Who is he?"

What the...? Oh, he was back to the pills. "Calm down, Vince. I just wanted to wait."

He stared at her, disbelief on his face. "Fuck!" His fingers dug into her arms. "I *knew* it. You been acting weird for months. You never want to go to my uncle's. And now I know why. You're fucking him."

Kate choked. "I'd rather slit my wrists than fuck your uncle."

"Then what the fuck is it?"

If he says "fuck" one more time, I'm going to kill him. If I say "fuck" one more time, I'm going to take a vow of silence. She had a Masters in social work, from Columbia no less, for Christ's sake. Why was she letting him drag her down to his level? She took a breath, deliberately lowering her voice. "All you do is yell at me these days. It's not like when we were first married. I'm worried about us."

"What does that have to do with my uncle?"

She couldn't meet his eyes. "I don't like him. That's all."

"Why the fuck not? He puts food on our table. You damn well better like him."

She looked at him this time. "Unlike you, I don't *have* to like him."

He flushed red. "You're not answering the question. You fucking my uncle?"

"For the last time, no!" She blew out fiercely, striving for control. She wanted to scream at him, to slap him until he saw sense.

He shook his head, his eyes turning mean. "You're lying; I can see it. I'm gonna kill him. And then I'm gonna kill you."

His hand came out of nowhere, backhanding her across the right cheek. The blow made her stagger, her hip striking the sink, her eyes instantly welling up with tears. She touched the spot where he'd hit her, the skin flaming hot and prickling beneath her fingers. Her stomach ached and she thought she was going to vomit up that damn pill.

She had one crazy idiotic thought: *Karma's a bitch. Serves me right for thinking of slapping him.*

No. That was Vince talking, telling her she deserved his lack of control, his anger.

With that slap, he'd just crossed her personal Rubicon. Now it was war. "What kind of limp-dicked loser hits his wife?"

Vince stared at her, his breathing ragged. "Who you calling a limp dick?"

"You, you pathetic, wife-beating, *loser.*"

She saw him shudder, knew he was furious, knew more slaps were coming. Knew she wouldn't back down, no matter the consequences. "Ever since we got here, Vince, you've changed. You've become someone I don't want to know anymore. You've turned into a big bully, just like your damn uncle. *That's* why I hate him. *That's* why I'm taking the pills."

He threw his hands up and she flinched. When he saw her recoil, guilt flashed across his face, his features softening. His voice fell to a whisper. "I'm sorry. You know I got a temper."

That old excuse. Anger roared up, making her stomach roil and her skin go hot, the pain draining away. "Face it. You're a wife beater. The lowest of the low. The weakest of the weak." She hissed her accusation, punctuating each word with the punch of her index finger into his bare chest.

"I'm not! Jesus!" He turned away for a second, then took a deep breath. "I won't ever do it again."

She narrowed her gaze. "You're damn right you won't."

He met her eyes. "What's that supposed to mean?"

Kate put her hands on her hips, her cheek throbbing. "Nobody hits me. *Ever*."

"Come on. It was a mistake. I got carried away." He reached for her arms, trying to pull her close.

She pushed him away. "Leave me alone."

He looked at her for a moment, his eyes wounded. "I'm sorry. How many times do I got to say it?"

"I can't forgive this."

"Damn it, Katie. You're my wife. We're married. That *means* something to me. Don't it mean *anything* to you?"

Some part of her wanted to say that it did. But if she gave in now, he'd just do it again. *I'm gonna kill you.* She'd never forget his saying that. She looked down at the marble tiles on the bathroom floor, her eyes idly tracing the honey-colored veins that ran through the creamy stone. Anything to keep from looking at him. Anything to keep him from seeing the truth in her eyes.

"Let me think about it," she mumbled. She needed him gone, ASAP, and if she had to lie, she would.

"Okay. But we got to talk about this later."

She nodded. She'd have to call her parents and ask them for money to get home. She could hear her mother now. "But Katherine, what did you expect? He's from *Jersey*."

"Katie, look at me." When she met his eyes, he said, "Look, I'm just a dumb fuck. I'm not thinking straight. I love you. I would never hurt you."

"But you just *did*."

He shrugged, his eyes sliding away. "I don't know what came over me."

She looked at him for a long time. "You are *not* the man I married. *That* man would never hit me. *That* man loved me." The words she spoke were thick and shaky, not the cool tone she'd intended. Her marriage was over. And it did mean something to her.

His chin came up and he met her gaze again. "Don't say that." His voice held a pleading note she'd heard too much of recently.

"Just leave."

He took a deep breath and looked like he wanted to say something else, but she pointed to the door. "I don't want to hear it."

Anger and sadness warred on his face. He took a step toward her, but when she moved back, his shoulders slumped and he put up his hands in surrender. "You're pissed. I can see that. You got to cool off, so I'm leaving—for now. But we got to talk this through."

"We will," she lied. She waited until he closed the door behind him, then she sagged against the sink, her arms trembling. Tears blurred her vision, and she stifled a sob, her throat aching, her eyes burning. She listened intently to the sounds of his moving around in the other room, waiting for him to leave. Finally she heard the outer door to their apartment close. He was gone.

She was alone. Again.

Kate rubbed her throbbing cheek and let the tears fall. How had their marriage degenerated so quickly? The first three months had been great, but the last six… and now this. She walked into the bedroom, her eyes going to the chair where the jacket had been.

It was gone.

A chill ran through her, instantly stifling her tears. It *had* been blood on the jacket.

If Vince was in the Mafia, if he'd killed someone, what reason would he have to let her go?

What was to stop him from hunting her down?

What was to stop him from killing her?

Not a damn thing.

END OF SPECIAL PREVIEW

Print and Ebook

www.danadelamar.com

Continue reading for a special preview of Kristine Cayne's first Deadly Vices novel

DEADLY OBSESSION

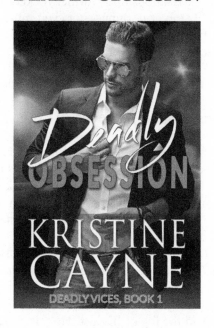

When an Oscar-winning movie star meets a department-store photographer...

Movie star Nic Lamoureux appears to have a playboy's perfect life. But it's a part he plays, an act designed to conceal a dark secret he carries on his shoulders. His empty days and nights are a meaningless blur until he meets the woman who fulfills all his dreams. She and her son are the family he's always wanted—if she can forgive a horrible mistake from his past.

A Hollywood dream...

Lauren James, a widowed single mother, earns barely enough money to support herself and her son. When she wins a photography contest and meets Nic, the man who stars in all her fantasies, her dreams, both professional and personal, are on the verge of becoming real. The attraction between Lauren and Nic is instant—and mutual. Their chemistry burns out of control during a photo shoot that could put Lauren on the fast track to a lucrative career.

Becomes a Hollywood nightmare

But an ill-advised kiss makes front-page news, and the lurid headlines threaten everything Nic and Lauren have hoped for. Before they know what's happening, their relationship is further rocked by an obsessed and cunning stalker who'll stop at nothing—not even murder—to have Nic to herself. When Nic falls for Lauren, the stalker zeroes in on her as the competition. And the competition must be eliminated.

An excerpt from *Deadly Obsession*

Lauren rolled her eyes. "Fine. Do it."

Nic bent down and brushed his lips against hers. For the first few seconds, she didn't kiss him back, but she didn't push him away, either. Then, on a sigh, she leaned into him and her arms locked around his neck. His tongue darted out to taste her bottom lip. Mmm… cherry—his new favorite flavor. When her mouth opened, he didn't hesitate.

He dove in. And drowned.

He'd meant this to be a quick kiss, only now he just couldn't stop. His lips traced a path to her throat. Cupping her bottom with his hands, he lifted her up, grinding against her. She moaned. It was a beautiful sound, one he definitely wanted to hear again.

A loud noise pierced the fog of his lust. He raised his head from where he'd been nuzzling Lauren's apple-scented neck to tell whoever it was to fuck off, but as the sexual haze cleared, he swallowed the words. The paparazzi had gathered around, applauding and calling out crude encouragements. Some snapped photos while others rolled film. Shit. He'd pay for this fuck-up and so would she.

www.kristinecayne.com